Back Stabbers II

By NYEMA

This Book belongs to
Jasmynn Hairston
please return
when done :)

ANEW QUALITY PUBLISHING
Published by A New Quality Publishing L. L. C
A New Quality Publishing
P. O. Box 589
Plainfield, New Jersey 07061
anewqualitypublishing.com
anewqualitypublishing@yahoo.com
Facebook/AnewQualityPublishing/ Facebook/NyemaTaylor

First Paperback Edition
Printed in United States

PUBLISHER'S NOTE

Acknowledgement

First and foremost, I must thank my Heavenly Father for continuing to prove me wrong. These last couple of years has been a struggle, not only for me but for my family and friends as well. But through His love, mercy and guidance, I've found the strength to get back at it and do what it is I was so gracefully sent here to do. Entertain! Lord, I wouldn't have been able to do it without you!

Special thanks go out to my Husband. I know I've been a handful these last few months while trying to get this project in order but you tolerated it all, and for that as well as all the good in you, I love you unconditionally. And to my Mom, the one who's been holding me down even before I was grounded enough to understand who I truly was. I want you to know I value the bond we share like I value my life. I love you! And to my Dad, it's been a ride for us both but look at us now, tighter than pit-bulls on a leash. I love you! And to my in-laws, Jackie, Beat, Jackia and Bruce, who accepted me from the beginning. Thanks for loving and holding me down like I was your own, especially when I've needed you the most. You've proved to me that blood isn't always so much thicker. And to my two special people in the cut that volunteered to help me put this project into motion. Aunt Sha, I know I worked your nerves but thank you so much for all your ideas with cover. We made it happen baby, I love you! And to my girl, Erika, thanks for the eyes. We definitely got a hit on our hands. Much love! And to the rest of my family and friends that have been so loving and supporting, even when times got tough. I love you all!

I want to thank my A New Quality Family and my big brother, J.M. Benjamin, for believing in me. There was no doubt in my mind that A New Quality wouldn't do big things. I'm just honored to be the 1st Lady. J-Rod Nider, let's get that "Breaking London" popping. FiFi Cureton, you killed them with "Have Your Ever..."Can't wait for the sequel. Randy "Ski" Thompson, Let's get it home team.

"Ski Mask Way II" was the truth. Cherie Johnson and Kathy, all I can say is "Around The World Twice." You ladies killed it. Kevin "Glorious" Gause, I'm waiting on "The Robbery Report II". Don't keep us waiting too long. Erica Kimberly, welcome to the family my sister. Can't wait to travel and do some numbers with you. Let's get it! And my girl Locksie "The Queen of Book Reviews" of ARC Book Club Inc., what would I do without you. Thanks for giving me that umph I needed to take this one right here to the bank. And like ANQP motto says, "A family that grinds together eats together..." And that we will do!

Many thanks goes out to all of the Readers, Vendors, Book Clubs, Book Sellers and Book Stores, especially Philly's Black & Nobel on Broad & Erie, (Hakeem & Tyson I love Ya'll), EMPIRE Books and Horizon, who've been holding me down faithfully since my journey began almost five years ago. I don't know where I would be without you all. Thanks from the bottom of my heart!

-NYEMA

Dedication

This book is dedicated to two special people in my life. First to my son, Shamir Taylor Jr., it feels like yesterday when I was rocking you to sleep in my arms. Now you're talking and running around the house like you pay the mortgage, and giving me orders like you're the boss. Where does the time go? I know you won't be my baby boy forever, but you will always be the best thing that ever happened to me. I love you Son!

And last but not least, to my step-father, David Crawford Sr., who helped raise and mold me into the beautiful woman I turned out to be. I know I haven't always been the easiest daughter to get along with, but we overcame all the obstacles and mounted a relationship that not a lot of young women get to cherish. You've shown me courage, you've shown me strength, you've shown me pain (with that belt) I didn't forget, but most of all you've shown me a life that was filled with all the finer things and I appreciate everything you've done for me. Unfortunately, a lot of girls are denied the chance to grow up with a father. I was blessed enough to have two. How can I be mad at that? Just make sure you hurry home before I send your grandson to you. I love you dearly!

Prologue

HOW IT ALL BEGAN
...REWIND (September 16, 2008)

Rashaud jumped to his feet, spun around like a professional break-dancer, pushed Keemah out of his way and sprinted out of his bedroom. He swooped his cell phone from the kitchen counter, scrolled down to the number listed as *Wifey* and pressed talk.

Azia said nothing when she answered, but he could hear her breathing.

"I know you on the phone! Where the fuck is my money?"

"I don't know what you talking about," she lied.

"Don't play games wit me, Azia! Where the fuck's my money?"

"I don't owe you no fucking explanation you owe me one," she spat. "How was your trip?"

"Girl, if you don't tell me where my shit is right now I'm gonna find you and rip your fucking throat out. Aint nobody but God gonna be able to save you!"

"How was she?" asked Azia, referring to Keemah. "Is she better than me?"

"You dirty bitch!" he yelled, startling Keemah who stood just a couple of feet away.

"I got your bitch alright. Tell her trick ass when I see her she better run."

"You tell her your muthafuckin' self." His blood pressure had noticeably begun to rise. "Tell me where my goddamn money is right now!"

Azia chuckled. "It should be ringing your bell at any second."

Her answer confused him. "What the hell do that mean?"

She brought her tone up a notch and repeated, "I said, it should be ringing your doorbell any second now."

He turned to look at the door. There was silence. He didn't understand what Azia was talking about. Then the doorbell rang and he walked over to peak out the peephole. "Who is it?" he ramped.

"It's the police!" Detective Joseph responded. "We have a warrant—Open up!"

Rashaud took five steps back away from the door. He snatched the phone away from his ear and stared down at it like it was diseased. "You dirty muthafucka."

BOOM! Azia heard the phone hit the floor just before hearing what sounded like an army of soldiers bursting into the place.

Mike stood behind her taking everything in. The smirk on her face informed him of how sheisty she could be, and she was enjoying every minute of it. Now he had to decide whether to keep his guard up, or trust and believe that she sincerely had his back. He tried his best to believe there was some truth to how she claimed to feel about him. It was possible. But out of fear of betrayal, like she had just done Rashaud, he made sure to keep one eye open. He had mad love for her for sure and was willing to take a chance and build a future with her. But he promised himself that he would never totally let his guard down.

Azia hung up the phone after hearing Detective Joseph and his team escort Rashaud and Keemah out of the apartment. She turned and wrapped her arms around Mike's neck. He lifted her from the floor and sat her on the countertop in the kitchen where they were standing. She smiled, gave him a kiss and said, "Game over!"

Mike stared into her eyes and asked, "How did that make you feel?"

Azia didn't answer the question right away. She knew she had to be careful with her response because although Rashaud had done her dirty, going as far as to turn him over to the police was farfetched. "I don't know how to feel right now" she frowned. "I thought I would feel good and relieved, but I don't."

"Are you sure you thought long and hard about this?" he asked. "Once you're labeled as a snitch, aint no taking it back."

"I just wanted him to feel some of my pain."

"I hate what he's done to you Azia, but everything that happened aint his fault." Azia knew Mike was right but said nothing. "Everything you told that Detective wasn't the truth. If you choose to take the stand just be prepared for them to dig into ya background too."

Azia failed to think about that part of the deal. Detective Joseph told her he would push for immunity for her as much as he could, but there was nothing in writing. The thought of being tossed in a filthy, diseased, roach and rat infested jail cell made her cringe. "So what am I supposed to do now?" she asked, feeling deflated.

"That's a choice you got to make on ya own. Whatever you decide, you're the one that's gonna have to live with it for the rest of ya life."

Mike gave her a peck on the forehead, grabbed a beer from the refrigerator and made his way out of the kitchen with nothing more to say.

■ ■ ■

Less than two months later, Azia's mind was made up. But after breaking the news to Detective Joseph, all hell broke loose. The police chief did everything he could to get Azia to change her mind and move forth with her testimony, but she refused. He even went as far as threatening to throw her in prison if she didn't talk. But seeing how frail and frightened she was, Detective Joseph stepped in.

"Chief, it's my fault. I'm the one that didn't get anything in writing--."

"I know it's your fault," he screamed. "Get her out of my precinct before I forget about all the laws of this screwed up justice system."

When they stepped foot out of the precinct, Detective Joseph turned to Azia and examined the tears in her eyes. "I know you're scared of what he may do to you if you go up against him, but you need to think about what he's going to do when he's set free because they can hold him for a little while, but they can't hold him forever. Your word would help out a hell of a lot."

Azia looked from the ground up to his eyes. "I'm not afraid of him and I don't need you to be afraid for me, goodbye Detective Joseph."

Detective Joseph watched her walk away shyly and climb into the passenger side of Mike's Jaguar. He watched the car intensely until it drifted beyond his eye's reach. "From one thug to the next," he mumbled, as he took his time heading back into the precinct. *Now I got to go back in here and deal with his bullshit.*

Back Stabbers II

By NYEMA

Chapter 1

A SAD DAY IN AMERICA

...Philadelphia, Pa· (Nine Months Later)

KoKa's Bar & Grill was luxuriant. It was very well established and had grown to become one of the most highly recommended restaurants, after being named one of the top ten new restaurants, in the city of brotherly love. Although it sat amongst other prestigious food chains, with its warm décor, upscale casual atmosphere and convenient location, KoKa's was the perfect spot for any occasion.

But when they say the heat is on, this hot summer day was every meaning of the phrase. It was June 29, 2009, a day the entire world would never forget. The restaurant was packed with grieving locals gathered around every flat screen television available. There wasn't a dry eye in the room amongst the silence as every ear focused in closely to every word from the commentator on the *CNN* network station. "Pop star Michael Jackson has been pronounced dead at the age of 50 after suffering a massive cardiac arrest," he sighed. "Paramedics rushed Jackson from his west Los Angeles home to UCLA Medical Center where a team of physicians attempted to resuscitate him for more than an hour, but unfortunately the famed singer was pronounced dead at 2:26 p.m." The entire place was in awe.

KoKa made her way through the crowd and into the office to be alone. She clicked the television on in search to find another station with better news hoping that all this was just a publicity stunt. It just had to be. *That man can't really be gone,* she thought. More tears crept down her eyes as she uncomfortably slouched down onto the chair and turned the volume up. *"For those of you just tuning in,"* the teary eyed spokeswoman squealed, *"The Los Angeles fire department was called to Michael Jackson's residence at 12:26 p.m. where paramedics performed CPR on Jackson, who was not breathing when they arrived at his home. He was rushed to UCLA Medical Center, just six miles from his home, where he has been pronounced dead at the age of 50."*

KoKa cut the TV off and cupped her face with her hands. With the indelible impact, Jackson left on music and pop culture, millions around the world was feeling the same grief and devastation KoKa felt at that very moment. "KoKa, we need you out here for a minute," yelled an employee, from the other side of the door.

After cleaning herself up, KoKa made her way back out Pinto the restaurant where she was approached by an unfamiliar face. The young man was fine and had KoKa been twenty years younger she probably would've been all over him.

"Hi," he said, extending his hand. "KoKa, right?"

His voice was enchanting, and his smile was intriguing. KoKa didn't know this man from a can of paint, but for some reason he seemed extremely odd to her. "I am," she responded.

"I know this may not be the best time," he said, scanning the distressed filled room. "But I just wanted to have the pleasure of shaking the hand of the person responsible for putting this smile on my face."

"And what off the menu blessed you with that smile?"

"Can't decide if it was the shrimp or the salmon," he grinned. He caught a glimpse of Mike coming through the entrance so he cut the conversation short. "I know you got a lot to handle so I'ma let you go. I'm sure we'll bump heads again."

"I hope so. We love new customers," she smiled, "And their money."

He returned a smile and headed for the exit passing Mike on the way. The two men stared into one another's eyes as they crossed paths. Mike stopped and turned to watch the stranger make his way out the door.

"You know him?" Mike asked, greeting his mother with a hug.

"Nope, this was my first time seeing him in here. Why you know him?"

"Nah," he smirked. "I seen him around a few times but I don't know that nigga, and you know that aint sitting too well with me."

"Baby stop being so paranoid."

"I aint paranoid, I'm cautious."

"Well whatever you want to call it," she said, kissing him on the cheek. "What's his name anyway?"

"His name Quadir," he blurted. "Why you need to know that?"

"In case I feel like snagging me a youngin' to get my swerve back," she joked.

"Don't get that lil dude f'd up Ma."

"Just teasing you." She directed her attention to the Michael Jackson tribute of all his videos that plastered the screens. "I need to find something to laugh about cause it's a sad, sad day in America."

Mike and KoKa posted themselves against the bar and watched the crowd imitate all of MJ's classics like they were their own. Mike produced his cell phone and answered a call.

"What?" he barked into the phone. "Where he at?" He paused for a moment and stared into his mother's eyes. "Shit, give me like thirty minutes, I be down there."

Mike barely ended the call before KoKa questioned, "Who was that?"

"I got something I need to go take care of," he sighed. "You gonna be alright?"

KoKa sensed something shaky in his voice. "What's wrong Mike?"

Mike didn't want to lie, but some things were better left unsaid. "Don't worry 'bout me I'm cool. I'll call you later."

Her intuition was telling her something different. "Stop lying!" she demanded, grabbing hold of his arm and eyeing him curiously. "Tell me what's wrong--"

"Ma, Ma..." he intervened, raising his hands. "Please let me go so I can handle my business." He was feeling at bit on edge after the call and the longer KoKa held him up, the longer it would take for him to go correct the problem. "I got this."

KoKa had to remind herself that he wasn't the same thirteen year old boy that she could control back in the day. He was a grown man now with grown man responsibilities. Although his choice of profession was one a mother would never prescribe for her child, she was thankful he was smart enough to make his way through that type of lifestyle.

"You better make sure you call me too," she warned.

Mike threw her a head nod and moseyed on out the door. The chill that crept down her spine begged her to follow and interrogate him some more, but her thoughts were distracted by a slew of customers bombarding her with goodbyes.

■ ■ ■

Twenty minutes later, Mike entered the smoke filled café with the mean face on. He strutted pass the mob of infested alcoholics and made his way over to his soon-to-be sorry excuse for a stepfather. With Camel, his muscle, on the other side of him, Mike snatched Anthony out of the face of another woman. She wasn't all that cute, but because of the size of her chest she was bound to catch the eye of any man. Had Mike been there under different circumstances, he would've been sure to catch a peek as well.

"Aye--son," slurred Anthony, staggering to keep his balance. "What you doin' on this side?" He tried to guide Mike over towards his lady friend. "Hey come meet," he leaned over to her. "Umm," he flagged. "I forget, but she aint from round here. I was tellin' her to--" He grabbed hold of one of the bar stools to keep his balance and spaced out for a moment. When he snapped back to reality he looked over at the woman and said, "Aint that right," forgetting that he never finished the sentence.

Mike was furious. "Bring ya drunk ass on before I forget about the love my mom got for you," he demanded.

Camel gripped Anthony by his collar and dragged him out the door. Everyone watched in amazement and laughter with no intentions on butting in.

Once Camel secured Anthony in the back seat of the car, he joined Mike in the front. "What you wanna do wit him?"

"Take his drunk ass home to sober up before my mom get there," spat Mike. He put the car into motion and sped off disturbingly. "I can't wait for the day that she's fed up wit his trifling ass."

"And-chu-woo-woo-woo...Woo---woo-woo—woo..." Anthony slurred the words to the song while laying, down in the back seat.

Camel laughed, but Mike didn't find anything funny. Had it not been for the unconditional love he had for his mother, Anthony would have been slurring his last song that night. This was the fourth time that month Mike had to embarrassingly remove Anthony from someone's establishment after he decided to drown his liver in *Southern Comfort* and make KoKa look foolish. As far as Mike knew, everyone was aware that Anthony got a little crazy when he drank, including KoKa, but Mike believed she was naïve to what extent he could go. He swore that if she did know there was no way she would continue to tolerate the man. Anthony was indeed what some women would call "sharp" when he wasn't drunk off the liquor, but the sight of him in his current state-of-mind made Mike sick to his stomach. He found it hard to understand what part of him made KoKa fall so deeply in love. The last thing he would ever want to do is break his mother's heart, but he promised himself that if Anthony didn't get himself together real soon he'd be checking out. Indefinitely!

■■■

On the other side of town, Azia took her time exiting her car in no rush to enter the upscale penthouse she and Mike shared on the outskirts of the city. She let her head fall back against the headrest and listened to the latest gossip in celebrity news playing on the radio. She closed her eyes in a desperate attempt to relax her mind after making it through yet another stressful day. The life she was living was one a young girl always dreamt of, but of course with more money came more problems. On top of school, she had been managing all of Mike's properties which were becoming more than a headache. Now that the semester was over, she assumed things would get a little easier. Shoot! That's why they say you should never assume.

The day Azia decided not to go through with testifying against Rashaud, Mike didn't hesitate to give her an ultimatum. If she was going to be a part of his life, there were changes needing to be made. It was either continue on with the life of independence she had created for herself, or give up everything to be with him including the hustle she had grown to love. Knowing the benefits of becoming his woman would never leave her wanting or needing for anything, she chose the latter. And in return, she was pushing a Porsche Cayenne, lived lavishly in a three thousand square-foot suite overlooking the Delaware River, owned a hell of a wardrobe, and had the means to more money than she could handle. Who could be mad at that?

All of a sudden, an unwelcomed presence overcame her. Her eyes pierced open as she leaned forward quickly and scanned the area twice. Her eyes stopped on a man and woman heading towards the elevator. They were all over one another. "Get a room," she smirked, with no intent for them to hear her. After killing the engine, she grabbed her pocketbook from the passenger seat and exited the car.

Nyema

With her heels clicking rapidly against the concrete, she scanned the area a third time while heading for the elevator.

This had not been the first time she felt like someone was watching her. It had been a few months since Rashaud was taken into custody, and Azia has yet to find peace knowing it was just a matter of time before he hit the streets again. She battled with herself over and over wondering if she'd made the right decision, but with Mike riding with her every step of the way, that secured all her doubts. If Rashaud was crazy enough to show his face and test the patience of one of the most powerful men in the city, he would just have to suffer the consequences.

Azia searched through the clutter in her pocketbook anxious to find her ringing cell phone. After reading the caller ID, she smiled and answered, "Hey babe."

"Hey Lady, I just left the restaurant, I'll be home shortly alright," said Mike.

She sighed. "I knew you weren't home yet," she whined. "What's taking you so long?"

"I was tryna beat you there but something came up so I'll be there in a few."

"Whatever--"

"I aint got time for all that Azia," he interrupted. "I'll see you as soon as I finish--up here—try--to wait up for--"

The phone began to fade in and out now that she had stepped onto the elevator. She looked down at the screen which now read *call failed*. Just before the elevator doors closed, she looked up and locked eyes with a man standing in the shadows amongst dozens of parked cars in the middle of the garage. Although he wasn't standing directly in front of her, something felt so familiar about the stranger, but she was sure she hadn't seen him anywhere in the building before. Every nerve in her body tensed up as she watched him walk towards the elevator. The closer he got, the more anxious she became. As if on cue, the doors slammed shut just before the unidentified man had a chance to step a foot close enough for her to register the face.

Azia pounded every button on the control panel in an attempt to get them back open, but instead the elevator ascended up. She fell backward allowing her body to rest against the wall with her heart beat well above the normal rate.

Ding! When the doors opened on the 2nd level, there were a few people waiting who took their time getting on. Azia would have dragged them on quicker if she could have. The ride back down to the garage level was antagonizing. The strangers beside her stared as she pushed the *G* button repeatedly like it was going to get her there faster. When it finally did, Azia rushed out ahead of them. Her head rotated back and forth several times in an attempt to capture every angle of the lot, but the figure her mind infiltrated just minutes ago was no longer there. *I know damn well I aint losing my mind* she told herself.

"Are you okay?" asked a stranger, walking up. Azia nodded her head *yes*. "Are you getting on?"

Azia walked into the elevator and slowly turned around. Standing in the same position she had been the first time, she looked out into the garage without thinking, blinking or swallowing only this time there wasn't anyone staring back at her.

Chapter 2

AM I LOSING MY MIND

Azia grabbed the small jar of Tylenol and a bottle of water from the refrigerator. She snatched up the cordless phone and passed out on the living room sofa. After consuming two pain killers, she kicked her shoes off and sank into the oversized plush pillows.

"Hey Sash, what you doing?"

"Sitting here wishing all these bills would just magically disappear," exhaled Sasha.

Sasha is Kane's girlfriend, Mike's right hand man. When introduced, both girls were reluctant to befriend one another, but after a little time and several weeks of a wardrobe competition, it turned out they shared a lot in common. Plus, Sasha was older and she and Kane had been together for over six years so Azia knew there was a lot she could learn from her.

"Stop acting like you worried when you know damn well Kane gonna take care of 'em."

"Shit his ass been acting real funny lately. He talkin' bout I got to pay my own credit card bills for a couple months cause he got some other shit to deal with."

Azia giggled. "Girl Mike did me the same way a couple months ago. He tryna make you spend ya own money to teach you a lesson. They tired of us maxing out those cards and depending on them to pay 'em off."

"I aint slow, I know what the hell he call his self doing but that's alright," she hissed. "He just aint getting no ass."

"Good luck with that."

"Did you decide if you gonna sign up for the summer semester?"

"Nah, I need a break. I'ma just knock my last two classes out next semester, and then I'll be done." Azia noticed a stack of mail on the table and began to sort through. "We still on for the gym tomorrow?"

"I aint got a choice the way my ass been woofing down everything in sight," she said, as the line beeped. "Hold on that's my other line."

Azia continued to sort through the mail until Sasha came back on the line. Two minutes later, she returned to the call. "Damn trick, you ignorant as hell for leaving me on hold like."

"That was Kane being a pain in my ass. Him and Mike at the boutique."

"How you know?"

"Cause I heard Kyla's loud ass in the background. I can't stand that whore. That bitch will fuck anything with legs. I was about to slap the bougieness out her skank ass the other day 'til Kane stopped me." Azia tried changing the subject but Sasha wasn't having it. "I know Kane fucked her triflin' ass. If you ask me every last one of them niggas ran up in that hoe."

"Sasha, I don't feel like hearing that nonsense.

"I don't know why you let the thought of that girl get under your skin like that."

"Bitch, you should too cause I know Mike done hit it once or twice before."

"Girl I'm hanging up I'll see you tomorrow."

"There you go getting all sensitive and shit. You know when I get to rapping I get into *tell it like it is* mode."

Azia didn't know if Mike had ever cheated on her before, but the mere thought of it gave her an attitude. "I don't feel like hearing about who Mike fucked or might'a fucked so I'ma let you go before I end up cursing ya ass out for talking shit."

Sasha laughed. "And what you think I'ma do after you curse me out?"

"Don't matter because I'ma let you go just so we never have to find out," giggled Azia.

"Alright Ms. Sensitivity, call and wake me up in the morning."

Azia ended the call and climbed from the sofa. She walked over to the other side of the room and tossed the stack of mail onto the dining room table just as her stomach began to turn in knots and a rotten taste filled her mouth. She gripped the water bottle and drowned it hoping to chase the uncomfortable feeling away but it only made matters worse. With one hand covering her mouth, she gunned for the bathroom and brought up the Jamaican dish she enjoyed a few hours back. After washing her face and brushing her teeth, she pulled out the *pepto bismol* from the medicine cabinet thinking *my ass better not be pregnant.*

■■■

By the time KoKa locked up the restaurant and made it home, she was exhausted. Her plan was to take a nice hot bubble bath and recoup a peace of mind. But when she stepped foot through her front door, she knew she was in for a hell of a lot more.

"Where the hell is my bottle of liquor at?" yelled Anthony, damn near pushing KoKa through the wall. "I'm tired of you touching my shit woman."

"I don't feel like your shit tonight goddammit," she squeaked. "I threw the shit in the trash so go fish for it if you want it that bad."

Anthony released KoKa from his grip and took a step back. Just when she thought it was safe to move he took her by the neck and dragged her into the kitchen. "I aint fishing for shit you gonna be the one fishing." He threw her head first into the trashcan. "And you bet'not come out without my damn bottle."

After seconds of sucking in the stench of old garbage, KoKa came up for air with the half filled bottle in one hand. "Here," she shouted, shoving it at him.

Anthony snatched the bottle, cracked it open and took five shots of it to the head. "That'll teach you to touch my shit," he said, smugly.

KoKa rolled her eyes and stormed upstairs to the bedroom. She jumped out of her clothes in a hurry and rushed for the bathroom. Anthony appeared just before she hit the bathroom door and blocked her path. "Move the hell out the way."

He grabbed one of her breast and squeezed it callously. "What you mad?"

KoKa tried pushing him but knew she had no chance at moving his two hundred and forty pounds of muscle. "I smell like trash," she said softly. "So please move out of the way so I can go take a shower--"

"You know how I feel about my booz KoKa." He tried to pull her in for a hug but she resisted. "I can't have a hug?"

"Anthony, move the hell out the way. Damn!"

He stepped to the side allowing her to enter the bathroom. She closed and locked the door behind her. After minutes of staring at the door, he took a few more swigs from his bottle and rushed down to the kitchen. Moments later, Anthony appeared back at the bathroom door with a phillips head screwdriver. Because the shower was running, KoKa was unaware that he had unscrewed the doorknob off to gain entrance until he snatched the shower curtain back startling her. "Why you lock me out?"

"Nigga you crazy," she replied, cutting her shower short. She had dealt with this type of nonsense from him many times before, but after the day she had she was well pass irked. "You gonna make me make a phone call in a minute," she warned. "Keep testing me."

"You call yourself threatening me now?"

"You too old for this shit aint you embarrassed?"

Nyema

"I tell you what I'm too old for," he said, snatching the shower curtain from the bar. With KoKa flinging her arms and legs, he managed to wrap in it from head to toe and carry her out to the patio. Once he had her outside, he snatched the curtain from her body leaving her butt naked for whoever walked by to see. "Are you embarrassed?" he said, mocking her.

KoKa tried to fight her way pass him for minutes before he gave in and let her run back inside. Fortunate enough for her, no one happened to walk by and witness the dispute. "You know what Anthony this shit here got to stop."

"What--" he sang, like it was all a joke.

"Please believe I put up with ya shit by choice but I'ma tell you something," she said, inching closer towards him. "You got one more time to put your hands on me--"

"And what, you gonna get ya son on me," he interrupted. "I know. I heard it all before."

KoKa bit her lip. She knew the conversation would never end had she said anything else because Anthony was the type that had to have the last word. She knew his fate was in her hands just as it had been for the last couple years. All she had to do was make one call and his life would be over. But she loved the sober, caring, compassionate part of him and that's what kept him breathing all this time. She was starting to question whether it was worth it.

Anthony glanced over at her cell phone, which was vibrating across the table. "You gonna get that?" KoKa darted for it but he beat her to it and checked the caller ID. "It's your son." He handed it over, and then snatched it back quickly. "Don't get cute you hear."

KoKa snatched the phone from him and answered. "Hey baby what's up?"

"I meant to call you sooner but I got a little tied up," Mike advised.

"It's alright as long as I know you're okay."

"I'm on my way in for the night I'll holler at you tomorrow."

"Okay baby."

Mike knew something was off because the normal KoKa would've been dead on his behind for not calling her sooner. "You alright you sound funny."

"I'm just tired I'm about to take a Motrin and call it a night."

"Where's Anthony at?"

KoKa looked Anthony in the face and replied, "He's upstairs sleep but let me go, I'll call you in the morning."

"You sure you cool Ma?"

"Good night baby, be careful going home." Anthony walked around the table and gently took the phone from her hand. He made sure the call was disconnected before speaking. "You know I love you right?" He knew how powerful of a man Mike was and if KoKa really wanted him hurt she could have said the word right then. He also knew that KoKa was not a weak woman. If she wanted to handle him herself she could have, maybe not physically, but in many other ways.

I know she like it when I rough her ass up he told himself, then leaned in for a kiss. She dodged it perfectly and met his lips with a bawled up fist. It wasn't a punch but it was something just to let him know who's really in control.

■■■

Mike stood quietly along the oversized king bed in their lavish master bedroom suite. He stared down at the smoothness of Azia's skin admiring her beautiful facial features as she lay asleep dressed in a laced nightgown with her long hair spilling onto the surrounding pillows, and her full lips seemed to pout at him. He smiled.

Unconsciously, she eased the sheets slightly off of her body seeking relief from the heat of the summer night air. After watching the wrinkles race across the red silk sheets, Mike's dark shadow spilled across the room as he glided towards the window to let some of the evening breeze inside. He then lit the three candles that were used as décor on top of the dresser. His movements were barely noticeable as he made his way back over to the bed. He removed his shirt, detached both cell phones from his hip and placed them on the nightstand. The lighting from the candles bounced off his skin making the muscles in his chest evident as he went on to remove his boots and slide out of his linen pants.

Mike crept up behind her and allowed his fingers to linger in the small of her back, making quick circular motions, and then moving them slowly across her thigh. She scooted back just enough for him to know she was awake.

"I knew you weren't sleep," he whispered. "I got you something for you," he said, dangling a diamond cross necklace that he pulled from out of nowhere.

Azia rolled over slightly allowing him to secure it around her neck. Showering her with gift after gift had become a routine, so she was the least bit surprised. She turned her entire body around to face him and stared into his panther-like eyes. Her nipples, now erect, strained against the nightgown seeking out attention.

Mike gently shifted his body causing her to roll beneath him. He cupped one of her breasts and gently brushed his teeth against her nipple through the lace. Brushing her hair aside, he began to delicately kiss on her neck, while she wiggled her way out the gown. He then cupped her breasts and showed them both the same amount of attention.

Azia moaned softly, her body warmed by his closeness and divulging excitement as he alternated between touching her stomach with his soft fingertips and caressing her inner thighs. As if he had all eternity, he slowly nibbled his way down to her feet and then back up to her face, his teeth now playing more boldly.

With incredible patience and still preferring to tease, he put his arm underneath her head to bring her closer and spent what felt like hours kissing, biting, licking and sucking all over her flesh as the scent of her sweet fragrance made him crave her more. His hands snaked down slowly towards the warm wetness between her legs, and his fingers gently fluttered up and down her clit occasionally running deep inside.

"Oh, Mike," she panted, her squirms becoming more intense.

Mike's arousal heightened as she pressed her body against him, and he dove in for a kiss. Azia's flirting tongue willingly hunted his while her body ached for every inch of him to fill her inner walls. One of her hands crept down between her legs and she began to fondle her own pussy. With her eyes closed, she reached out her fluid coated hand and began to spread her juices along his stone, gripping and squeezing his balls all at the same time. Seconds later, she scooted her hips up to his level and positioned his erection to enter her dome.

"Mmm…Mmm…Not yet," he advised, pulling back from her raging hot desire.

Again, the two began to kiss with passionate hunger, and then Mike kissed his way down to her hairless pussy lips. He sucked her already moistened clit while she thrashed wildly all over the bed.

"Why are you doing this to me," she cried, over and over again.

Moments later, she began to convulse as Mike flickered his tongue in a way that brought quivering orgasms out of her glistening body. Taking control of the situation, she pulled him up, rolled him over and turned herself around into the *69* position. Her tongue wasted no time to run up and down his shaft as he grabbed her ass with both hands and invited her pussy back down to his face.

Azia was no professional, but she was no slouch when it came to bringing her man to ecstasy. She deep-throated him, wavering between sucking his dick and engulfing his sac until Mike couldn't stand it any longer.

Nyema

"A'ight...Hold on," he squealed, with the feeling of cum boiling in his balls.

Coming up for air, she spun around, straddled him, pulled her sopping wet pussy open with one hand and guided him inside of her with the other. Her dazed eyes closed briefly while her walls adjusted to his thickness. After reveling in the feeling of him being inside, she leaned back, grabbed both breasts and began a rhythmic grind on top of him. Minutes later, there was no holding either of them back. Mike gripped her waist forcing her to pick up the pace. She whirled and twirled them both to their peaks.

"Damn..." he groaned, digging his claws into her ass. "Fuck..."

"OHBABYILOVEYOUSOMUCH..." she screamed, grinding her clit against the base of his dick. All of a sudden, she pitched forward and covered his body with hers. "Damn this some good dick," she huffed, as both their bodies fell limp.

Mike could feel the hot stream from her river of juices ooze down his balls and drop to his inner thighs. "A nigga sure can go for a hot meal right now," he exhaled, smacking her on the ass as they both closed their eyes trying to enjoy the afterglow of the sexcapade.

Chapter 3

THE HEAT IS ON

Sasha and Azia were in the gym getting their aerobic workout on. After the hour session lead by an instructor came to an end, the girls headed over to the elliptical to burn a few more calories before quitting for the day.

"So are you gonna say something to Mike about the letter you found about the paternity test?" questioned Sasha. "I tell you one thing, you better than me cause I would'a been up and down Kane's ass had it been me."

"I'm waiting on him to say something."

"Evidently he don't feel the need if he aint said nothing by now."

"He's probably waiting on the results."

"The hell with that girl," she said, tooting her lips. "You need to grill him and find out what's up with that. You the one about to be playing stepmom so you got a right to know what the hell's going on."

"Just keep your mouth shut Sasha. Don't say nothing to Kane cause all he gonna do is run back to Mike."

Sasha used to fingers to slide across her lips as if she were zipping them shut. "I aint getting in that, I got my own damn problems."

"What problems you got?"

"This goddamn baby momma of his is tryna drive me off the edge but I got a trick for both their asses."

"Girl don't go do something that's gon' land ya ass in jail cause it aint worth it."

Nyema

"Worth is the last thing on my mind. Kane know I will stab a bitch in a minute so I pray to God he aint stupid enough to be fuckin' that loud mouth hoe behind my back."

"Aint you the same one that always tell me it don't matter what they do out in the streets as long as they keep the drama and disrespect away from home."

"That bitch don't count, I can't stand her ass. She been giving me her ass to kiss since me and Kane got together. According to her I broke up their," she said, using both hands to imprint quotation marks, "Happy home."

Azia cut the elliptical machine off and sat on the bench beside it.

"You know what I told her," Sasha went on, "He aint know what happy was until he found me." She looked over at Azia who looked a little out of it. "You alright girl?"

Azia slowly stood from the bench and started stretching. "Yeah, I just got a little lightheaded cause I aint eat nothing this morning."

"Oh alright…" said Sasha, staring at her friend strangely and knowing it was more to the story than her just missing breakfast. "You ready to go?"

"Yeah I got to head over to the boutique you gonna ride with me?"

"No can do," she smirked. "Kane told me I had to keep my ass out of there unless he was with me. He already knows if Kyla say one more thing to me I'm going to take her tall lanky ass and use her as a broom to sweep up ya'll store."

"Mike won't let me get rid of her. He said she handles business well so I need to put my personal feelings aside."

Sasha sucked her teeth. "Hmm…She's handling business alright!"

■ ■ ■

Azia had just pulled into the Walgreens parking lot when her cell phone rang. It was Detective Joseph calling. Her heart picked up speed. She hadn't heard from him since she last seen him at the precinct so she knew whatever it was couldn't be good.

"Is this Azia?" the scratchy voice asked.

"Hey Detective," she said lightly, heart racing. "What can I do for you?"

"It's been a while, how are things coming along?"

"I can't complain." Her fingers began to twitch. "It would be nice if you were calling to check up on me but I know that isn't the case."

He took a deep breath. "I wish I were calling just to check up but I have some other news as well."

Azia shifted her weight on the armrest and peered out the front windshield. "What is it?" she asked, nervously.

"I received some papers on my desk today about the status of--"

"Just tell me, is he getting out?" she intercepted.

"It looks that way Azia. He won his appeal and without your testimony there was nothing more they could do." The air was filled with silence. "Azia, are you still there?"

She gazed out the window and drifted into la-la land for a moment. "I'm here."

"You know you always have the option to--"

"I'm not taking the stand. I refused to do it then and my mind hasn't changed so I guess I'll just have to take my chances."

"I figured you would say that, but I still had to try my hand," he sighed. "I like you Azia. You remind me a lot of my daughter. I just wish there was a way I could help change your mind."

"I appreciate everything you've done. You never judged me. But you have yourself a good day detective and try not to worry too much," she said, feeling an anxiety attack coming on.

"I'll try my best but you make sure if you need anything you call me." He cleared his throat. "Watch out for yourself young lady."

She dropped her head onto the steering wheel. Her stomach felt like twelve midgets were inside playing tug-a-war. Minutes later, she looked over towards the entrance of the store forgetting why she was even there in the first place. When she finally remembered she contemplated on running inside to grab the pregnancy test but decided it could wait. Instead, she sped out of the lot recklessly almost sideswiping a car on her way out. *Move out the damn way old lady.*

Twenty-five minutes later, she was driving through an industrial part of the city. Parking was always a hassle in the middle of the afternoon and she hated it. After five minutes of searching for a spot, she finally lucked up. It was tight but she refused to look any further. She climbed out the car, disregarded the parking meter like it was invisible and bustled through the afternoon pedestrian rush like a salmon swimming upstream.

Finally, she arrived at *A*Style Boutique* irritable and annoyed. It was no fun walking a three block stretch in six inch heels. Before entering the store, she spotted Kyla through the cracks between the mannequins displayed in the glass window. She was bent over the counter smiling in the face of a male customer. *Fuckin' whore!*

Azia headed straight for the counter where her target was located. She looked at the guy and said, "Excuse me," then directed her attention to Kyla. "Don't you have some work to do?"

Kyla looked into Azia's eyes long enough to say, "I'm aware of what need to get done," she stated, then continued on with her conversation.

"Kyla, I'm not gonna keep coming in here explaining how this store supposed to be run," spat Azia. "If you not capable of operating this business like it needs to be then aint no need for you to be here."

"I know how to operate a business," said Kyla, with the snap of her neck. "And if ya man thought otherwise I wouldn't be here now would I."

Azia had to laugh to keep from taking her head off. "Okay Miss *I know how to operate a business*. I'm happy for you. But I'm not talking about *a* business, I'm talking about *this* business," she pointed. "So I tell you what, take ya operating a business ass up out of this one before I make a mistake and stick my foot down your throat."

Kyla didn't know what to make of Azia's threat. She knew they weren't the best of friends but this was the first time she'd ever came at her like that before. And what puzzled her most was that Azia never raised her voice. Was she serious? Because all eyes in the store were on them, she weighed her options. Not one to be labeled a coward she called Azia's bluff.

"You call yourself firing me," she snickered. "The only one around here holding weight is Mike." She rolled her eyes and cocked her head to the side. "And the last time I heard you don't carry his last name so." She sneered, leaning forward with both arms folded on the counter. "Tell me how you plan to get me up out this joint cause it aint gonna be on my two feet."

There were only two options at that point. Azia had the choice to walk away and let Mike address the situation later, or do things her way. Because of the few customers lingering around store, she considered option number one, but after thinking back to all the bull crap Sasha told her, option number two sounded a hell of a lot better.

"That's your call then bitch--"

Kyla never saw it coming.

With a mouth full of blood, Kyla's tall frame hit the floor instantly. Azia stepped behind the counter before anyone could stop her and dragged Kyla out of the store, head first.

Nyema

She dropped her on the sidewalk and spit on her. "That's for fucking my man bitch."

Kyla laid there holding her jaw with tears in her eyes.

"What you thought I aint know?" she barked. It never bothered Azia too much because she knew the girl meant nothing to him, but it was only so much of her lip she was willing to take.

"I don't give a fuck what you know it aint gonna change shit." Kyla boasted, while being helped up by a bystander.

Azia broke free from one of the customers that had followed them out. "Bring ya ass back in this store and I'm gonna let you taste the bottom of these Jimmy Choo's you wish you could afford." She pushed through the small crowd of whispers and made her way back inside the store.

Once the customers were back inside, she apologized to them all hoping her actions wouldn't turn them away from doing business there again.

"Better you whip on her than me," a blonde-haired lady chirmed. "Every time I come in this store she got an attitude. If it weren't for Mike I would've stopped giving ya'll my hard earned money a long time ago."

"Well from now on feel free to come with a peace of mind because she won't be back, and if any of you ever have a problem with any of our employees please be upfront about it."

Azia stepped back behind the counter to finish ringing up the customers while the other two employs straightened up the little bit of mess that was made. The last customer to get rung up was the same guy Kyla was talking to when Azia arrived, the same guy that approached KoKa at the restaurant, the mysterious Quadir. This was the first time she got a good look at him and in a weird kind of way he reminded her of Mike. He stepped up to the counter and smiled but she didn't smile back.

Azia started to ring up his items. "Your total is Two-thirty-five."

"I know I can get some kind of discount after what I just witnessed," he smiled.

I be goddamn she thought. "No problem I can take off ten percent," she said, working her fingers on the register. "Two-hundred-eleven dollars and fifty cents."

Quadir reached in his pocket, pulled out a wad of hundreds and smiled. "You could've made it an even two hundred and eleven."

Azia held out her hand to collect the money irked. She gathered his change and as friendly as she could sound replied, "Have a good day."

"Seems like you the one having the bad day. You not supposed to let nobody take you off ya square. You look too damn good for that," he winked. "But don't worry about it we all get caught up from time to time."

"I hope what happened doesn't stop you from doing business here."

"Absolutely not," he advised, gently grabbing hold of her hand.

She snatched her hand back. "No offense but I need to handle my other employees."

"None taken," he chuckled. "I'll see you around." He headed towards the exit and turned back just before walking out and said, "Mike's a lucky man."

Azia smiled weakly and glanced over at the other two employees who were watching out the corner of their eyes. *Look at their nosy asses.* She waved them over. "Let me holler at ya'll for a minute."

Mel and Sophie quit folding the stacks of clothes that had fallen onto the floor during the tussle. Mel, who was the quieter one of the two lead the way. She was short, chubby in the face and had big poppy eyes that spotted pretty much anything that moved. Sophie was short as well but more petite. She wore her hair back in a ponytail so much "Ponytail" became her nickname. It did nothing but reveal her shiny ass forehead and big toothed smile.

Nyema

"Just like I apologized to the customers I feel the need to apologize to ya'll," stated Azia. "I tried to keep the matter under control long as I could but I refuse to be disrespected." Azia collected the cash from the register and placed it in a money- bag. "I said that to say this, I show ya'll nothing but respect so I expect the same in return." She stepped from behind the counter with the bag in her hand and stared at them both. "You look like something's on your mind, Sophie?"

Sophie stood silent and expressionless. Mel was cool but Kyla was her ace in the hole so she was feeling some kind of way. She had a lot she wanted to say but her job meant more.

"Did you really have to fire her?" she asked, with a straight face.

Azia sat the money- bag down on the counter mentally preparing herself for the next beat down. "If you don't like how I manage this store you can leave too Sophie. Ya hands aint tied."

"I was just asking a question."

"And I answered it so is there anything else you wanna say?" Sophie nodded her head *no*. Azia turned to Mel. "You?" Mel shook her head *no*.

I'm sick of these damn young girls. Azia snatched the bag from the counter. "After ya'll straighten up you can go home for the day I'll see you tomorrow, regular time."

On her way to the office she could hear the phone ringing off the hook. She knew it wouldn't take long for the news had traveled back to Mike. After tossing the money bag onto the desk, Azia came out of her heels and flopped down in the leather swivel chair. She stared at the phone, her eyes growing more intense with each ring. After collecting her thoughts, she picked up. It was Mike and he was far from his usual humble self.

"What the hell is wrong with you?" he barked.

She held the phone away from her ear while he spoke. "Can we talk about this later?"

"No, I wanna know why you thought it was okay to show ya ass in the store while customers were shopping."

"I don't feel like this right now," she growled. "If you would've kept your dick in your pants we wouldn't be going through this now would we."

"Watch what you say to me before you get slapped in your mouth alright. Now I don't know who the hell been giving you false information but you playin' yaself."

Azia rolled her eyes. "Whatever, Mike."

"I might not bitch about it, but I definitely pay attention," she advised. "The dizzy bitch runnin' round here like she the head bitch in charge. How can you--"

Mike cut her off. Arguing with a woman and all that going back and forth was something he could never tolerate. "Pay close attention 'cause I'm only gonna say this once," he warned. "The reason why she runnin' round there like she the head bitch in charge is because she wanna be and you done slipped up and let her steal some of your shine by reacting. Yeah, you might'a laid the bitch out but she got your attention loud and clear," he frowned. "The next time you decide you wanna act like a park ape out in public, think about what you're gonna lose because if I wanted a monkey I would be at the zoo picking the little muthafucka out." Between clenched teeth he said, "Don't ever embarrass me like that again in life," and hung up in her ear.

Azia slammed the phone down. She massaged her head trying to soothe the splitting headache that had just arrived. Her day couldn't get any worse. She would never deny loving Rashaud, but her love for Mike was on a whole different level. It was the kind of love that frightened her, the kind of love that she had heard of many times before but promised to avoid only to find out there's no running from it, when it hits you you're stuck. Mike was the only one she counted on to have her back no matter what, but at that moment she felt alone. Tired of playing the tough role she broke down, and didn't care who could hear.

Chapter 4

LIVING LIFE LIKE IT'S GOLDEN

...Atlanta, GA

Welcome Home Soldier was splashed across all the banners that hung from left to right across the massive amount of space Bilaal rented out for a dear friend's welcome-home party. After spending close to fifteen years in prison, Omar was finally a free man and he couldn't have been happier. He smiled and took a moment to stare around the recently renovated warehouse grateful of the outcome. Bilaal had really out done himself with the decorations and so many old friends had come out to celebrate the lost time. Waiters and waitresses swarmed the place serving wine and h'orderves while the DJ had the crowd locked on the dance floor grooving to his old school choice of tracks.

Bilaal approached Omar from behind. He gripped the wine glass from his hand and said, "What you sipping on soda?" He laughed. "Let me show you how us real grown men get down."

"I've waited almost fifteen years for a stiff one so c'mon and show me the way," chuckled Omar.

Both Omar and Bilaal headed over to the oversized bar where two females were tending to the partygoers. They were dressed identical in black spandex short-shorts and tuxedo tail jackets. Omar found it almost impossible to keep his eyes off of their bottoms.

Bilaal gripped two bottles of Patron and passed one to Omar. "Don't worry yourself. I got something real nice lined up for you," he assured him. Bilaal popped the top to his bottle and took a swig. "This is that smooth shit right here."

Omar raised his bottle, read the label and then took a swig, longer than Bilaal's, and slammed it down on the bar. "This is my kind of shit right here. Now all I need is a P.Y.T and I'm good."

"A pretty young thing huh?" laughed Bilaal. "I don't know about young but I definitely got something real special for you," he advised, patting him on the shoulder. "But before we get into all that, I got something else I need to show you."

The two headed out through the dense crowd. Omar's eyes roved up and down all the huge breasts and bare thighs that blanketed the place. He was more than ready to sink himself into something warm and welcoming. "C'mon man I'm growing a little impatient here after seeing all this ass jiggling around this joint."

Once they arrived out front, Bilaal turned and tossed a set of car keys to Omar all in one motion. "Just a little welcome home present," he grinned. "If you're anything like you use to be I know you don't deal with nothing but the best."

Omar examined the brand new burgundy custom made Escalade and smirked. "I was hoping for a Maybach but I guess this'll have to do," he teased.

"Whatever nigga, you'll be able to afford ya own Maybach soon enough but until then ya ass better settle on this for now."

Omar crossed around to the driver side examining the 26-inch chrome rims and low profile tires before climbing inside. He took in the new car scent as he studied the two-toned leather seats with the letter O embroidered in all the headrests. He rolled the window down, stuck his head out and shouted, "What you couldn't afford to get my whole name?"

Bilaal laughed and flagged him before turning to walk back inside the warehouse. Omar hopped out his new toy, hit the chirp to lock it up and followed behind Bilaal ready for the next surprise.

"So that's what the streets been missing," said an unfamiliar face.

Omar swooped the female's hand up to his lips and kissed it. The woman was fine and he was hoping she was the special someone Bilaal had mentioned earlier. "And you are?" he asked.

"Hoping you don't have anything planned after the party," she smiled.

Omar noticed Bilaal approaching the two of them and smiled. "Is this me big fellow?"

"Nope," said Bilaal, nudging him on by the shoulder. The woman scornfully watched him escort Omar into a private room. "After you Mr. Love Machine," said Bilaal, with his arm extended.

Omar slid pass Bilaal and gave him a slight bump. When he entered the office, he lost himself after setting his eyes on one of the most beautiful women he'd ever seen. She was heartwarming, breathtaking and mind-blowing all in one. He looked back at Bilaal, but said nothing.

"Now," Bilaal boasted, "This is you."

The woman ascended from the seat and glided across the room so smooth it looked like she was sliding across ice. Her long legs led the way. Omar could smell the scent of her Burberry perfume before she landed next to him. "Welcome home Omar," she smiled.

Never had Omar been at a loss for words over beauty before in life. He had been with plenty of women back in his day and although some would blame it on his time away from the outside world, that was hardly the case. The woman was a goddess. "Well now that I see you have my name established how about you sharing yours."

She extended her hand and said, "My name is Gisele, but you can call me whatever you want for the night."

Omar glanced over his shoulder at Bilaal who was still posted by the door with his arms folded. "So does this mean you're my other surprise?" he asked, redirecting his attention back to her.

Gisele smiled and stepped closer, close enough to kiss him if she chose to. "I can show you better than I can tell you," she winked, and led the way out.

Chapter 5

CASUALTIES OF STREET WAR

Kane tried his best to hold in his laugh, but he couldn't hold it in any longer. He was standing at Mike's parked car on the West side of the city where their main stash spot was located. The whole fight between Azia and Kyla was amusing to Kane, and he was glad Sasha wasn't the one who was cutting up for once.

"I swore Sasha was gonna be the one to whip her ass," he said, leaning into the window "My girl Azia gained ten points for this one."

Mike stared at his friend who was damn near rolling over in gut crunching laughter. Although he was still furious with Azia, he had to laugh himself. "You silly as shit man."

"I told you to leave that dumb ass girl alone before she got you in trouble. You were supposed to hit it and split. Ya simple ass wound up plating seeds and giving the bitch a job and shit."

"I don't even know if the kid is mine."

"I'm surprised Kyla aint running her mouth bout the whole baby thing."

"Because her ass aint sure if he's mine. She know as soon as she go running her mouth she aint getting shit else from me." A light bulb went off in Mike's head. "Hold the fuck up nigga cause you ran up in it too so he might be yours."

"Umm-Umm, nigga don't be tryna pin him on me." Kane took a moment to be serious. "On some real shit do you think he yours?"

"I don't know but my mom say he is. Kyla be taking him by the house to see her tryna get on her good side but if he aint mine that shit gonna break her heart."

"That's fucked up."

"Fuck it," said Mike, stepping out the car.
but wait on the results." He scanned the a
The block was dotted with cars, hustlers a
no threats, he headed for the three-story row 瑞...
Kane following close behind.

"What them niggas in there doing?" asked Mike, as they
made their way up five paved stairs.

"Tallying up," replied Kane. "I told 'em to hurry up and get
back out there on the block." Kane saw something unusual
in Mike's swag. "Stop sweatin' that shit my dude."

Mike ran his hands down his face. "Nah, I got some other
stuff on my mind."

"Something I can handle for you." Mike shook his head *no*.
"I need to holler at you bout one of them knuckleheads too.
I think it's time to cut him loose."

"Which one?"

"Deuce," he informed, before coming into audible range of
the men inside the house. "He don't listen and he be out
here doing his own thing."

"I'll holler at him," advised Mike. He then respectfully
greeted the three workers and headed upstairs to the third
level, alone.

Mike strolled down the narrow hallway to the back
bedroom. He punched in a six-digit security code outside
the thick wooden door to gain entry. Once inside, he
headed over to a hidden and very well secured wall safe
and punched in another code. The safe containing five kilos
of cocaine and fifty thousand in cash popped open almost
instantly. He snatched up a blue duffle bag from the closet
and stuffed it with three of the kilos and twenty thousand
dollars. After locking the safe and securing the room back,
he jogged back downstairs and tossed the bag over to Kane.

"Hit me when you in the clear," said Mike. Kane nodded
his approval and went on his way. Mike then focused in on
the other three guys. Two were sitting on a small floral sofa

...ng out money stacks while the third rubber banned ... stacks and separated them into zip-lock bags. "Everybody good?" he asked the young hustlers. The men nodded in unison trying not to mess up the count. "Call if ya'll need anything."

Mike was on his way to his car when he spotted Deuce, the guy Kane had concerns about. He zeroed in on him discreetly from a distance for nearly five minutes before approaching the corner he was posted on. Standing with Deuce was two other guys, Sammy and Lox, who were undeniably reliable and loyal when it came to Mike. All three men looked hammered, as if they'd been slinging rocks for days without a break.

"How the streets looking?" asked Mike, shaking all three of their hands.

"Everything's slow motion right now," said Lox. "But we killed 'em earlier today," he boasted.

"Alright, just make sure to keep your eyes open." Directing his attention to Deuce he said, "Let me holler at you for a minute." Deuce followed Mike back across the street to his car without hesitation. Leaning his back against the driver door Mike tucked his hands into his pockets and said, "We haven't had the chance to touch base in while. Wassup wit you?"

"I'm good," he shrugged. "Out here doing what I do."

"Anything you wanna talk to me about?"

"Nope!"

Mike nodded his head. "You got anything personal going on right now that's drying ya pockets out?"

His pride wouldn't allow the truth to be revealed. "Everything straight but what's all the hundred and one questions about?"

"I like to stay on top of what's going on in my circle. You got a problem with that?"

Deuce knew he had out stepped his boundaries. "Naw Mike, I aint mean no disrespect."

"Listen, if you having problems that don't pertain to me or my business that don't mean I won't help. But a closed mouth won't get fed, you got me?"

The two men knocked knuckles.

"I feel you," Deuce responded.

Mike opened his car door. "I'm glad you do." He climbed inside, started the engine and rolled the window down. "I heard you can be a hothead sometimes. Make sure you choose your battles wisely cause everybody aint gonna be as friendly as me," he informed.

Deuce presented a weak smile, which quickly faded after Mike pulled off. He watched with envious eyes until the red tail lights disappeared around the corner. He wanted to be the one pushing a Jag not slinging rocks on a corner. He believed in his heart that he was designed to be a Boss just as much as the next man and was willing to do whatever it took to get there.

Deuce took his spot back on the corner with his nose up in the air. Sammy and Lox were in the middle of a *Celtics* vs. *Lakers* debate.

"What was that about?" Sammy asked. "Everything good?"

Deuce grinned, looking like a skinny ass Craig Mac. "Look like I might not be on these corners wit ya'll niggas too much longer. I feel a promotion coming," he lied.

Sammy and Lox looked at one another and burst into laughter.

"Get the fuck outta here you lying ass nigga," teased Sammy. "Only thing ya ass gettin' promoted from is puberty."

Sammy and Lox laughed as their hands collided. They knew damn well he was far from being promoted after the information they had just passed on the Kane.

Deuce was burning up on the inside. He hated having to put up with their little boy jokes just because he was the youngest of the three. He produced a blunt from behind his ear, sparked it and took a puff to calm himself. "Ya'll niggas gonna stop disrespecting me alright," he whined, childishly. "I might be younger but I bet my dick bigger than both of you muthafuckas."

Sammy looked at him oddly. "If you don't get ya nut ass outta here."

Deuce looked at them both and clutched onto a handful of his pants between his thighs. "I can show you better than I can tell you," he said, unzipping his pants.

Lox stood quietly. He didn't like Deuce nor did he trust him and it was no secret that he wasn't one of his favorite people. He just dealt with him on the strength of Mike.

With every bit of six inches of pure nakedness plastered in his hand he instructed, "Matter fact from now on just call me mister big." He took another puff of his blunt and stuffed his sex symbol back into his fruit of the looms.

In a matter of seconds, Lox leaped pass Sammy with his gun out and kissed Deuce's testicles with the barrel of it. A dope fiend that was speedily approaching caught sight of the beef and made a quick u-turn back down the block like it was on fire.

"C'mon man ya'll runnin' the money away," cried Sammy. He tried sliding in between the two men but realized he was too close to Deuce's object for comfort. "Ya'll cut this shit out," he said, dusting his clothes off like they were out of place. "Ya'll blowing my high."

Deuce stood frozen as the fire from the blunt made a puddle of ashes on the ground.

Lox stare grew intense. "What you got to say now mister big?"

"C'mon Lox, stop fuckin' around before that shit go off," begged Sammy.

Lox could tell Deuce had stopped breathing. He enjoyed watching him squirm. Then out of nowhere, Lox broke his stare and started cracking up. "Ya nut ass can breathe now," he said, between breaths. "You probably shitted on yaself didn't you?" He grabbed for the back of Deuce's pants but he resisted.

Sammy shook his head in disbelief. He knew how his brother felt about Deuce and would never side against him, but if Mike found out, he was on the corner acting ruthless they'd all be in hot water.

Lox snatched the blunt out of Deuce's hand. "Puff puff pass my nigga."

Chapter 6

WHERE'S THE LOVE

···*Back in Atlanta*

Omar turned out of the sleeping position and spun upright to plant his feet on the floor. He ran his long thick fingers down his face and smiled when he turned to his left. Gisele was spread across the bed wearing nothing at all. Her beauty was stunning, her persona was breathtaking and her sex was therapeutic. But he knew nothing about her so he had no choice but to take it for what it was. Sex!

Omar stood up from the bed and went into the bathroom. After releasing his morning run, he went over to the washbowl and admired his well-sculptured body in the mirror. Lifting weights in prison had finally paid off and boy was he happy to be a free man, ecstatic. Spending nearly fifteen years inside put a damper on his parade. It brought all the money and power he'd worked long and hard for to an abrupt halt. Now that he was free man, it was time to get back into the swing of things. But first, his mission was to make things right between him and his daughter.

Omar washed his face, brushed his teeth and gargled before re-entering the presidential suite he'd grown to love. Just as he entered the bedroom and reached for the remote, Gisele rolled over after feeling the emptiness beside her.

"I would've loved to roll over to some company," she grumbled, with squinted eyes. She clutched on to another pillow and changed positions. "You know I have to fly to LA today or did you forget?"

Settling on a news channel, he sat the remote down and joined her on the bed. "How could I forget, I've been dreading the day. I was just starting to get use to you being around."

"Well I guess that means we need to make plans for me to fly back real soon."

Omar snickered. He'd only been home for a little while and hadn't had his share of playtime with the women yet, but he had a good feeling that she was a different kind of woman. "I can arrange that," he smiled. "Hopefully it's sooner rather than later."

Gisele didn't have to dignify his comment with a reply. Instead, she smiled. She could tell by the look in Omar's eyes that he was falling for her, and had she been there under different circumstances she may have actually given him a chance. But her guard was up because she was there for one reason only, and in due time she planned to show him exactly what that reason was.

Omar watched her crawl to him, seductively. "Are you sure you have to leave today?"

"I wish I didn't but you know how it goes, business first."

"What am I chopped liver?" he joked.

"As much as I love partying with you," she said, nibbling on the small of his back. "And I definitely love fucking you," she admitted, working her tongue up to the back of his neck. "I got some things I need to tend to, but I promise I won't stay away for too long."

Omar had no choice but to respect her decision. "How 'bout we do breakfast before you go?"

Gisele straddled him and positioned all ten inches of his thickness inside of her. "I was thinking more like," she whispered, winding her hips rhythmically. "Dessert."

■ ■ ■

After hours of Gisele sexing him in every part of the two thousand square-foot suite, Omar was officially pussy whipped. She had already showed him a dozen tricks, but evidently, she made sure to save the best for last.

"You need me to drop you off at the airport?"

"No, I have some loose ends to tie up before I fly out," she said, putting her earrings on. "But I'll make sure to call you before my plane takes off just to hear that sexy voice of yours one last time," she said, walking into the bathroom.

Damn she sure knows how to get a nigga open he thought, before the ringing of his cell phone gripped his attention. He grabbed it from the bed and screened the call. It was an anonymous call so he contemplated on answering, then against his better judgment he took the call. After hearing the voice on the other end, he was glad he did. "Talk to me."

"I heard somebody at this number was looking for some valuable information..." the hard, scratchy voice spoke on the other side of the line. "Would that somebody be you?"

"First off you need to make yaself known," Omar replied, coolly.

"The name's Shiz. I was referred to you by an acquaintance of yours, Misty, I'm sure you know who I'm talkin' 'bout."

"And?"

"I got some valuable information I'm sure you'd be interested in."

"And what would that be?"

"I'd rather not say over the phone. Call ya girl Misty check me out. If you're pleased with what she has to say, meet me outside of Club Crucial tomorrow night, 9 PM. I'll be in a black Audi."

Omar and Gisele locked eyes when she returned from out of the bathroom. The smile that she once possessed was gone.

"I'll see you then," Omar advised, and then ended the call.

Gisele was at the bed packing up the rest of her clothes when Omar approached her. He took the clothes from her hands, spun her around to face him and wrapped his arms around her waist.

"Where'd that pretty smile run off to?" he asked.

Gisele perked up those Angelina Jolie-like lips of hers and said, "You could at least wait until I get out the state to make plans." She tried her best to reassemble her smile, but it wasn't the same.

"You look so sexy when you pout."

"I guess you got a lot of catching up to do huh?" she questioned, fishing for information.

"You just focus on your schedule and find out when you can get back here to me," he said coolly, and then walked over to the mini-bar to pour a drink.

"Don't waste your time. I doubt very seriously if she's better than me."

"Who said it was a she?" he giggled.

Gisele didn't want to press the issue and make him suspicious, so she decided to change the subject. "I'm going to miss you while I'm gone," she flirted, positioning herself behind him.

Omar allowed her soft silk hands to roam down to his pelvic area. "Alright now, don't start something you can't finish."

"I never do," she hissed, turning her back to him and arching it so that her ass could tease his growing erection.

Omar slid the shirt from over her head and allowed the fingertips from one hand tease her flesh while the other fondled her breasts. He leaned forward and used his lips to trace a path from her shoulder and around to her collarbone, lightly nibbling on the areas in between.

Gisele twirled around and hopped up on the desk. With her legs spread wide, she pulled Omar in, unzipped his pants and yanked them to the floor. She then slid her hand into his boxers and pushed her tongue into his mouth.

"Keep it up and you gonna miss that flight," he warned, breaking free from the kiss.

"Just shut up and fuck me," she ordered, throwing her legs straight up in the air like a gymnast, and snatching off her shorts in one quick motion.

Nyema

Omar grabbed her down from the desk, spun her around and bent her over, doggy style. His hands led her hips to form an arch as his tongue ventured along the small of her back. Gripping her by the neck, he pulled her body back to his and sent his hands to roam mischievously across her stomach while his thumbs brushed her nipples. Working his way back down to her wetness, he stroked three fingers in and out of her slowly before bringing them up to her mouth so that she could lick them clean.

Placing soft kisses between her shoulder blades he whispered, "Let me hear you beg for it," then slid his fingers back inside of her, gently.

She relaxed into his embrace and gave herself over completely to his probing fingers. "Fuck me baby…" she whisked, positioning his rock at the entrance of her vagina.

Omar grabbed her ass cheeks and plunged his way inside of her so hard he elicited a "Yesssss…Fuck me harder you big dick mutha--" from her.

Gisele fiercely fucked him back while rotating her hips desperate for another orgasm. She covered his hands with her own, both massaging her breasts as he drove in and out of her tunnel, each moan becoming louder with every stroke. Feeling the desire to climax, she leaned forward over the desk and scratched at the wood while the sound of sweaty bodies smacking echoed in her ears.

Omar licked the sweat from her skin, relishing the salty taste of her flesh, never missing a beat. "Yeah," he growled. "Just like that." He was on the verge of exploding, and after feeling the muscles in her pussy contract, it sent him over the edge. "GODDAMN…" he huffed, feeling like his insides were being milked dry.

"Mmmm…" they exhaled in unison.

Omar slid out of her and fell back into one of the chairs with Gisele falling down on top of him. She could feel his chest rising and falling rapidly against her side as her muscles continued to twitch.

"That was just a little something extra to remember me by."

Omar let his head fall back on the chair and replied, "Woman, maybe it would be best for you to keep ya ass in Florida. I'm scared of you."

She kissed him on the forehead and replied, "You definitely should be!"

Chapter 7

UNSOLVED CHEMISTRY

It had been weeks before Azia finally came to terms with the possibility of being pregnant and finally made it around to scheduling a doctor's appointment.

Although she and Mike were still beefing behind the fight, she still gave him the option to accompany her to the appointment, or not. She knew he would be angry for a couple days because she chose to fight the girl in front of customers, but damn, he'd been holding the grudge for way too long. She had to actually talk herself into believing, more than once, that the reason he was so upset had nothing to do with him catching feelings for Kyla. *Nah, he aint loving that hoe* she told herself.

After setting things up with the nurse down at the clinic, Azia decided to take a long hot bubble bath before meeting up with Sasha at *KoKa's Bar & Grill*. She spread out in the Jacuzzi with only her head above water and allowed her body to succumb to the jets varying pressures trying hard to relax her mind. There was way too much stress weighing on her brain and being pregnant was one of them. There was nothing more she'd rather have in the world than the opportunity to birth Mike's child, but she wasn't too sure if he felt the same way.

■■■

Two hours later, Azia was dressed and heading out the door. When she stepped off the elevator and into the garage, she couldn't help but scan the perimeter while heading to her car. Paying close attention to her surroundings had become more of an obsession than a necessity. As soon as she brought the engine to life, the gas light came on. "Dammitt," she barked.

Chancing on making it to the city to get gas because it was a lot cheaper, Azia exited off *95* and crept towards Spring Garden with her fingers crossed. Thankfully, the gas station was just a few blocks away. *Thank you Lord* she exhaled pulling into the Sunoco. After slipping on her oversized designer shades, she grabbed her pocketbook from the passenger seat and hopped out of the car.

A dozen eyes followed as she switched into the convenient store, but this was not surprising to her. Azia was the property of a *Boss* and she flaunted his money well. Ignoring the stares and perverted comments from a few dirty old men, she strutted into the store and headed for the candy isle. Chocolate and bubble gum had become a craving and she was up for eating anything that would keep that nasty taste out of her mouth.

Because she was looking down, Azia never noticed the guy that had seemingly snuck up behind her. But when she turned and bumped into him, she was ninety-nine percent sure that their collision was no accident.

"You stalking me now?" she smirked.

"I never been labeled as a stalker before," Quadir smiled, angelic.

She stared into his dark piercing eyes and melted at his enchanting personality. "You should keep it that way."

He followed her over to the cashier's booth. "I didn't get a chance to ask when I saw you in the store but what's your name?"

"Taken!" she frowned.

"Damn, it's like that," he said, grabbing her hand as she dashed for the exit. "This is our second meeting and you still aint catch mine."

"On purpose," she winked, and continued on to her car.

Nyema

Azia didn't know who he was or where he came from, but what he did have was a lot of balls for pressing up on her like that.

Again, he followed behind her, over to her pump. "Can I take care of that for you?"

"Listen because the last thing I wanna do is waste your time or mine. I'm spoken for, I never stepped out on my man nor do I plan to, so please go try ya luck on the next chick."

She stood tall and confident as he inched towards her and whispered in her ear, "Do I make you that uncomfortable?" He took a step back and looked into her eyes. "Or is that you're afraid I may be the one to make you slip?"

Holding her ground and without hesitation Azia replied, "I refuse to even dignify that with a response." After screwing her gas cap back on, she slid her sunglasses from the top of her head back onto her face and pushed him out of her way. "Better luck next time."

■■■

Azia walked into KoKa's and greeted the hostess, which was also Mike's Aunt Val, with a hug then followed her through the large front bar down to the main dining area where Sasha awaited in a corner booth. Aunt Val and KoKa looked so much alike. The only difference was Val had a lot more to love around the hip and thigh area. And she loved Azia for Mike because the girl reminded her so much of herself about twenty years back.

Azia got excited when she saw Sasha sitting there sipping her cocktail. Even though the girls made an effort to talk at least once a day, it had been weeks since they last time seen one another.

"Girl you don't waste no time do you?" smiled Azia.

"You already know I can't come in here without having Missy hook me up one of her famous concoctions." Sasha pushed her drink aside. "Look at you glowing."

"Shut the hell up. I know damn well aint nothing glowing about me the way I feel."

Sasha studied her friend for a moment longer. "I don't care what you say. I'm reading something right now and it aint got nothing to do with morning sickness."

Azia laughed it off and poured herself a glass of water from the pitcher on the table. It was true. Her insides had been tingling ever since she left the gas station. "Anyway," she started, before taking a gulp of the water. "I finally scheduled a prenatal appointment."

"Bout time, I can't believe you waited so long. Is Mike going with you?"

"I don't know what he's gonna do, we aint the best of friends right now."

"I know he aint still mad about you whipping that bitch ass," she said, with her nose turned up.

Azia opened her menu and scanned through it like she hadn't seen it many times before. With her eyes glued on the lunch specials she responded, "I don't know what the hell his problem is."

"Chil' he'll get over it. Him and Kane need to cut that shit out. I don't understand--"

Sasha replaced her criticism with a smile when she noticed KoKa approaching the table. "Ms. KoKa, look at you looking marvelous as usual," said Sasha, sarcastically. "I wanna be just like you when I grow up."

KoKa slid in the booth beside Azia. "Quit sucking up you lil hussy," she grinned. "Why didn't you tell me you were coming down today?" she asked, swapping a quick hug with her daughter-in-law.

"I didn't plan on it."

KoKa picked up Sasha's cocktail from the table. She looked over at Azia and said, "This aint yours is it?"

Azia felt it was safe to assume that Mike opened his mouth about the pregnancy. "You No KoKa, it aint mines."

Nyema

KoKa didn't hesitate to confirm the assumption. "You just make sure you take care of my grandbaby," she said, sliding out of the booth. "And I'ma tell you like I told my son. Ya'll planted the seed, deal with it."

"That's right," Sasha intervened. "Time for him to man up"

"Don't make me tear your lil ass up about my baby," warned KoKa. "Don't nobody talk shit about him but me."

The last thing Azia heard was *grandbaby* before she drifted off in a daze. Someone else weighed heavily on her mind and she couldn't stop thinking about him. Was it the sweet scent of his cologne, the way he squinted his eyes when he smiled at her, his sexy deep voice or just his all around swagger? She didn't know the answer, but she knew the best thing to do was stay far away from...Damn she didn't even know his name. Maybe it was best that way. The less she knew the better.

"Azia," KoKa repeated for the third time. If KoKa was a mind reader she would've been a dead woman. "What the hell you in la-la land about?"

"I'm trying to fight this nauseous feeling I got," she lied, snapping out of her trance.

KoKa didn't quite believe it but gave her the benefit of the doubt. "I'm gonna send you over some ginger tea, it'll help."

"Alright," whimpered Azia. She clutched onto her stomach to help sale the lie. "Some soup too, please."

"And the salmon lunch special for me," added Sasha.

"You just make sure you got your money ready after you get finished eating your salmon special."

Once KoKa was out of hearing range, Sasha leaned across the table and said, "Ya mother-in-law is a piece of work how do you deal wit her?"

"When dealing with a woman like KoKa, you learn to just shut up and listen cause the more you talk, the longer the conversation will be," she said, rumbling through her purse in search of her phone. She scanned the caller ID but didn't recognize the number. "Hello."

There was silence on the other end of the line for seconds before the hard voice said, "I'm back!"

Azia recognized the voice right away. Every bone in her body tensed up and the back of her throat dried up. She couldn't respond if she wanted to.

Rashaud giggled. "Now that's the kind of response I was hoping for. I'll see you soon." And with that, he ended the call.

Azia put her phone away avoiding eye contact with Sasha. The last thing she wanted to do was alarm her knowing the first person she would run back and tell was Kane. She figured that as long as she ignored Rashaud's calls and kept her distance everything would be okay.

"Who was that?" Sasha asked.

"Somebody dialed the wrong number," she lied, twirling the straw in her drink.

■■■

Thirty minutes later, Azia and Sasha were in the middle of demolishing their lunch choices for the day. "Damn this salmon is on point!" exclaimed Sasha.

At that moment she just happened to glance up towards the entrance and caught KoKa escorting Kyla out the door. At first she thought nothing of it, but then she became curious. Was Kyla there trying to track Mike down or what?

"What the hell is she doing here?"

Azia shifted her body around to see whom Sasha was referring to, but there was no one there but a couple waitresses and the hostess. "Who are you talking about?"

"I just saw KoKa and Kyla walking out the front. I know she aint here tryna start no bullshit."

"I don't know but I'ma damn sure find out."

Both Sasha and Azia rushed through the restaurant to make it out before she was gone. But when they got out there,

Nyema

Azia wished she would've kept her ass inside. KoKa was in the parking lot holding a baby that looked to be around two years old. She had no idea the girls came out, but Kyla sure did. She looked at Azia with a look on her face as if to say, "Now what, bitch."

"You got to be fuckin' kidding me," blurted Sasha. "Don't go over there," she said, trying to pull Azia back. "Azia," she repeated.

Against the advice of her friend, Azia approached them. She looked KoKa dead in the eye and asked straight up, "Is this Mike's baby."

KoKa was so upset with herself. She had no idea they had seen Kyla enter the restaurant because she rushed her back out the door as soon as she arrived. *Mike is gonna kill me* she thought, shaking her head. "Azia just go back inside and I'll be in there in a minute."

"Just tell me if it's his." She turned to Kyla. "This Mike baby?" she pointed.

Kyla sucked her teeth and rolled her eyes. "Hmm…" She knew better than to answer that question, but she was cool with that because it felt damn good watching Azia go through the motions. She took the baby boy out of KoKa's hands and secured him in his car seat. "I'll talk to you later Ms. KoKa."

If it were ever possible to transform from a cub to lion in the blink of an eye, Azia had coined the phrase that hot summer day. She leaped pass KoKa so quick you would have thought she was a bolt of lightning. "You fucking bitch--"

Kyla never seen what was coming to her before her face was slammed against the hood of the car, and then against the rim of the tire and almost through the window.

Sasha loved nothing more than to see Kyla get her butt whipped but she couldn't sit back and watch Azia do something that would result in a record for the rest of her life. She and KoKa both had a tough time pulling them apart. It was like trying to separate a hawk from a pigeon.

"Get her off before she kills that girl," shouted KoKa.

With the help of a couple staff members, they were able to keep the girls apart. KoKa snatched the baby from out of the car seat trying to stop him from screaming at the top of his lungs while Sasha tried to talk Azia back into the restaurant before someone called the cops.

"Yeah, bitch, what you thought it was going to be a repeat of the last time," shouted Kyla. "Go check that lump out and then come holler at me."

Azia might've been a little scratched up but she knew damn well she didn't have no lumps because the chick didn't hit hard enough. Sasha finally got through to her and led her back into the restaurant.

"Take your baby home Kyla," KoKa demanded. "We'll straighten all this mess out later."

"Aint nothing to straighten out," she said, storming around to the driver's side. "Her ass is going to jail for attacking me."

KoKa pulled her cell phone from her pocket and dialed Mike. "Calm down aint nobody going to jail."

"You watch and see," she screamed out the window, then sped off.

Chapter 8

Fifteen Years-n-Counting

···Back in Atlanta

| |

You sure you don't know what I'm talking about?" asked Omar. "Because my man here assures me that you know exactly what I'm talking about. You callin' him a liar?"

"Look," the man spat, hanging by his neck from the ceiling post in his unfinished basement. His hands and feet were tied with duck tape, and blood was leaking from an open wound on the side of his head, compliments of Omar. "I don't know who the fuck you are or what the fuck he talkin' 'bout. You got the wrong mutherfucka."

"Is that right?"

After Omar received the call from Shiz a couple weeks back, he headed straight over to Misty to get some answers. He and Misty had been friends for over thirty-five years, and he knew that even after all the years he'd been gone, she was someone he could trust. She was the first woman he ever truly cared for before Michelle, Azia's mother, came along. The only reason their relationship didn't survive was because, at that time in his life he loved the streets more than he loved her.

Misty clarified who Shiz was and vouched for him and the information he was willing to provide. After Omar heard that Shiz knew something about the men that set him up, he was itching to hear what he had to say and didn't want to wait until the following night so he called him back and the two men agreed to meet the next morning instead.

Omar sat attentively on the other side of the booth inside of a local restaurant listening to Shiz inform him of the whereabouts of one of the men that was responsible for the death of his wife. Had it not been for Misty, he would've been suspicious. But something inside of him wanted to believe Shiz. Maybe it was desperation. He promised himself a long time ago that he would find whoever was responsible and make them pay for the life they had stolen from him, and now the time was near.

"This mutherfucka's lyin'," blurted Shiz. "He was there."

"Fuck you," the man yelled, sending a mouth full of hawk spit his way.

Shiz took the two-by-four posted against the cracked cemented wall and flung it at the man's knee caps like they were baseballs.

"AHHH…" the man screamed out in agony.

"Tell 'em the fuckin' truth," ordered Shiz, positioning the lumber to swing it again. "Tell 'em right now or I'ma make sure the next swing dislocate a bone."

The man declined to answer. He took the blood that had oozed down his face and accumulated in his mouth and spit it out on the ground.

Just as Shiz attempted to swing the two-by-four again, Omar used one hand to stop it mid swing. He knew trying to beat the information out of the man could take hours. He didn't have hours to waste so he went in for the kill.

Omar gave Shiz a head nod and said, "Bring her down." He then took the two-by-four and started to twirl it with sarcasm. "I know how to make 'em talk."

The man's eyes followed Shiz's movements up the stairs, curiously. When he disappeared, he redirected his attention to Omar with a puzzled look.

Omar strolled across the floor to a small black crate and cocked his foot on top of it. He took that time to examine the basement thoroughly for the first time. "I see a lot of potential here in this basement," he said, sarcastically. "Too bad you won't be around long enough to make it happen."

"Brother, I'm tryna tell you, I don't know who you are. He don't know what he talkin' 'bout--"

Nyema

"Save ya breath…You're gonna need it in a minute."

Shiz struggled his way back down the steps, but he wasn't alone. He had a thirty-something year old woman wrapped in his arms with her mouth and hands duck taped. Her eyes were swelled from crying and her face was drenched with tears. She locked eyes with her fiancé and began to cry harder.

"She aint got shit to do wit this," he barked. "Let her go mutherfucka."

"It's funny that you say that," replied Omar. He took his foot off the crate and slow walked back over to where the man was hanging. "I remember saying the same thing when I was in your situation. But ya'll mutherfuckas aint care. Ya'll were sent to do a job and that's all that mattered, right?" He gripped the two-by-four as tight as he could and said, "All I want to know is who sent you."

"I told you I don't know---"

WHAM…Omar sent the two-by-four smashing into the woman's chest. She dropped to her knees, all the wind was knocked out of her. Tears formed almost instantly in the man's eyes, and at that point Omar knew he'd found his weakness.

"Beautiful woman you got here my man," said Omar, watching Shiz pull the woman's limp body up from the floor.

"You aint got--to-do-this," the man whined, all choked up. "Please Omar," he cried.

Omar walked up to the man and guided his head up with the two-by-four so that their eyes could meet. "You know it's funny that you called me by my name," he said, softly. "Since you claim you don't know who I am."

Shiz snatched the woman by her hair and said, "I told you he was lyin'. Now you gonna pay you rotten mutherfucka."

"Who sent you to kill me and my family?" growled Omar.

"It wasn't supposed to go down like that," he admitted. "She wasn't supposed to be there."

"That's not what I asked you."

The man fell silent so Omar took the two-by-four and sent it crashing upward between his legs. Again, the man screamed out in agony from the chilling pain that shot from between his legs all way up into his chest. His testicles felt like they were on fire.

"I will torture the shit out of both of ya'll if you keep playin' wit me," Omar advised. "Who the fuck sent you?"

"C'mon man--"

"You know what," said Omar, retrieving his pistol from the back of his pants. He aimed it at the woman's head. "You think I'm a fuckin' joke?"

"Alright...Alright..." he whimpered. "I'll tell you just take the gun away from her head." He watched Omar lower his weapon to his side and started shaking his head with shame. He never dreamt the day would come that he'd be labeled a snitch. "Bilaal was the one that sent us. He wanted you out of his way so he could take over--"

In one swift motion Omar stuck the barrel of his gun damn near down the man's throat. "You fuckin' wit me," he snarled. "Nigga, you better not be fuckin' wit me."

Whatever the man said next was inaudible because of the gun that was stuffed in his mouth, but as soon as Omar removed it he was ready to spill the beans.

"He paid us, fifteen hundred a piece, to come lay you down and collect whatever money and drugs you had at the spot. It was supposed to be a clean sweep, but when ya woman popped up from out of nowhere it complicated things."

"Fuck you mean it complicated things. Ya'll aint have to kill her," he shouted, digging the gun into the man's skull. "You better find a better way to convince me that Bilaal was behind it or I'ma make you watch me paint you wit her brains."

"I swear I aint lying. It's the truth!" he exclaimed. "He told us that ya wife left for a couple days so that was the best time to get at you while you were alone. Ya'll had a big argument, something like that. She went to her mom's right? Think about it. How would I know all that?"

Briefly, Omar thought back to that night and remembered everything like it was yesterday. He was hemmed up by two of the assailants while the other interrogated him, at gun point, about where the money and drugs were hidden when Michelle walked in and interrupted. When the triggerman took the gun off him to shoot at her that gave Omar the opportunity to free himself and draw his own gun, which in turn brought down only one of the assailants before the other two got away. But the man was absolutely right; Michelle wasn't supposed to be there. Omar recalled the conversation he had with Bilaal that same day advising that he and Michelle had a fight about another woman, and that she was going to stay with her mother for a few days. So he couldn't help but to think *could this mutherfucka be tellin' me the truth?*

"Bilaal was mad about her getting caught up in it. He asked which one of us was responsible for doing it and when Kev told him he did it, he put three bullets in his head."

Omar's adrenaline began to pump. "You think that shit supposed to make me feel better? Huh, mutherfucka?" He rushed over to Shiz, yanked the woman from his possession, and dragged positioned her face-to-face with the man, less than two inches away. He started desperately trying to wiggle his way free knowing what would come next. "Now just because he let you live, another mutherfucka got to die."

"Don't do it man...Please don't do--"

Omar could feel the woman trembling in his hands. Her heart was beating so hard he could feel the quickness of it pulsate. The scent of her sent a chilling sensation through his soul. He was no monster, but the man that was strung up in front of him had a price to pay so her blood was on his hands.

Omar thought about Michelle one last time, and the smile she used to possess. And then, *POW*...The bullet shot through the side of the woman's face, traveled downward, and exited out of the side of her chin. She was dead before her mind could process the thought of her actually being shot.

"You mutherfucka..." the man yelled out, face covered with the blood of the woman he planned to make his wife. "You mutherfuckers..." He quit trying to break free, his body felt numb. "You aint have to do 'er like that," he screeched.

"And you aint have to do mine like that either you coward," advised Omar, and then he sent two bullets through the man's dome; one in the eye and the other through his forehead. With his gun still raised, he pointed it at Shiz. "Should I be worried about somebody finding out what went down here tonight?"

Shiz raised both hands in the air and replied, "If you didn't have any faith in Misty, you wouldn't be here right now. If you don't want any witnesses, then kill me. But just to let you know, we both here for personal reasons and have our own agendas for wanting to see Bilaal go down."

"You saying it like you already knew who was responsible."

"I did!" he exclaimed. "But would you have just taken my word for it? Hearing it from the source made it a lil' more convincing don't you think?"

"So you say ya reason is personal, how personal is it?"

"Bilaal's the reason my mom and pop aint here no more, and it's up to me to make sure they get the justice they deserve."

"Sound like we headed for a war youngin'," said Omar, lowering his weapon. "You ready for that?"

With every bit of determination in his eyes he replied, "Ready as I'm gonna be."

Chapter 9

ANOTHER SOMETHING IN THE WAY

...Meet Quadir

I I

It was a hell of a crowd posted up outside of the pool hall on Oregon Ave. When one car pulled off another pulled up almost instantly, but it was much worse on the inside, nearly packed with groups of men high off testosterone and half-naked women scavenging the place like blood suckers. All twelve pool tables were in motion, beer bottles were flowing like frequent flyers and everyone was betting big.

"What it do home team," said a white boy sitting at the front door as Quadir entered. He extended his hand for a shake.

Quadir looked at him curiously for seconds before addressing him. "Do I look like a friend of yours?" He smacked his hand out the way and continued on inside.

The boy leaned over and whispered to his friend, "Fuck he think he is--"

"Shut up fool you just played yourself," his friend responded.

Both guys stared at Quadir from behind as he made his way across the laminate flooring to where his crew had created their very own private section. He smacked hands with folks on the way until one in particular stopped him dead in his tracks. Her smile was vibrant but the set of double-D's protruding through the top of her tube-dress is what snatched his attention.

"You smiling like you know me," he stated.

"Maybe it's because I wanna get to know you," Kendra blushed.

He checked her out for a minute longer. She wasn't a ten but she'd do for the night. He grabbed her hand and led the way over to his bunch.

As soon as the two of them were close enough for Fritz to witness, he brought himself to an upright stance rather quickly, cue stick in hand. He was on the other side of the room but Quadir still managed to capture a glimpse of the man's rapid behavior. He nodded his head in that direction and asked Kendra, "Is that ya peoples over there?"

She looked Fritz square in the eye and said, "He's yesterday's news."

"Enough said." Quadir grabbed a couple bottles of beer from the bucket of ice and yelled over to his man Pooch, "I got next."

■■■

Two pool games and six beer bottles later, Quadir was in the men's bathroom with his pick of the night getting some wild, crazy head. His hands roved through Kendra's hair as she bobbed up and down on his shaft in the two-foot stall like it was going to be her last meal. But before she could finish completing the job she'd been sent down there to do, the stall door flew open and the feather weight was ripped from her knees by her hair and dragged out of the bathroom.

The interruption offended Quadir. He was livid for not getting the chance to get his shit off. By the time he got his pants up and made it pass the onlookers in the bathroom, Fritz had managed to drag her over to the section he and his clique claimed for the night.

"You's a scandalous ass hoe," he said, smacking her into one of his boys. "You aint embarrassin' me, you embarrassin' yaself."

This wasn't the first time he'd roughed his lady up out in public nor was this the first time she'd used another man to make him jealous. That was just the kind of games the two played. But what she didn't know was that the pawn she decided to use for the night was no gamer and ruthless was his middle name.

Pooch was bent over the pool table in the middle of a game when Wayne, one of his soldiers, hipped him to what had just gone down in the bathroom. Aiming for the *8* ball with one eye open and the other closed, he knew it was about to be total mayhem up in there. "Where he at?" he asked, forcing the stick into the cue ball which in turn popped the *8* ball in the corner pocket with ease.

"There he go right there," Wayne pointed.

Pooch stood upright and tossed the stick on the middle of the pool table and headed in the direction of the commotion. Just as Quadir went to lunge at Fritz, Pooch jumped in between the two men. "Hey," he intervened, "Now is that necessary?"

"I don't know who this nigga is Pooch but you need to let 'em know wassup," Fritz warned. "Cause I know damn well he don't wanna stir up no beef." He looked at Kendra and said, "Especially over this whore."

"Nah, we don't want no trouble." He looked over his shoulder at Quadir. "Do we?"

As bad as Quadir wanted to rip the man apart he knew it would cause too much street heat and that would only slow up what his real angle was, so dealing with Fritz would have to get pushed to the back burner, for now. "Nah, we cool," he said, twisting his upper lip. "But you could'a let a nigga buss a nut before dragging the bitch away." He made his way through his army of men back over to his pool table, snatched up the cue chalk and applied it to the stick thinking *a bunch of fuckin' faggots.*

■■■

On the other side of town, Mike and Azia were in the middle of a heated debate. After KoKa texted him *911* advising that he get to the restaurant *ASAP,* he stop what he was doing and damn near ran every light to get there knowing that whatever it was, it had to be serious.

"If you keep attacking that girl like that she aint gonna keep letting me talk her out of pressing charges on you Azia," barked Mike, all up in her face.

"Fuck that hoe," she hollered.

"You need to sit ya ass down somewhere and chill the fuck out. That shit between me and her happened before we got serious," he reminded her, in a more tender voice.

Disregarding all the curious eyes that were zoomed in on them from the kitchen staff, Azia stood frozen in place drowning in tears. So what it happened before her, he kept it a secret for way too long. "You should'a been told me Mike. Had you been honest none of this shit would've happened so if you wanna blame somebody blame yourself."

KoKa felt like crap after seeing Azia that torn apart. Had she been able to meet Kyla at the door one minute sooner, things could have turned out a whole lot different. "Ya'll need to keep it down in here." She unclipped a set of keys from her waist. "Matter fact go talk in the office, aint no need for everybody to be up in ya'll business they done seen enough already."

"I'm done talking," said Azia. She went to walk away but Mike yanked her back towards him. She looked him coldly in the eye and repeated, "I said I'm done talking."

Mike let her go, but of course KoKa had to try her hand. She was partly to blame with the way things went down. "I think instead of running away from this now is the time to sit and talk about it Azia."

Azia stopped, turned and said, "I don't recall me asking for your opinion." She rolled her eyes and stormed through the double doors leading into the dining area and out of the restaurant.

Shocked, KoKa looked at Mike with her hands on her hips. "Oh no—who the hell--" She could barely get the words out. "That little winch better be happy I feel sorry for her ass."

Mike looked at his mother and shook his head. How could she let this happen? "I can't believe you let this go down."

"Oh now it's my fault," she said, offended. "Ya ass should've been told that girl instead of tryna be all sneaky like ya fuckin' father." After the words left KoKa's mouth she wished she could send them in reverse back down her throat. "I didn't mean--"

Mike threw up his hand and kissed his mother on the cheek. "It's cool Ma. I holler at you later."

KoKa stood there frozen in place knowing that for the first time in his life she had actually made her son feel like the shit bag his daddy was. She cursed herself for doing it and promised that she would do whatever it took to make it up to him.

■■■

Quadir smacked hands with his boys outside of the pool hall before making his way back to his car. He climbed into the 06' Pontiac Grand Prix, and pulled his cell phone from his hip. He punched in a number and let his head fall back on the head rest. "What up?" he spoke, into the receiver.

"You tell me," Bilaal's heavy voice replied.

"I heard you wanted to holler at me."

"Wanted to touch base," said Bilaal. "Everything cool up there."

Quadir wasn't surprised that word had got back to him about the incident in the pool hall. That was Pooch's job. He was Bilaal's eyes and ears in Philly. "You know how it can get up here at times but don't worry, I'm focused."

"I hope so," exclaimed Bilaal. "The plan was for you to stay under the radar, remember that and just know that by the time this is all over you will get the revenge you been itching for."

"I aint gonna have it no other way."

Although Quadir didn't have everything in place, he knew it was a matter of time before he'd have Azia up under his wing. Bringing down her man was his mission, but taking her from him was going to be icing on the cake.

When he was just ten-years-old, the only man he'd ever grown to love was robbed of his life way before his time. He and his father did everything together. He kept him laced in all the latest fashions, taught him to ride his first bike and shoot his first gun. Although his father had another family to deal with, he never neglected the fact that Quadir and his mother remained a priority. It took him a long time to get over his father's death. He struggled through elementary school, quit in his third year of high school and gave his mother nothing but hell the whole ride through. Quadir was straight up hood, loose cannon. He trusted no one, answered to no one, said what he wanted to say and did what he wanted to do. As soon as he was of age, he left his mother's house and never looked back. He felt that she was to blame for allowing his father to choose to stay with his other family instead of them. Had she put her foot down maybe he'd still be alive.

From New Jersey to New York, Philly to Baltimore, Virginia to Atlanta, living on the go had become a part of who he was. Wherever there was money to be made he was there to make it, which placed him in the company of Bilaal. According to them both, it must have been fate.

After finding out that they shared some of the same friends and were in the same circle, it turned out that they both were after one thing, but for totally different reasons. Mike!

With him out the picture, Bilaal was sure he'd be able to take over Philly as well as the tri-state area. At that moment, Mike was the only thing standing in his way. But for Quadir, it wasn't about the money. His beef with him was more than a power stricken temper tantrum. It was about devotion. Loyalty! And he was willing to do whatever he had to do to avenge the death of the only man he was ever able and willing to call *Dad*.

Quadir ended the call and brought his engine to life while laughing to himself. Bilaal could think he was in control of the situation all he wanted to, but Quadir was past the point of reasoning. He glanced down at his watch. It was just after one o'clock in the morning, still early to him. In no rush to call it a night he rolled, licked and sparked a blunt. Catching the back view of two cuties that just walked by, he rolled his window down. "Wassup shawdy?" he said, blowing smoke. Distracted, the girls stopped and looked back at him. "What ya'll gettin' into?"

One of the women sucked her teeth. "Girl c'mon," she urged, tugging at her friend.

"Hell naw," her girlfriend squeaked, freeing herself from the grip. "I peeped that nigga in the pool hall." She walked over to his car. Her girlfriend followed. "I hope you calling us over to share," she smiled, sniffing the aroma of what smelled like some good ganja.

"That depends."

"On what?"

"What I'm gettin' in return."

"See, he got to be crazy if he think his lame ass gettin' some ass for some fuckin' weed," the girl spat, pulling her friend away from the ignorance.

Quadir laughed. He heaved on the end of his blunt and dropped his head back on the headrest until something extremely fascinating caught his eye. It was Fritz and Kendra stepping out of the pool hall hand-in-hand. He didn't know what kind of sick twisted relationship they had going on, but she left a job undone and he wasn't having it. After watching the couple climb into a maroon Dodge Magnum and pull into traffic, he pulled off behind them.

Staying at least two cars behind, Quadir followed them to a little block less than fifteen minutes away from the pool hall. Quadir pulled to the side of the curb on the corner and watched the two argue and scuffle their way into one of the row homes. Ten minutes later, Quadir had finished his blunt and was on his way down the block to finish what was started. Before hitting the step, he could hear loud bickering coming from inside the house. He used his finger to cover the peep hole and knocked on the door.

"Who is it," Kendra shouted.

"It's police," he said, disguising his voice.

"Who?" She swung the door open with her hand on her hip. "What you think you doing here?" she asked, looking Quadir square in the eyes.

He produced a gun from behind his back and placed the barrel up to his lips. "Shhh…"

Kendra attempted to dive back inside the home, but Quadir grabbed a handful of her hair and blanketed her mouth. "Scream and I'ma shoot you." He jammed the gun into her back and used his foot to close the door.

"Who da fuck at the door?" Fritz yelled, from the living room. He was on the sofa catching up on the NBA highlights when they entered the room. "What da fuck?" he said, diving for his gun but Quadir was too quick.

He flung Kendra into Fritz to distract him and leaped over the small glass coffee table towards the weapon. "Back the fuck up," he growled, aiming both guns at them. "Sit the fuck down and relax. This won't take long."

"What the fuck you want?" barked Fritz.

"According to you what I don't want is beef," he smirked. "Right my nigga?" Fritz went to get up. Quadir shook his head. "Nah," he said, cocking the hammer on his .357. "I don't think that's a good idea."

Tears had already begun to water Kendra's eyes. "I'm sorry," she cried.

"You aint got nothing to be sorry for boo cause you was doing a hell of a job," he giggled. "This nigga's the one that interrupted." He dropped one of the guns down to his side. "Matter fact, c'mere." Kendra hesitated. "C'mon, I aint gonna hurt you," he lied.

She walked over to him, shaking tremendously.

"You want the hoe you can have her--"

"Shut the fuck up," Quadir said, aiming the gun in Fritz face. Without taking his eyes off of him he said to Kendra, "Get on ya knees and finish what you started." Her tiny five-foot-one frame looked up at him with shameful eyes. "Don't make me repeat myself."

Fritz turned his head away from the horrific sight of Kendra performing oral sex on another man.

"Nah brother, I need you to witness every bit of this," he said, looking back and forth between him and Kendra. She had positioned herself on the floor in front of him and took all of him into her mouth. "C'mon now you gonna have to do better than that," he advised, aiming the second pistol on top of her head. "Yeah, that's how you do it," he moaned.

Minutes later, Quadir tried his best to refrain from totally succumbing to the sexual pleasure that he was receiving, but Kendra worked her tongue like magic. Just as he was about to cum, Quadir briefly let his head fall back and his trigger finger clinched. The gun went off sending a bullet straight through the top of Kendra's skull. It happened so fast both Quadir and Fritz jumped.

"What the fuck--" Fritz shouted in disbelief. He stared at the blood leaking from Kendra's lifeless body that stretched across the floor.

"Aww shit," Quadir said, trying to get himself together after that explosive orgasm. "Damn dogg," he grinned. "That was my bad."

Fritz knew he was in a no win situation so he tried his luck. He jumped to his feet, leaped over the table and charged at him.

Quadir pulled the trigger, but unfortunately for him the gun jammed and his right eye met Fritz's fist. He staggered back, but managed to stay on his feet. Just as Fritz went to dive back in two bullets connected with his chest in mid air stopping him dead in his tracks. The heavyweight fell backward onto the coffee table sending both, him and it, crashing to the floor.

Chapter 10

LOST IN THE NIGHT AIR

It had been a couple days since the incident at KoKa's and Azia still couldn't manage to control her emotions. She was sitting in the middle of a full-size bed in Sasha's guestroom crying hysterically. Sasha sat beside her and wrapped her arms firmly around her friend. She didn't know what she could possibly say that could help take some of the pain away so instead of saying anything she just gripped her tighter. She was just glad that Azia had no idea that she'd known the truth long before things hit the roof. But it wasn't her place to tell and if she had decided to, Kane would've put his foot in her ass for doing so.

"I was able to handle the fact that he may have had a son out there somewhere," Azia sniffled. "But for him to let that girl smile all up in my face and the way she was disrespecting me behind my back." She cried harder. "That's the part that hurt so bad. Why didn't he just tell me?"

"I'm sure he had his reasons hunny, they always do." Sasha handed over some *Kleenex* and stood up from the bed. "There's some clean washcloths and towels in the closet. Go take you a nice hot shower and try to relax ya mind girlfriend." Azia took the box of tissues and grabbed a few. "You can stay here as long as you need to, okay?" Sasha gave her one last hug and headed out the room, closing the door behind her.

Kane was standing outside their bedroom impatiently waiting on her to finish playing mother love. With his arms spread out to the side of him he asked, "What the fuck Sash--"

Nyema

Sasha threw up a finger to her lips. "Shhh…" She pushed him in the bedroom and closed the door. "What the hell you standing there wit the mean face on for? She needs somewhere to stay," she whispered.

"It aint had to be here."

"I aint sending that girl to no hotel by herself."

"You always tryna play captain save-a-hoe. I told you bout getting in the middle of that bullshit between her and Mike. Her ass know damn well she aint leaving him so she might as well go home."

Sasha threw a pillow at him. "Shut up Kane. Aint nobody say she was leaving him. Damn!" she said, stripping down to her underwear. "And what the hell you yelling at me for what done crawled up your ass?" She switched across the room and stood in front of him to block his view of the television.

Kane paid no attention to her or the low cut boy shorts that laid perfectly between the crack of her cheeks. "Move out the way."

"Make me," she said, snatching the remote. "You really gonna sit here and act like you mad cause she here. Naw nigga," she pointed in his face, "You mad at ya baby mom and tryna take that shit out on me but I aint having it." He didn't respond. "Yeah, I know I'm right. Your ass thought I aint know you was over there earlier today. Ya daughter was in school nicca so what the fuck was you there for?"

Kane jumped up from the bed and slid a shirt over his head. "I don't feel like dealin' wit ya shit right now Sasha--"

Her red-boned frame stood tall with long auburn colored hair running down the small of her back to match the all around beauty. She placed both hands on those brick-house-hips of hers and watched him lace up his boots. "You aint got no damn choice but to deal wit it--"

Kane gripped her off of her feet and pinned her to the wall, but she wasn't afraid. She loved the attention and how dangerous and twisted their relationship could be. Sasha was gangster, and he knew it.

"What I tell you 'bout talkin' to me like you the man of the house?"

"If you wanna be wit the weak ass bitch go on and be wit her then."

Kane released his grip and allowed her feet to hit the floor. "You better be lucky I aint got the strength to fuck ya red ass up right now." He pushed her aside and went to walk out of the room.

Sasha leaped between him and the bedroom door like a human grasshopper. "Ya ass aint leavin' up outta here."

He wrapped his strong hands around her neck and with a sexual overtone he whispered, "What you want? Huh? Some attention?!?" He caressed from her thigh up to her breasts.

The smoothness of his voice sent a chill through her clit. The more his fingers twirled across her soft skin, the more electrifying her hormones became. "Get off me," she whimpered.

"You know you don't want that." He whipped up one of her breast and sucked it ever so gently, and then brought the other up to meet his tongue and give it the same attention.

Sasha let her head fall back surrendering to his passion. "OHHH…" she gasped.

Kane released his tongue from her flesh and grabbed her gently by the hair. "This is what you wanted right?" he teased, nibbling on every one of her hot spots.

Kane was a monster when it came to the streets, probably the most vicious individual Mike had on his team. But when it came to Sasha, she had the kind of effect on him that would make a grown man cry. The two were made for each other, lovers and best friends, ruthless and down for whatever. Needless to say, whenever he needed her to ride she was there. If it meant risking her own life or freedom, then so be it. It was her loyalty and will to love him and him only that had him open. She was his everything and had proven on several different occasions that it was them against the world.

Using the door and the back of his neck as leverage, she wrapped her legs around his waist. "Baby, please don't make me beg," she squirmed. Her panties were so wet you could wring them. She rocked her hips in motion with the two fingers he held deep inside of her and flinched with every bite he sank into her skin. Minutes later, her body was convulsing like it was hit with electricity from a stun gun. "Ughhh…Kane I love you so much," she panted.

Still in the standing position, their tongues intertwined as they walked as one over to the bed. He released her, spread her legs apart and dove in, face first. Sasha arched her back and submitted to the pleasure of making love to his tongue. She had been with other men before, but from what she could remember, he was the best that ever did it.

"I wanna feel you inside of me," she chirmed. He ignored her plea and kept at it. "Please put it in, I'm bout to cum," she squirmed, twirling her hips with each lick.

"Umm…Umm…" he muttered, sucking her clit like it was a jolly rancher.

At that point it didn't even matter. She was ready to explode with or without him inside of her. *Damn I love this man* she thought as her pussy muscles began to contract. She grabbed his head with both hands and pinned his face into position. "I love you Kane," she cried out, reaching another orgasm within minutes.

■ ■ ■

The evening had just begun to dwindle down for some and was just getting started for others. Lox and Sammy made their way up the block towards the stash house counting the handful of money they'd just came up on at a neighborhood crap game. It was almost time for them to change shifts and Deuce was still nowhere to be found.

"Fuck that nigga Deuce at?" blurted Lox, sticking his winnings into his pocket.

"I aint heard from him today," replied Sammy.

As soon as the two men stepped foot inside the house and closed the door, the door was violently kicked back open, almost instantly. Knowing that if any of them reacted by reaching for their gun could cost them their lives, Sammy, Lox and the two other hustlers that were already inside counting money stood at attention with their hands in the air.

Three crooks entered rushed in wearing ski masks to hide their identities. One of the crooks, the tallest of the three, darted across the room aiming his gun while another crook, the shortest of the bunch, forced Sammy and Lox to the ground by shoving two pistols damn near down their throats. The third crook never said a word. He was the one who emptied the tables of all the money, cocaine, marijuana and any weapons they possessed into a trash bag.

"Which one of you muthafuckas wanna play hero?" asked the tallest crook. "I'm dying to buss a cap in somebody's ass tonight."

"Hurry the fuck up nigga," shouted the shortest crook, to the man that was filling the bag with both pistols still jammed in Sammy and Lox's mouths. "Time to bounce." He nodded his head at the tall crook ordering him to back his way up out of there. "If any of you dick suckas move I'ma blow these two niggas tonsils through the back of their fuckin' necks," he barked.

As the tall man crept his way out the door followed by the man with all the goods, the last crook used one of his pistols to knock Sammy out cold. He then kissed Lox's forehead with both pistols and looked over at the other two men.

"Get the fuck down and kiss the floor," he demanded. When the men were face down he mugged Lox with the pistols. "You too muthafucka." With all their faces glued to the floor, the gunman started to back his way out, pistols drawn. "Now I wanna hear ya'll sing Old MacDonald," he directed, before getting out the door.

Nyema

Lox cocked his head slightly to the side with his face twisted. Old MacDonald!?! Was he serious?

"You heard me," the crook barked as if he could read Lox's mind. "Get to singing before I blow ya face off," he growled. "Old MacDonald had a farm, EE-I-EE-I-O…" he sang.

Chapter 11

IF THESE WALLS COULD TALK

...Back in Atlanta

Omar met Bilaal over at his luxurious single-family estate located just outside of Buckhead in Atlanta. Bilaal showed him to a scarcely furnished room with nothing but two leather chairs, a small coffee table, widescreen television and mini-bar. Bilaal retrieved the remote control from the table and powered the television on before flopping down in one of the chairs.

"I take it your time with Gisele went well. I haven't heard from you in days."

Omar shrugged his shoulders and strolled across the room to the mini-bar to make them both a drink, two vodkas on the rocks. Then he took a seat in the other chair and propped his feet up on the coffee table.

"I guess you can say that."

"Watch out for her, she aint nothing to be played with. Your game might be a little rusty, it's a brand new world and the game has definitely changed."

"If she was too much trouble you would'na threw her my way," he said, taking a sip of his drink. "I hope!"

"Hey, if you still got it like you say you do I'm sure you can handle it," he advised, extending his drink for a toast. Omar let his feet hit the floor, leaned forward and the two men clinked glasses. Bilaal sat his drink down and began to rub his temple. "We haven't really had the chance to talk business since you got home. A lot has happened since the last time we spoke when you were behind bars."

A look of concern crossed Omar's face, but he was all ears.

Nyema

"Our man Mike is up North doing big things," Bilaal sighed. "Damn near got the whole city on lock, even our Italian friends."

Omar nodded his head, slowly. "That aint nothing that can't be changed."

"Don't do what I did and sleep on the nigga," warned Bilaal. "I knew he had a few people in his pocket, but I gave him less credit than I should have."

"What about the girl?"

"They're definitely an item." Bilaal smirked. "I don't know how in the world she got him to settle down. She must mean something to him."

Omar smiled. "Sound like to me we got us some leverage."

"You sure you wanna go that route?"

"What's the problem?"

Bilaal sighed heavily. "As bad as I wanted to get at her because of all the money she cost me behind that bullshit with Twin and Mustafa, I let it ride on the strength of you." Bilaal slid to the edge of his seat and looked Omar dead in the eye. "I mean, that is ya flesh and blood."

Omar slid to the edge of his seat to meet Bilaal's stare. "I waited a long time to get out and get back on top where I belong," he stated. He took back the last of his drink and slammed the glass on the table. "And I aint letting nothing or nobody get in the way of it."

Both men stared at one another intensely until Bilaal laughed trying to lighten the mood. "I just need to make sure we're on the same page regarding that before I touch base on other things." He was itching to get around to the real reason he'd asked Omar to come over. "But that's not the only reason I asked you over," he advised. "We never got a chance to talk about the night all that shit went down before the cops took you in."

Every muscle in Omar's body tensed up. Had Bilaal been able to see through all that toughness he would have sensed the pain Omar was clinging onto, but he was a professional at keeping his cool which is how he managed to always stay two steps ahead.

Omar stood and collected both of their empty glasses, then moseyed on over to the bar to refill them. "That was a long time ago," he said, passing Bilaal another drink.

"You're right, but I still wanna know what went down."

"Some niggas broke in. They tried to rob me so I handled it, end of story."

"Who were they?"

Omar felt like his insides were turning raw. He didn't know how much longer he would be able to play it cool. "I don't know," he lied. "Like I said, it was a long time ago, I'm over it."

Bilaal flagged him. "You don't get over a muthafucka runnin' up in ya spot and killin' ya family." He hopped out of his seat. "What drug you on?" Bilaal produced a large envelope from beside his chair and slid it across the table towards Omar. "What if I told you I found out who planned the hit and I handled it?"

Omar emptied the contents onto the table. He sat cold and expressionless while staring down at the gruesome photos of a twenty-something year old guy that had been executed. *This must be Kev* he told himself, thinking back to the information he was given. *Three bullets in his face just like he said.*

After looking over the pictures, he looked up at Bilaal with a smirk etched across his face and replied, "I would say that's what friends are for." He reviewed the pictures one last time trying to see if there was anything familiar about the victim. "There were three men. I killed one of them myself, what happened to the other one?"

"Never got my hands on 'em, but I'm sure if he still out there you'll find him."

The wise man was doing a hell of a job acting as if he wasn't the brains behind the whole operation. Omar was hurt, but not surprised. He sensed disloyalty in Bilaal before everything went down, but before getting the chance to act, it was too late. He'd be damned if he lost that chance twice.

"You know that wife of yours was a good woman," said Bilaal, "I made sure that fagot suffered before I pulled the trigger," he lied. "Does your daughter still blame you for what happened?"

"Why wouldn't she after everybody told her I was responsible?"

"You'd think she'd still reach out to hear your side of the story."

"She doesn't need to be anywhere 'round me, I'm poisonous."

"That's the way to be," smiled Bilaal. "And just to let you know, I got a guy up there on the inside that's gonna help turn Mike's world upside down and when it happens, it aint shit he gonna be able to do about it." Bilaal walked over to Omar and raised his glass in the air. "Welcome home my brother."

■ ■ ■

Omar climbed into his car with one thought in mind. Bilaal's head on a platter! Just as he removed his cell phone from his hip and tossed it into the cup holder it rang. He took a second to screen the call before answering. "Talk to me!"

"What's happening ol' timer," said the heavy Italian voice on the other end of the line. "It's been a long time. What fourteen-fifteen years?"

Omar cracked a smile at the sound of Georgio's voice, but it quickly fell dry. "Close enough my brother," he said. "How's the family?"

Georgio was an old friend of Omar's. The two went as far back as bell bottoms and finger waves. When he heard about Omar getting busted, it broke his heart because although he was Omar's connection to the purest cocaine Philadelphia had to offer, he was also like a brother to him.

"Living!" the big man huffed. "I heard you down there chasing them Georgia peaches," he teased. "When you heading back up North?"

"To tell you the truth I was already there, but I didn't stick around too long. Just had someone I needed to check in on, but I'll be heading back real soon," he advised. "I need you to line something up for me."

"You know I'm not one to ask many questions, but I just can't help myself," Georgio chirmed. "Would this have anything to do with Azia 'cause if so I must say she's very well taken care of?"

"Hey, Georgio, you know me. I'll forever appreciate your opinion, but I'm a fact checker."

Georgio chuckled like he should've known better than to expect different. "She scored one of the good ones Omar. Mike's powerful and very well respected. He does more than just take care of himself. He takes care of his team and he takes care of his community, knows how to keep everybody happy." He sighed, heavily. "I heard about the plan your friends are down there mustering up. Should I be concerned?"

"Absolutely not!"

"Enough said! Call me when you're ready to head back this way and we'll set things into motion."

"Sound like a plan. We'll talk soon…"

Chapter 12

FROM HELL 2 HOT WATER

How the fuck them niggas get up in here," barked Kane, storming through the front door of the stash house. "All this muthafuckin heat in here and them niggas left up outta here breathing." Kane was furious. After he and Mike received the call they hurried over to count their losses. "I don't understand this shit."

Mike entered the house a few minutes after Kane had arrived. The men feared Kane, but the thing that worried them the most was how Mike would react. All five set of eyes followed as he calmly closed the door behind him and glided across the living room floor towards Kane.

"I'ma need you to stop yelling before you cause an unnecessary scene on the outside," he whispered in his friend's ear. "I can hear you all way down the street." He took one look at the lump on Sammy's head and asked, "You cool?"

"I'm straight," Sammy lied. His head was killing him.

Mike waved the four men over to the sofa. "I know ya'll still a little shook, but come sit down and give it to me how it happened."

"And where the fuck Deuce at?" blurted Kane.

"I tried calling him," said Lox. "He late."

"How fuckin' convenient," Kane growled. He snatched his cell phone from the holster and strolled into the kitchen, vexed. He was nothing like Mike when it came to maintaining his composure. Kane was ready to hunt the perpetrators down and skin them alive. "Them muthafuckas gon…"

When Kane's loud voice disintegrated behind the kitchen walls, Mike continued to address his team. "What's the count?"

"S-S-Seventeen and some change," TyTy chirped, unable to look him in the eye. In the seven years he'd been working for Mike, this was the first time he'd ever got caught slipping.

Mike sighed deeply. Seventeen thousand dollars was a grip to lose, but it wasn't about the money. He was more concerned with finding out who had the balls to run up in his spot. It bothered the hell out of him. He lifted his eyes from the floor and said, "Ya'll did right by lettin' them ride. What you choose to do for me out here in these streets aint worth losing ya life, remember that cause had one of you tried to play hero I'd probably be paying to bury ya ass right now and sending roses to ya momma's house. And the last thing I feel like dealing with is unnecessary heat from the cops." He threw a friendly backhand into TyTy's chest. "No need for you to feel like shit right now, we good."

"Whhhhh..." The four men exhaled like they'd been holding their breath for hours instead of minutes.

"But ya'll gotta give me something to work wit," continued Mike. "Ya'll recognize any of 'em?"

"On some real shit," replied Sammy. "I think Deuce had something to do wit it."

"No doubt," Lox added. "The way he been ridin' the corner like he the Boss give me more reason to believe that shit--"

"I aint sayin' one got anything to do wit the other," TyTy interrupted. "But I heard the dude Rashaud back out here on the streets. You think he still got beef wit you for pullin' his shawdy?"

"He aint the first or only nigga wit beef. What I need for ya'll to do is lay low for a couple days 'til I get this shit figured out."

"And what about Deuce?" asked Sammy. "I think I can get at him, get in his head for you."

"If you cool wit that go on and do what you need to do." Mike climbed from the seat just as Kane returned. "He answer?"

"Yeah that fagot answered," spat Kane. "Said he around the corner, be here in five."

"Alright, let me holler at you for a minute."

Mike and Kane made their way upstairs to speak privately while the others clowned on Sammy getting, knocked out trying to make light of the situation. Minutes later, Deuce came strolling through the door. Tension instantly filled the air as he locked eyes with Sammy, then Lox and the other two guys. He closed the door behind him and walked over to where they were seated.

"Fuck happened to you?" he asked Sammy, curiously.

Sammy tried to be as cordial as he could without letting anger reside. "Some fools ran up on us, got us for a few stacks and some work."

"Get the fuck outta here," responded Deuce. "Who?"

Lox had no intentions on playing Mr. nice-guy with him. "If we knew who it was do you really think we'd be sittin' here right now lookin' at ya ugly ass face?" He jumped to his feet only seconds away from ripping the traitor apart. "Where the fuck was you at my dude?"

Things were definitely heating up in there. After hearing the ruckus, Mike and Kane rushed back downstairs to stop Lox from ripping Deuce to shreds because they needed him alive. If he did have something to do with the robbery, he was the only way they could get to the bottom of it. Mike threw his arm up in front of Lox's chest while Kane crossed over to where Deuce stood nervously.

"Where was you at when those niggas ran up in here and robbed the joint?" asked Kane, smacking Deuce in the back of the head. Deuce stepped back with a dismantle look on his face. "You should'a been here over two hours ago," he said, backing Deuce into a wall with his pistol drawn.

"I-I-got caught up wit my moms," he stuttered, staring down the barrel of the gun. "I got here soon as I could."

"Call her," ordered Kane. "And she better tell me the same muthafuckin' story chump."

There was no need for Deuce to make that call because Mike saw straight through his game, but he didn't want him to know that. "Nah," said Mike. He walked over to Kane and placed his hand over top of the gun to lower it. "It's cool Kane," he advised, and then looked deep into Deuce's eyes. "You on our side, right?"

Sammy inched towards them. "He cool Kane, I can vouch for that." Kane shot Sammy a stale eye. But Sammy didn't hesitate to reiterate, "He's good."

Kane stuffed the pistol back in his pants. "You lucky this nigga stood up for you, but luck aint gonna save ya ass next time." Kane brushed pass Deuce and left out of the house.

"I need ya'll to lay low until I find out what the fuck's up," demanded Mike. "Give it a couple days before you get back at it. If you need something to hold you over just let me know."

"Fo'sho," said Lox. He bumped knuckles with Mike and bumped shoulders with Deuce on his way out the door.

Mike exited next followed by TyTy and the other guy.

Deuce exhaled and bumped knuckles with Sammy. "Good lookin'."

"Aint no good lookin', ya ass owe me big time."

■■■

Mike and Kane watched intensely from behind the tint of a parked LeSabre as Deuce and Sammy headed up the block. The smile on Deuce's face had them both tingling on the inside, but there was nothing they could do except wait it out.

"You think Sammy gonna get that little nigga to run his mouth?"

Nyema

Mike brought the engine to life and pulled away from the curb. "I don't know but Sammy stepping in was on point."

"Hopefully Deuce will feed off of it."

"Shit, you had me thinking you was bout to put one in him."

"I almost forgot I wasn't supposed to."

"I aint really tryna wait it out and depend on Sammy. I'ma need you to come up with something," said Mike, coming to a red light.

"No doubt, I'm on it."

"I need the team to eat, shit and breathe Deuce for breakfast, lunch and dinner for the next few weeks, his dumb ass bound to slip up."

"Damn," blurted Kane, unknowingly rubbing the bulge between his legs.

Mike stared at his friend like he was diseased. "Fuck you doing man?"

Kane looked down and realized he was living what he thought he was privately thinking. He released himself and laughed. "Oh shit, my fault family. But every time I think about that trifling ass bitch for a baby mom burning me, I start feeling fucked up all over again."

Mike laughed. "I hope you got some medicine for that shit," he said, pulling into traffic. "That'll teach you to stop fuckin' around. Sasha gonna whip ya ass."

"I know, I aint been slinging no dick her way lately. She aint crazy, she gonna start that inspector gadget shit pretty soon," he sighed. "The doctor told me not to have sex until I finish these damn meds and if I do make sure I strap up."

"Sasha aint tryna hear that shit," he giggled.

"Who you tellin'." Kane didn't know if he was more nervous for himself or for his baby's mother because if Sasha found out his visit over there earlier that day was to whip her ass for giving him the clap, she'd probably kill them both.

Mike pulled behind Kane's parked car. "Alright homie, go on and get ya dirty dick ass up out of my ride," Mike chuckled. "That shit might be contagious."

Kane threw up his middle finger. "Fuck you nigga."

Mike waited for Kane to secure himself inside of his car before grabbing his cell phone from the cup holder. He dialed Azia's number for the fourth time, and again, he was sent straight to voicemail. Frustrated, he threw the cell phone back into the cup holder and yanked the lever into drive."

Chapter 13

ONE THING AFTER THE OTHER

$\dagger$ $\dagger$

Azia broke out of the bedroom early that next morning. She felt like the walls were closing in on her. On top of getting little to no sleep at all because her mind kept drifting all night long, she couldn't help but glue her ear to the wall and listen to Sasha and Kane's beef. That was until Sasha's loud mouth was replaced by a shit load of moaning.

She peaked out the bedroom door, head first. Assuming Sasha and Kane were still in the room asleep, she made her way downstairs after washing her face and gargling. She grabbed the orange juice from the refrigerator and slammed it on the counter top trying her best to control her anger. *Lord, please give me the strength* she thought, while gulping down the glass of juice.

"Did that orange juice do something to you?" asked Kane.

She never heard him come up behind her. "No! Why'd you ask that?"

"Cause you slamming shit like somebody owe you something." Azia grinned and went to walk out the kitchen. "Don't leave on the count of me," said Kane. "You aint gotta hide the fact that you mad."

"I aint trying to."

Kane sighed. "You know I'm the last one to butt in ya'll business right?"

"So you say," she answered, sarcastically.

"See," he said, pointing. "That smart shit aint gonna get you nowhere. It's time for you go home and set shit straight wit ya man."

"Kane, I know that's ya homie and all, but if you aint feeling the extra company I don't have a problem with going to get me a room."

He paused for a minute and poured himself a glass of orange juice. Azia stared at his facial expressions knowing he had some more to say. "Azia, you so busy walking around here wit ya nose in the air and ya ass can't even see straight."

"What?" she asked puzzled.

"You heard me," he muttered. "If you had any real sense ya ass would be waking up to ya man right now mapping out a plan to make shit more comfortable and convenient for the both of ya'll cause that girl don't mean shit to him. And Mike would probably kick me in my ass if he heard me say this, but you the only woman that ever won his heart. Believe that. And I'ma let you know something else. You better get ya shit together because love or no love he will find a way to tune ya ass out and if that happens," he said, punching her gently across the chin. "It's gonna be painful trying to work ya way back in."

Azia stood miserably as he exited the kitchen. She heard him loud and clear. But what was she to do? Run back in his arms after ignoring him for only one night. Hell no! She had to tough it out and teach his ass a lesson.

Azia was standing at the sink rinsing her glass out when Sasha appeared in the kitchen wearing nothing at all, butt ass naked. "Oh goodness, if this is how it's gonna be I just might have to go get me a damn room. I aint never gonna have no luck."

"Girl please," said Sasha, wiping cold from her eyes. "I aint putting no clothes on for you, you aint no damn guest. She bumped Azia out of her way. "You staying in or you wanna ride wit me down to the club? I gotta go holler at D for a minute."

Sasha had been dancing at D's Gentleman's Club, one of Philly's most notorious gentleman's club, on and off for the past six years. The club housed only the best of the best and in order to get your name on the list you had to either know somebody that knew somebody, or have pockets that hung low. The owner of the spot was D, short for Demetrius, a short nerdy type dude that played no games when it came to making money which is what earned him much respect. He'd recruited Sasha when she was just eighteen-years-old, fresh out of high school. With no intentions on going to college, she wasn't sure what her next move would be until being introduced to D. After hearing how much money she could make in a week, she was game and eventually turning into one of his highest profited dancers since the opening of the club.

"I'll ride wit you but first I need you to swing me home so I can get some of my stuff."

Hearing this was a big shock to Sasha. She was sure Azia would be running back to Mike by now. "You sure about that?"

"I just wanna make him sweat a little bit that's all. His ass will think twice before playing me like that the next time."

"O-kay," Sasha sighed. "Well don't make him sweat too long pumpkin because the water might run dry."

Azia listened to Sasha go on, but in her head, she knew what she had to do. Jealousy could be a deadly weapon at any given time, and she was willing to try her hand just to see how deadly it could be.

■ ■ ■

Cherry Hill, NJ. Sasha and Azia were sitting in a restaurant talking over some bar-b-cue and frozen daiquiris. After swinging Azia home to grab a few things while Mike wasn't there and dropping by the club to get a few things squared away, the girls agreed that the next stop would be to conquer their hunger.

"Mike would never let me go shake my ass in front of a room full of niggas. I'm surprised Kane alright wit you doing it."

"He alright wit it cause my man knows me," she smiled. "Shit, my hustle aint no different than his. I may take off my clothes and shake my ass but at the end of the night I'm going home to my man and he knows it."

"But still, I know he be a little uncomfortable when he in there watching all them men drooling over you, and not to mention the ignorant ass ones calling ya'll hoes and shit."

"Hey what can I say," she shrugged. "They can call me all the hoes they want, but you best believe I'm an ambitious ass hoe so they aint got no choice but to respect it."

"What ya freak ass need to respect is the fact that you got company and keep ya voice down at night."

"Girl his ass been act'n like he too busy to give me some dick," said Sasha, nibbling at her Cajun burger. "Little do he know I'm taking that shit tonight."

"It damn sure aint sound like he wasn't in there dick'n you down last night with them thins ass walls ya'll got up in there," giggled Azia.

"Oh, no hunny, that's how loud he can make me howl just wit his tongue alone. Had he been laying the pipe you would'a definitely decided to go get you a room last night." Sasha wiped her mouth. "But guess what," she said, switching to serious mode. "One of the spots got hit last night."

"One of the spots," repeated Azia.

"Would you stop acting slow and read between the lines."

Azia's jaw hit the floor. "Get the fuck outta here."

"I can't believe all this bullshit is going on. Something wicked done hit the circle and this is gonna be one of those times we gonna have to sit back, shut the fuck up and do whatever they tell us to do."

Azia watched Sasha stir the frozen daiquiri that was now melted at that point. She respected all the wisdom Sasha instilled in her but she was still her own woman. She stared down at her cell phone thinking back to Rashaud's phone call. She hadn't heard from him since but ninety percent of her was feeling like he had something to do with it.

"Don't worry about it too much cause people don't know how to keep their mouths shut. Whoever's responsible will be found out and they will be dealt with. Simple as that!"

Azia laughed. "You swear you's a gun," she joked.

"I aint a killer but don't push me," she sang, in her Tupac voice.

Both girls burst into laughter, so hard it took a minute for them to regain their composures. Sasha used the wet wipe provided by the restaurant to wipe her hands, then pulled out the Mac to gloss her lips while Azia busied herself with texting.

"Who you texting?"

Damn she nosy as hell. "Are you going with me to my appointment tomorrow?" asked Azia, changing the subject.

"Mike need to be the one going wit you."

"I aint heard from him so he probably on some stubborn shit right now."

"Girl stop trippin', he going," she advised, tossing the dirty wet wipe into the half empty plate. "C'mon, I'ma run back to the club to see if D made it back yet."

Azia stood from the table. "Can you run me to my car first, I got something I need to go handle."

■■■

A little over an hour and a half later, Azia was pulling onto an all but familiar block. She pulled up to a curb and stepped out of her car amongst dozens of other cars with the engine still running. She scanned the area, no one was out. She leaned back into her car to grab her cell phone when out of nowhere, a set of hands appeared around her waist. Startled, she spun around frantic and came face to face with Rashaud.

"I always wondered what this would feel like," he smiled, holding her tightly.

In no position to move, she stared him in the eye. She too wondered what it would feel like to see him for the first time, and she felt everything but what she thought she would. Fear!

"You missed me?" he asked, going in for a kiss which she resisted. "You called me so you must miss me a little bit."

She tried pushing him off of her but his grip was like a pit bull's lockjaw. "Can you let me go please?"

"I can't," he smirked. "If I do I might lose you forever."

Azia used all her might to push him away and he finally let go. She leaned into the car, popped the trunk and walked around to open it. Rashaud watched her grab something out and slam it closed. Then she walked back around to where he stood and dropped a bag at his feet.

"What's this?"

"What's left of ya money," she spat. "Hopefully you'll take it and we'll call it even."

He laughed. "Who put you in charge of making business moves?"

"I'm not laughing Rashaud," she said, sternly. "Stay away from me and please stay away from Mike before somebody wound up getting hurt."

"Is that your way of telling me you still care?" he smirked, looking down at the bag at his feet. "What make you think da money gonna keep me away from you?"

"Because I gave you the benefit of the doubt and assumed that after sitting in that two inch cell you had enough time to think and realize that life's too short to waste." She picked the money up from the ground and shoved it into his chest. "Take the money Rashaud and like I said, stay away from Mike and his businesses before you start something you can't finish."

Rashaud didn't know what she was talking about or what she thought he did, but he didn't feel the need to question it because whatever it was is what got him the meeting he'd been waiting for. When he received the text message from her asking could they meet, it caught him off guard. He swore with all his being that Azia would try to fly under the radar in order to avoid bumping in to him. And for a minute after getting the text, he thought it would be the perfect opportunity to choke her which was something he'd dreamt about doing for the last several months. But after looking into her eyes and feeling her touch, he had to admit he was still deeply in love with the girl.

"You keep it," he suggested, never grabbing hold of it. "That's my gift to you."

Azia looked across the street and caught Helena standing in the door of one of the row homes holding a baby on her hip. "I don't want nothing from you." She nodded her head towards Helena and Rashaud turned slightly to follow her stare. "So this where you gonna be playing house at huh?" she asked, still a little bit bitter that he made that baby on her.

"Hey, I aint got no choice but to man up and take care of my responsibilities."

Azia let the bag go and it hit the ground, again. "Well maybe this'll give you a head start," she said, climbing back into the car. "Stay the hell away from me."

"Just answer me this one question," he said, yielding her from closing the door. "What made you choose him over me?"

Azia looked him square in the eye and replied, "Because he looks at me the way you used to." She grilled him a second longer and tried to shut the door.

Again he stopped it from shutting. "What he got that I aint got?"

Azia slapped his hand out of the way and said, "He got *Me*."

Chapter 14

PEACHES AINT ALWAYS SWEET

···Back in Atlanta

ǁ

Gisele stepped out of her two-door Maserati and into the back of a black Lincoln Town Car. As soon as she secured herself in the seat, Ralphie, his driver, pulled off into traffic. She turned to her left and smiled at the sight of Bilaal who in turn handed her over an envelope filled with cash. She remained silent while he finished up on a call.

"Yeah, they hit him and his girl up. Robbed his spot and left them both for dead. Now I got to deal wit the shit." He paused. "I need you to meet me over on Peachtree at seven so we can handle it." He paused again. "Alright, I'll see you when you when you get there."

"Something wrong?" asked Gisele, twiddling her thumbs.

"Nothing that I can't make right," he replied, sparking his cigar. "How was Florida?"

"Sunny..." she replied, crossing her legs to get more comfortable. "What has our boy been up to since I've been gone?"

"He's been pretty quiet, not making too much noise. But you need to jump back in and pick up where you left off, immediately."

"That won't be a problem."

"I'm going to tell you now, the only way you're gonna be able to get back at Omar in the worse way possible is if you get close enough for him to trust you with his life. He's no fool. Working your way to his heart so that you can pull the strings is the only way to do it."

Nyema

"It wasn't hard to pull his daughter up under my wing. I doubt if he'll be a problem," she boasted.

Gisele gazed out of the window and drifted into deep thought back to the last time she'd seen her brother. When she heard that he was killed during a home invasion, her whole world had fallen apart. And on that day just a little over fifteen years ago, she vowed that if she ever got the chance to revenge his death, it would be done. After Bilaal tracked her down and told her that Omar was the one responsible and was being released from prison, she felt that in some weird way it was God's work. And after finding out that Omar's daughter and her Ex-Angel was one in the same, she couldn't help but think *what a small world!*

Gisele directed her attention back to Bilaal. "I'm no amateur, I know what needs to be done," she said, smugly. "But he's your friend. How can I be sure that you won't turn the tables on me?"

"Gisele, Sweetheart, money will always trump friendship in my world. Don't forget that if you get Omar out of my way, I'll end up a winner behind this too."

The Lincoln came to a complete stop beside Gisele's Maserati and Ralphie came around to open the door for her.

"If you don't think you cut out for the job…"

She stuffed the envelope into her pocketbook, stepped out of the car, bent over slightly into the car and said, "It's not the job I'm afraid of. It's you!"

■ ■ ■

Later on that night, Ralphie, Bilaal and Tone, one of his trigger-happy soldiers, pulled behind an abandoned warehouse into a dark field that was filled with nothing but dead grass and debris. Tone and Ralphie retrieved a body from the trunk of the car and dropped it face down just inches away from Bilaal's feet. The victim was bloodied, battered and bruised, barely breathing.

Tone stuck his pistol in the young man's face and poked at him so he would awake while Ralphie walked back around to the driver's side of the car and flicked the headlights on. Bilaal watched intensely as Shiz cracked open his swollen eyes and cocked his head up slightly to look back at him. He knew he was counting down to his final breaths of life, but the only thing he could think about was leaving Omar out there to bring Bilaal down on his own.

"Now that you had you a lil' nap," Bilaal said, sarcastically. "Hopefully you're ready to talk?"

"I aint--got-shit to-say," Shiz coughed, through a bloody mouth and painfully cracked ribs.

"Well that's too bad," said Bilaal, using his foot to kick Shiz over onto his back. "I guess I'll just have to torture you like you tortured my nephew to get some answers."

Shiz grabbed at his aching ribs wishing there was a way for him to get inside and rub them down. "I don't know what the fuck you talkin' 'bout," he squirmed.

"Aint no need for you to lie boy," advised Bilaal, kneeling down beside him. "You the only one been runnin' 'round town asking 'bout him and then he end up dead. What I want to know is why you did it and who the nigga was that helped you."

"Fuck you—you piece of shit--"

Bilaal punched Shiz in the mouth so hard he knocked two of his front teeth out and damaged his own knuckles. "Fuck me? No fuck you…" He climbed to his feet and shot Tone a look that told him exactly what to do.

Tone walked over to Shiz's body and shot him in both legs. "Who the fuck was you wit?" he asked, and shot him another time in his left leg.

Shiz was in so much pain he couldn't scream, all he could do was cry and grab at his wounds and pray that he was strong enough to sit through it all without telling them what they wanted to know.

Nyema

"Who the fuck helped you do the job?" shouted Bilaal, snatching the gun from Tone and sending another bullet further up his thigh.

Shiz cringed. Just as he went to caress his last wound Bilaal grabbed hold of his hand and sent a bullet straight through the middle of it. "Soothe that you cock suckin' mutherfucka…" He then grabbed his other hand and put a bullet in it as well. "I can stay here all night--"

His sentence was cut short by a set of headlight sweeping up the rubble that jerked all of the men's attention. The driver pulled into the field and parked directly beside Bilaal's Lincoln Town Car. It was Omar! With the engine still running, he stepped out of the car and headed their way. He didn't know why Bilaal wanted to meet him there, but with two pistols stuffed on each side of his pants, he was ready for whatever.

Omar caught sight of the body that was sprawled out in front of the three men, but it wasn't until he got closer and zoomed in could he tell that it was Shiz. With his antennas up and adrenaline pumping he asked, "Fuck goin' on out here?"

"You remember that situation we talked about the other day?" asked Bilaal. "Well this here is number three," he lied. "Finally found the lil' nigga."

Omar took a moment to examine Shiz's body while trying to come up with a plan. He wasn't sure if Shiz had ratted him out and he was being set up, or if Bilaal was really trying to sell him a dream so he decided to play along.

"Nah," said Omar, shaking his head. "Never seen him before, he wasn't there."

Bilaal threw his arms up in the air. "That was over fifteen years ago brother," he growled, frustratingly. "I'm tellin' you it's him…"

Omar glanced at Shiz another time and for the first time the two men locked eyes. This was not how Omar planned for things to go down. He'd envisioned getting Bilaal one on one and making his back stabbing ass suffer before taking him out of his misery, but there was no way that he could just sit back and watch them take Shiz's life just for his selfish reasons.

As if Shiz could read Omar's mind, he looked deeply into his eyes and slightly brushed his head from side to side. He was willing to take one for the team knowing the odds against Omar were three to one.

"You one of the lil' mutherfuckas that killed my wife?" grilled Omar, but Shiz declined to reply.

Bilaal inched in closer and aimed the gun down. "Don't you hear this man talking to you? I told you I can stand here all night and put fifty more bullets in you if you wanna die slow so I suggest you tell 'em what he wanna hear," he ordered, in a convincing tone.

Had Omar been a fool, Bilaal would've definitely won him over.

"I'll see you in hell you fat mutherfucka," Shiz slurred, and spit at Bilaal's feet.

Bilaal looked over at Omar and smiled. "You wanna handle it or you want me to?"

Omar looked down one last time, and then turned as if he was heading back to his car. "You handled it thus far, you might as well finish."

Just as Bilaal was about to return the gun to Tone so he could finish the job, Omar spun around with one pistol, dropped Tone with two shots while reaching for his second pistol, which dropped Ralphie with three shots just as he was about to run for cover. In one quick motion, he ran up on Bilaal, aimed one of the pistols at his head and aimed the other down at Tone who was crawling his way to where his gun had fallen.

"Fuck you think you doing?" barked Bilaal.

*POW...POW...*Omar sent two more shots into Tone's back, which stopped him dead in his tracks and sent his body crashing to the ground. He then shoved Bilaal down to his knees, just feet away from Tone.

Nyema

POW...He sent one last bullet in the back of Tone's head to finish him.

The closeness of the blast startled Bilaal. He turned his head slightly back towards Omar and said, "What's this all about?"

"Shut the fuck up you shady ass mutherfucka," growled Omar. "Don't sit here and front like you don't know."

"Know what brother?"

"I aint ya mutherfuckin' brother," said Omar, clocking him upside his head with his pistol. "You thought I wasn't gonna find out you was the one that put the hit out on me? You should know me better than that."

"Somebody done told you wrong--"

Omar jammed both pistols into the top of Bilaal's head so hard it left impressions. "You wanna keep playing stupid? Huh? Get ya fat ass up..."

The heavy weight pulled him-self from the ground.

"Turn the fuck around and face me," ordered Omar, and Bilaal did as he was told. "I aint gonna shoot you from behind 'cause I aint no coward."

Despite the pain Shiz was in, there was no way he was going to miss what was about to happen with his own eyes. He used the little energy he had left to shift his body.

Bilaal raised both arms out to his side. He knew his life was over and tried his best not to go out like the coward he was. "So what now?"

"I treated you like a brother and you do me like this?"

"Money trumps friendship! No hard feelings my brother."

"Is that ya final answer?"

"I aint afraid to die--"

With each pistol aimed at Bilaal's eyes, Omar pulled the triggers simultaneously sending the heavy weight plunging backward onto the rubble. He then stood over top of him and emptied every last bullet he had left into his face, center mass, splitting it into two.

"I bet you wish you would'a changed ya answer now mutherfucka…"

Chapter 15

A TEST OF FAITH

The following morning was a beautiful one, no breeze at all. Rolling out of the sleeping position Azia opened her eyes and sighed feeling that it was gonna be a bad day before it even began. She glanced over at the alarm clock trying to shake the feeling. It was just before eight and her doctor's appointment was scheduled for ten-thirty that morning. She rolled over and reached for her cell to see if she had any missed calls from Mike. Nothing! After blowing her phone up the day everything went down, he hadn't called back since. Not even to let her know whether or not he was still going to make the appointment. The thought of him abandoning her brought on some emotion. She embraced a pillow and cried softly.

After an hour of drowning in her own self-pity, she forced herself up out the bed and into the bathroom for a hot thirty-minute shower. Now more relaxed, she managed to put her emotions into place thinking *it is what it is*. She hopped into a pair of tights and a tank top and swung over to the dresser to finish applying her make-up. Satisfied with the final touches, she slid on some shades anxious to see her baby on the screen for the first time. Nobody was going to steal her joy, at least that's what she thought.

Finally making it downstairs to the living room, she zoomed in on Sasha who was sitting on the sofa in some cut-off jean shorts and bra. "Sasha," she sang, "I told you my appointment was at ten-thirty why you aint dress yet?"

"I gotta get caught up on this paper work," she lied, using the coffee table to straighten a stack of papers.

"I told ya ass I aint wanna go by myself," mumbled Azia. "You should'a told me that last--"

Sasha stood from the sofa and said, "Girl hush, you aint going alone ya ride outside waiting on you so get the hell out and stop whining."

Azia walked over to the window and peaked through the blinds. It was not hard for her to guess who Sasha was talking about when she saw the Jag parked directly in front of the door. She spun around to Sasha like she wasn't happy to see him sitting there. "You aint have to call him."

"Get the hell out and go see about my God-baby," she ordered, pushing her towards the door.

Mike moved a small brown paper bag from the passenger seat when he noticed Azia approaching the car. "Alright, we'll talk later," he said, ending his phone call.

Azia climbed in and tried hard to keep her game face on. "You aint have to get off the phone on the account of me."

"How about good morning," he said, passing her the brown paper bag. "I figured you'd be hungry."

As bad as she wanted to play tough, the smell of that bacon and egg sandwich won her over. "Thank you," she spat. "I didn't even think you were coming."

"If you really believed I would do you like that," he said, pulling into traffic. "Then you don't know me like I thought you did."

Azia cut her eye at him with a smirk etched across her face but Mike did a fine job of ignoring it. He looked over at her for a split section and giggled to himself. She was something else and he loved every bit of it. But sometimes he regretted the way he felt about her, it was frustrating. He's never had that much love for anyone before, except his mother. The reason he hated it so much was because to him, it was a sign of weakness, something any enemy could use to get at him. And with her bringing a baby into the world would only further complicate things. But, she was his woman and would probably become his wife, so there was nothing he could do but take it how it came.

■ ■ ■

Nyema

Mike had his hand stashed under the cotton hospital gown the nurse had ordered Azia to put on before exiting the room. They were in the middle of playing make up when then Doctor came in and interrupted. The fifty-something year old foreign Doctor entered the room looking down at the clipboard in his hand.

"Ms. Elliston," he smiled. "It's been a while since the last time we've seen each other. You call yourself hiding from me?" he joked, shaking Mike's hand. "I'm assuming you're the father." Mike shook his head yes as the Doctor to a seat in front of Azia. "So, what took you so long to get in here to see me?"

"I just found out a couple weeks ago," she lied.

"Hmm...I'm sure you had an incline," he grinned. "There's very few woman who make it through thirteen weeks without some kind of symptoms."

Mike looked at Azia strangely but said nothing.

"I'm that far along?" she blurted.

"According to your last menstrual but when I get some measurements from the ultrasound I can give you an exact," the Doctor stated. He stood from the stool and began collecting some equipment. "Are ya'll ready to see your baby."

"Ready as I'm gonna be Doc," said Mike, stretching.

Azia reclined backward on the table and allowed the Doctor to rub cold jelly all over her belly. He pulled the ultrasound machine a bit closer and panned across her belly with a small wand. Both Mike and Azia's eyes were pinned to the monitor. As soon as what appeared to be the fetus popped onto the screen, all three of their hearts melted.

"There's your baby," the Doctor hesitated, his look of warmth turning drastic.

Mike caught the look of concern and asked, "Is everything alright Doc?"

"I'm a little concerned with these measurements but no worries," he said, grabbing another tool. "I need to check for a heartbeat."

Azia sat quiet as her heart started fluttering close to two miles a minute. Mike swooped her hand into his and they watched the Doctor run the small microphone slowly across her belly fishing for a sound, any sound, something, but there was nothing.

The two minutes it took him to search brought Azia into panic mode. "What's wrong Dr. Levy?"

The Doctor connected the microphone back to its base and slid the monitor out of the way. "Azia, I'm afraid I have some terrible news," he sighed. "I was unable to find a heartbeat."

She heard him loud and clear but because it wasn't what she was looking for him to say, denial kicked in. "I just saw my baby on the monitor," she said. "I'm definitely still pregnant."

Mike looked at her in awe. He knew how much she was looking forward to the baby and his heart felt for her.

"The fetus stopped growing a couple weeks ago. Had you not come in you would've miscarried soon. Unfortunately, there's nothing that can be done in the first trimester."

Azia refused to believe it. "You tryna tell me my baby been dead for two weeks but I been sick as a dog." She looked up at Mike with tears in her eyes. "Mike tell him--"

The Doctor stepped in closer. This was the part of his job he hated but somebody had to do it. "I'm sorry Azia. I'll go ahead and schedule you for a D & C on Monday. If you happen to miscarry over the weekend, you'll need to go to the closest emergency room."

I'm sorry Azia was the last thing she heard before drifting off into the zone. She felt so empty inside, a feeling that she had felt only once before, many years ago when she lost her mother. She watched the Doctor shake Mike's hand and exit the room. *How can he be this calm* she thought, shifting her anger towards Mike. He extended his hands to help her down from the table but she pulled away. "I don't need any help," she spat. She was angry inside and he was the only one around whom she could take it out on.

Mike grabbed her clothes from the chair and handed them over. "This shit aint my fault," he advised.

She snatched the clothes from his hand. "You could at least act like you care."

"I'm here aint I--"

"You only here cause you tryna act like you half-ass happy. From day one you act like this baby was gonna be the one to fuck up ya world when the whole time you already had let a rundown ass tramp fuck it up--"

"I aint tryna hear that shit right now, I'll be outside waiting," he said, with a no nonsense attitude.

Mike was right, it wasn't his fault, but who else was she to blame. Azia rolled her eyes and continued to dress. As many times as she told herself she would never have any kids, when she found out that she was pregnant she couldn't remember a time she'd felt happier. And just like that, it was all taken away in the blink of an eye.

Chapter 16

SOME KIND OF CHAIN REACTION

...Back in Atlanta

ǁ

Gisele quickly sat upright on the bed and grabbed the remote control so that she could turn the volume on the television up. She thought her eyes were deceiving her when she saw Bilaal's picture flash across the screen, but when she heard the Reporter verify his name she knew she wasn't tripping.

"Sources say the massacre happened sometime late last night and, and again the three victims have been identified as 39-year-old Ralph Turner, a local resident of Brookhaven Township, 22-year-old Antoine McTyler, and 42-year old Bilaal Westbrook, a well-known drug lord that has been rumored to have dealings with over fifteen recent murders that have taken place around the city of Atlanta. Details has yet to be confirmed--"

Gisele hurried and turned the volume on the television down when she heard the shower cut off. Omar exited the bathroom a few minutes later with a towel wrapped around his waist. He could tell by the look in Gisele's eyes that something extremely terrible was wrong.

"You alright?" he asked, approaching the side of the bed where she was sitting.

"Have you spoken to Bilaal today?"

"No, I haven't. What's up?"

She turned the volume back up and said, "They found him murdered last night in the back of a warehouse."

Omar took the remote from her hand and cut the volume up some more. "Can't be, I just talked to him last night."

Nyema

The news was now showing snap shots of the field, markers where bullet casings had landed, and where the three bodies were found. Omar grabbed his cell phone and dialed Bilaal's number, which went straight to voicemail.

"Nah, this shit can't be right."

Gisele watched him dial Bilaal's number three more times while pacing around the room.

"Shiiit, that's fucked up!"

She stood from the bed and walked over to comfort him. Even she couldn't see through his act. "Bilaal did a lot of dirt to a lot of different people. Anybody could be responsible for this."

Omar shook his head as if he was in denial. "They aint have to do the boy like that," he sighed.

"Don't worry yourself. You knew the old Bilaal, but I knew the new Bilaal," she said, hinting about his disloyalty. She thought that this was the perfect time to play *confessions* as if she was another statistic caught in Bilaal's web. "He wasn't for nobody but himself."

"Apparently not, he did me a favor by sending you here to me," he replied, coolly, "Unless he had a motive behind that too."

Gisele wrapped her arms around his neck. "I don't know what his reasons were, or if there was a reason. I'm just glad that he did," she said, stealing a kiss.

Omar's antennas flew up, immediately. *The boy just died and she flippin' the script on him already. What is this chick really into?* Omar thought to himself. She may have thought he was sweet because he'd been away for awhile, but she didn't know the real Omar.

"Now that Bilaal's gone," she said, planting small kisses all over his chest. "I'm sure that my friends will be looking for someone to fill his spot."

Omar couldn't believe what he was hearing. He had been kicking himself in the ass since the killing because he never got the chance to have a sit down with Bilaal and find out who his drug connect was, and here she was staring him right in the face, a wolf in sheep's clothing.

"I'm sure we can make that happen," he said, flipping her over onto her back.

Gisele snatched his towel off and tossed it over her head. "I'll make sure to give them a call but first," she said, positioning her body under his. "You got to work for it," she smiled devilishly pulling him closer in to her by his manhood.

Chapter 17

LAYERS OF LOVE

KoKa was at home alone sitting in the kitchen when her phone rang. She had decided to take a day off from the restaurant so she could catch up on some bills around the house that she'd been neglecting for weeks. Anthony was gone for the day and she wasn't the least bit upset about it either. She was finally able to get the peace of mind she been wishing for.

"Hey baby," she said, after hearing Mike's voice. "How's the appointment go?"

"Not good at all. I'll be over to talk to you about."

"Something wrong with the baby?" she questioned, concerned.

"I'll fill you in when I get there. I gotta make a run then I'll be over."

KoKa put the phone back on the receiver and tried to figure out what could've possibly gone wrong. Tired of playing the guessing game, she grabbed her cell phone and called Azia. No answer! She called again. Still no answer so she left a message advising her to call back. Just as she went to make another call, she heard the front door open. Knowing there was no way in the world Mike could've got there that quick she jumped up to go and check it out.

Anthony dropped a pair of work boots from his hands in the middle of the living room and passed out on the sofa. He looked over at KoKa when she appeared in the living room and turned his head like he'd never even seen her.

"I thought you were gonna be gone until later tonight?" she asked, removing his boots from the middle of the floor.

"And?" he asked, sitting up. "What am I intruding on ya plans or somthin'?"

"Don't start ya bullshit," she said, leaving the room before he could even get started. She never realized he was tailing her until a heavy blow connected with the back of her head landing her on the floor. "What the hell is the matter wit you?" she squirmed. She looked into his eyes and could tell he'd been drinking. "Take ya drunk ass on up outta here I aint going through this bullshit wit you no more," she said, picking herself up from the floor. "I'm sick of it."

"I aint going a muthafuckin place," he yelled. KoKa made her way into the kitchen and he followed. "Why the hell I got to hear from Toni that he was at the restaurant being catered to by you?" he raved. "You had the nerve to give that fool a free meal. You fuckin' him aren't you?"

"I know damn well you aint talking bout cross-eyed ass Toni," she shouted back. "I aint give him shit for free you asshole."

The backhand smack he delivered across her face knocked her up against the refrigerator. He then opened the refrigerator door and started yanking food out from the shelves. "Since you wanna embarrass me and give away free meals and have them niggas laughing behind my muthafuckin' back, I aint doing or buying shit else up in this muthafucka. Go buy ya own damn food cause all this shit right here I paid for." He stormed across the room to a large KoKa's Bar & Grill take-out bag that was sitting on the counter. He snatched out the two platters and was about to smash them on the floor until she ran over and stopped him.

■■■

Mike spotted Anthony's Benz parked in the driveway at KoKa's house when he pulled up. He remembered her saying he would be working late, that was the only reason why he decided to come over. Although he had to respect his mother's personal life and let her live, he tried his best to avoid bumping heads with Anthony just to keep things kosher. For a minute, he thought about just leaving and hollering at her later but something inside of him wouldn't let him go. He stepped out of his car and used his set of keys to make his way inside.

No sooner than he stepped foot through the door, Mike caught the tail end of Anthony smashing a plate of food in KoKa's face so hard it forced her to the floor. And like a bat out of hell, Mike flew to the dining room where they were located and spun him around into a wall. Anthony threw both hands in the air as if to surrender, but it was too late. Mike hammered the man's face with his fist.

"Jesus Christ," slurred Anthony.

Mike grabbed the other plate of food and smashed it in his face. "You like beatin' on my mom you fagot?" He punched him in the gut which broke him down to his knees.

KoKa flew over and tried to break the two men apart. "Ya'll stop it." Mike kicked him in the ribs ignoring his mother's demands. They watched Anthony spit a mixture of vomit and blood on the floor. "Please stop Mike before you kill him," she cried, trying to help him to his feet.

As soon as Anthony was good and on his feet Mike snatched him from KoKa and dragged him to the front door by his neck. "If ya pussy ass step foot back in this house I will put a bullet in ya muthafuckin' head," Mike roared. "You hear me?"

Anthony landed on his knees and hands after Mike mugged him out the front door. He was scared half to death. He was never afraid to admit that he'd lost a couple fights back in his day, but this was no ordinary fight. This was a plain ol' ass whipping that deserved no explanation. He knew he was wrong for putting is hands on KoKa but he was a man of pride and always let his pride get the best of him. So what could he do but pick his ass up, get in the car and take it as a loss. What he damn sure wasn't going to do is run back up in that house and play *billy bad ass* with Mike, not with the mental state he was in. The look he witnessed in his eyes was enough to make Floyd Mayweather take a walk.

Mike was still standing in the door but KoKa had already disappeared back in the house. "I suggest you move a little quicker ol'head."

"A'ight...A'ight...I know I fucked up--"

"I aint tryna hear nuttin you got to say," advised Mike, stepping down off the steps. "Get in ya ride and roll the fuck out."

Mike waited until Anthony got in his car and pulled off before making his way back into the house to find KoKa. He tracked her down in the kitchen cleaning up the mess that was made.

"He put his hands on you?"

"No--"

"Don't lie to me mom."

"I said no," she lied. After seeing what her son was capable of for this first time in his years of living, there was no way she was going to tell him the truth so he could go hunt Anthony down and do something that would land him in prison for the rest of his life. "You alright?"

"I'm cool I need to be asking you that."

"I'm good things just got a little out of control that's all."

"Nah, it was more than a little out of control. The nigga smashed a plate of food in ya face," he said, still steaming. "Matter fact..." He leaned over to hug KoKa. "I see you later."

She grabbed hold of his arm so tight you couldn't slide a nickel through. "No, baby, please just leave it alone. Do that for me," she begged. Their eyes locked. "Please do that for me." Mike nodded his head in agreement and secured his mother in his arms.

Chapter 18

NEVER DOWN FOR LONG

...One Sunny Saturday Afternoon

Sasha burst into her guestroom and jumped up and down on Azia's bed like a four year old. She had been trying to talk Azia out of the bed for over a week now only to get bombard with excuse after excuse about why she didn't want to come out. So instead of letting her continue to sleep the days away, she mapped out a plan refusing to take *no* for an answer.

"Get ya ass up or I will jump up and down on this bed all day if I have to," said Sasha, tiring herself out.

"Pa-leaz leave me alone," Azia begged, throwing a pillow over her head.

Sasha bounced one last time and landed on her behind. She rolled on top of Azia. "C'mon A, get up. I'm eighty-eight percent sure shopping will make you feel a little better."

Azia took her head from under the pillow and looked at her friend like she was speaking a different language. "Please tell me how you came up with eighty-eight percent."

"It's more than eighty-five, thought I'd make it sound better," she shrugged.

Azia threw the pillow at Sasha and rolled back over. "Please leave me the hell alone.

Sasha climbed out of the bed and said, "Alright, keep ya little funky attitude." She slipped back into her slippers and headed out of the bedroom.

Without opening her eyes Azia yelled out, "And stay out."

Five minutes later, Azia was awakened by an enormous amount of cold water being poured over her face and hair.

She jumped up out the bed furious. "Bitch, have you lost ya damn mind," she shouted.

"And you done lost ya damn hairstyle so get up and get dressed so we can go get it fixed," Sasha taunted. She walked out of the room with the empty glass in her hand knowing she had won.

■■■

The unisex salon was filled with men and women, some being serviced, others waiting their turn. There was a television mounted to the wall showing a sitcom but no one was really watching. Azia and Sasha walked through the door and just looked at each other. They knew one or the other had a lot of work cut out for them because getting their hair done without an appointment was going to take a lot of talking into, a wing, and a prayer.

"Look who the wind done blew in," said Lenny, their gay friend.

Sasha flopped in the empty chair at his station. "I hope that means you're happy to see us."

"Umm-Umm huzzy, don't even try it I aint foolin' wit ya'll," he twirked, with sass. Azia stood by giggling. He always seemed to amuse her. "I got too many heads in here today."

"Don't do us like that Lenny--"

"Us?!?" he asked, taking a step back. He looked over at Azia. "I aint got time for the nonsense," he mumbled, stepping around his chair and over to Azia. He ran his fingers through her hair and smelled it. "You I'll do," he said, switching back to his station. "Only because it looks like you got some kind of wet animal on top ya head." He spun the chair Sasha was sitting in around and said, "But you need to get up out my chair cause you just got yours done a few days ago, so you can wait."

Azia gave Sasha a wicked grin and pulled her out of the chair. "Excuse me--"

Nyema

Lenny interrupted before her butt could hit the cushion. "Hold on now sweetie, you still gonna have to wait ya turn," he teased, waving a client over.

Azia sucked her teeth. "You aint gotta be so rude." She grabbed a magazine from the bin and slouched down in a seat amongst the other clients that were impatiently waiting their turn.

■ ■ ■

While waiting for Lenny to get through with some of his clients, the girls decided to waste some time by walking around the corner to a nearby breakfast store to go bust a grub. But after seeing the thick mob that swarmed the place it may not have been the best idea.

"Shoot, I aint leaving I'm hungry as hell," said Sasha, excusing her way through the massive crowd of hungry people. "See if you can find us a table while I order the food."

Azia knew the odds of finding somewhere for them to sit were slim to none, but she went to look for the heck of it anyway. While sliding her way through any available opening in the air tight crowd, Azia caught the sight of Quadir sitting at a table all alone. He had his head submerged in the plate of French toast, eggs and bacon in front of him so he never seen her coming until she stood in front of him. With her *True Religion* jeans wonderfully emphasizing the gap between her legs, Quadir looked up in suspense.

Azia couldn't help but question the black eye he was sporting. "I would love to see what the other guy look like," she giggled.

"Nah, I don't think you wanna see him," he snickered, with his eyes glued to her ass as she took the empty seat across from him.

Quadir was definitely caught off guard. Had he bumped into her on a different day and was actually alone, he would have felt a hell of a lot better than he did at that moment. "How you know that seat aint taken?"

"Well if it is I guess I'll just sit here long enough for her to come back and get jealous."

"That was cute," he chuckled.

"And so are you."

Quadir dropped his fork in the plate and pushed it aside. He stared at her awkwardly trying to figure out what it was about her that had Mike all raddled.

"You had so much to say the last two times we bumped heads and now you aint got nothing to say at all."

"I was just waiting on you to bend a little. I knew it was gonna happen sooner or later."

Every nerve in her being was telling her to walk away from the danger sitting in front of her. *Oh he is really feeling himself* she told herself, swallowing the full essence of his swag. *Damn he is fine though.* "And now that I have bended a little, what's next?" she asked, before being rudely interrupted by the rattling of the dishes on the table.

Kyla appeared from out of nowhere and slammed her pocketbook on the table so hard it startled them both. They were so caught up into one another they never saw her coming. "I'm ready to go," she informed, gritting on Quadir.

Azia was surprised, confused, curious, and delighted all in one. Azia remembered seeing them talking at the boutique the day she and Kyla got into it but assumed it was a casual conversation between an employee and a customer. But this was the happiest she'd ever been to see Kyla since she'd known her, happy because she was killing two birds with one stone. It was safe to assume her and Quadir had something going on even if it wasn't serious seeing them talking was enough to ruffle her feathers. And on the other hand, Azia knew Kyla would run back to Mike and make up a bullshit ass story like she was all up in Quadir's face or something of that nature. She was hoping she did so it could stir up some jealousy in Mike.

"Well I guess my mission here is accomplished," she smiled, referring to the previous comment she made to him about making the woman he was with jealous. Finding out the woman was Kyla was icing on the cake.

Sasha stepped up to the table setting two platters on the table and eyeing Kyla like a hawk. "Is there a problem?"

Quadir stood from the table. "Naw, everything's good. Ya girl was just asking was I done so she could get this table," he lied.

Sasha surveyed his eye. "Damn, who blacked ya eye?"

Kyla sucked her teeth and started to respond for him until Quadir stopped her. He smiled trying to ease the awkwardness and said, "You ladies enjoy your food."

■■■

After eating and getting caught up with some of the folks they hadn't seen in a while, Azia and Sasha made their way out of the store and headed back towards the salon. They were laughing and joking about Quadir's black eye when someone behind the wheel of a *Grand Prix* honked the horn to capture their attention. Quadir stepped out of the car and waved Azia over.

"Damn, could you get rid of her any quicker?" she asked, meeting him half way.

"I did whatever I had to do to get back here to you," he smiled. "Hopefully you meant what you said."

"I don't speak just to hear myself talk," she sassed. "But now I might have to reconsider, especially after finding out the kind of company you keep."

Quadir glided towards her, smoothly, stopping when they were just inches apart. The sound of his voice and the scent of his cologne were so soothing it made her moist. Had he moved in for a kiss she probably would've allowed it.

"Make sure you use this," he said, sticking a folded piece of paper between their lips. It was the only thing standing between her and the kiss she was thriving for. "You won't be disappointed."

She watched him stroll back to his car conceitedly as Sasha made her way over.

"I know what you thinking Azia, but I'm telling you don't do it to yourself," she advised. Azia stuck the number into her jean pocket and smiled. "I know that smile girlfriend. I held the same one too many times before and I'ma tell you like this, if you decide to step out and go hoe-bounce thinking it's the best way to get back at Mike, you gonna wound up losing him forever."

"Girl I was a hoe way before Mike came along," she joked.

The girls shared a moment of laughter before continuing on to the salon. "On some real shit, if you decide to make moves make sure you don't tell me shit," Sasha exclaimed. "I don't need nothing coming in between me and my dick again after I finally got me some."

"Damn you finally got you a piece? That's why ya ass was all giddy jumping up and down on beds early in the damn morning."

"I had to rape his ass but hey, I take it how I can get it," she shrugged.

Chapter 19

GOING STIR CRAZY

Rashaud stood at attention while Helena tugged at his pants from below. She looked up and smiled at him seductively, and then went to work with her tongue like she was sucking milk from a cow.

"Damn, girl," he moaned. "You got a nigga trippin'." Caught up in the groove of things, Rashaud lost himself in the past. With his eyes closed, visions of him and Azia clouded his mind. He missed her terribly and although she had stolen his money and was the reason behind him going to jail, she still and would always be the love of his life.

Rashaud squeezed Helena's head so tight she was no longer in control. He guided her head back and forth, left to right, and around in circles. She hung in there for as long as she possibly could, but after gagging uncontrollably and almost out of air, she ripped herself from his grip and jumped up from the floor.

"What the hell is your problem Rashaud," she shouted, gasping for air.

"What the fuck are you talking about?" he asked, pulling his pants up. "All of a sudden you can't handle suckin' a nigga dick." He knew he was dead wrong but he didn't care. "And you always wanna question why I've always treated her better than you," he barked, referring to Azia.

Helena stood frozen. Not only did she feel stupid, she felt deflated, embarrassed. She could feel her knees getting weak as thoughts of everything she'd done for him while he was down raced through her mind. *He got the audacity to throw that bitch name in my face after all I have done for him*. She took a seat on the edge of the bed and dropped her head in her lap, knees bouncing and heart thumping.

"You's a weak ass bitch," he spat. "There, you wanted to know why I aint in love wit you, now you know."

Helena picked her weight up from the sofa and threw herself at him. "I fuckin' hate ya ass," she screamed.

Helena wasn't a bad looking female. With her five-foot-seven coke bottle shape and beautiful long curved legs, she never had a problem pulling a man. Not even after she birthed her and Rashaud's baby because breastfeeding slimmed her right back into shape. But her only down fall was falling in love with a man that didn't know how to love her back.

Rashaud focused his attention on the darkness in her eyes. It was something he had never seen in her before. "Bitch is you crazy?" he asked, flinging her off of him.

And again, she rushed him like a defensive end rushing a quarterback and went to smack him but he blocked it. "How can you treat me like this after all I've done for you?" she cried. "I would do anything for you and you running around here chasing after a bitch that don't want your no good ass. And I heard about how you out there fuckin' all these other bitches too while I'm sitting in here taking care of ya son."

Rashaud was amused. This was the most excitement he had since he'd got out, and seeing this feisty side of Helena made him proud. "What you want me to say I was just fuckin' them hoes I was gonna get right back?"

"Don't give me that Jay-Z bullshit--"

"When you act like you don't wanna be fucked I make moves. End of discussion." He sat on the bed to put his Tim's on, guiltless. "Now just be happy I don't tear ya ass up for punching me in my fuckin' face."

Helena wiped the tears away from her face and watched him stroll over to the dresser. He picked up his brush and started brushing his hair, smoothly. "All that crying shit is for the birds," he smirked. "Suck that shit up and go clean ya face off." He flung the brush on top of the dresser. "And go shut that crying ass baby up."

■ ■ ■

Mike was in the office at the boutique counting money and updating the books, something Azia had always taken care of and to be honest, he was missing her. At first it was because he'd gotten so use to waking up to her in the morning, but now he was missing her for a lot of other reasons. On top of dealing with KoKa's man problems and handling all of his street business, he had to find a way to keep on top of everything else together, the boutique as well as all his other properties. Now that he had to do it all by himself, he was kicking himself in the ass for letting things between he and Azia get so far out of control. They had been beefing long enough and it was time to make shit right.

"What up pimpin'," said Camel, voluntarily busting into the office.

"I guess you really don't know how to knock do you?" quizzed Mike.

"I knew you wasn't in here getting' no ass so--"

"Next time I'ma greet you wit something real special if ya ass don't knock."

Camel flagged him. "Kane said he gonna meet up in a hour. You ready to ride?"

"Yeah, I just gotta drop this by the bank," he said, stepping from behind the desk with the moneybag in his hand. "What are they out there doing?"

"Flirting wit every dick that swing through the door," he laughed.

Mike shook his head. He knew he had to get Azia back in there fast because dealing with Mel and Sophie was something he didn't want to do. He and Camel made their way out of the office and back onto the store floor. Mel was ringing a couple customers up and Sophie was in the corner acting like she was straightening up.

He waited for Mel to finish with the customers and joined her behind the register. "I gotta make a run but I'll be back," he said. "Ya'll cool in here by ya'll selves?"

"It's been slow today so I'm sure we'll be okay," she said, breaking her neck to see who had just entered the store.

Sophie's eyes followed Helena as she walked straight up to the counter with purpose. Being the news box that she was, she moved in closer and started to refold another pile of clothes and she and Mel glanced at one another with curious eyes.

"I'm looking for Azia," Helena stated.

Mike looked up at the unfamiliar woman. "And you are?"

"Tired of her ass," she spat. "Is she here or what?"

"No she's not here and I'm gonna have to ask you to please leave my store."

"Oh," she blurted, sucking her teeth. "So you Mike?"

"Last time I checked."

She shifted all her weight up on top of the counter. "Do me a favor and tell ya whore to stay away from my man."

"And who would that be?"

"Rashaud," she smirked, thinking the name would cause a reaction.

Mike crossed from behind the counter and stepped in front of her. "Do I look like I have time to get in the middle of you and that nut ass nigga bullshit?" he asked, in a threatening tone. "Now I asked you the first time but now I'm telling you to step on the other side of that door and don't come back in here unless you looking to buy something."

Helena rolled her eyes and switched her flat ass out of the store.

Mike watched until the door closed behind her, then he directed his attention to Camel. "You ready man?" Camel nodded. "I'll be back in a few," he advised, and they were out.

Nyema

■■■

Going against her gut, Azia allowed Sasha and Lenny to talk her into hanging out with them after leaving the salon that night. It was just after ten o'clock and she was already irked because she ended up being the last one to get her hair done. The only reason she survived was because of all the folks that came in and out, including a DVD bootlegger, costume jewelry pusher and bean pie slinger that managed to keep her entertained.

With Sasha being the designated driver, they turned onto 3rd off of Callowhill and pulled into the congested parking lot across from a Saloon. The bass from the music coming from inside lingered amongst the night air, busy streets and cheerful crowd. "I don't believe I let you talk me into coming out," muttered Azia. "I aint even dressed."

Sasha surveyed Azia as she stood tall in a white fitted button up shirt, her denim washed True Religions and a chic pair of red pointy-toe pumps that match her red clutch perfectly. She locked arms with her as they headed across the street and said, "Girl don't worry about it, it's only *Buckhead*," she smirked. "Just c'mon, I got something that's gonna make you feel so much better."

■■■

Less than an hour later, Sasha had lived up to her word. Azia wasn't a heavy drinker but that night, she drank in the worse way and sure she'd live to regret it the next morning. After her second drink, the liquor had already begun to send a calming sentiment through her body. Not only was the thought of losing the baby clouding her mind, they distance between her and Mike bothered her deeply. For the first time in a long time, she felt like her world was sinking.

Using the alcohol to wash all the problems away for the night, Azia gulped down her fourth cocktail. She didn't know what was in those drinks, but whatever Sasha had the bartender concoct had her ready to ride the mechanical bull stationed in the back of the club. Accompanied by Sasha, she bypassed the line of people waiting to ride like she was a celebrity getting stardom treatment. There were some loud whispers and stares, but no one stepped forward to stop them.

"You better ride that monkey," blurted Lenny. He appeared out of nowhere and stood beside Sasha with three drinks in his hands. He handed Sasha one of them.

Azia handed over a five dollar bill to the attendant and stepped into the inflatable bull pit. The man helped her up onto the bull and from there it was chaos. At first she held onto the rope like a born pro thinking she had everything under control. Then suddenly, the bull took off, quick, fast, and undefeatable. It swung from left to right, back and forth, up and down until forcing her to fly aimlessly onto her face. The crowd erupted in laughter, including Sasha and Lenny before they hurried over to help her out of the pit.

Lenny threw her a high-five. "Ya drunk ass lasted longer than I thought you would," he said, handing her another drink.

Azia threw it back, her fifth one of the night. The more drinks that came, the stronger they were. After while, she said to hell with cocktails and started taking straight shots.

"Slow ya ass down it aint going nowhere," yelled Sasha. "You probably can't even see straight."

"I can see just find," Azia slurred, and a large hand landed on Azia's shoulder from behind. Startled, she spun and tried to register the face. *What the hell is this fool doing here* she wondered.

"Enjoying the view from the back," he said, reading her mind.

"Stalker," she grinned. "I thought I told you to stay away from me."

"You know Philly aint but so big. We're gonna run into each other."

Sasha whispered into Lenny's ear, "Stay here and watch her."

Nyema

Lenny sipped on his drink while cutting his eye discretely in their direction. *He sure is fine I wonder who he is* he thought.

Sasha stepped into the restroom and retrieved her cell phone from her pocketbook. She scrolled through her contacts and stopped on Mike's name. "Hey Mike, I think you need to get down here. Azia been drinking and the dude Rashaud is in here."

"Alright…" is all he said before ending the call.

Sasha made her way back over to where she'd left them and scanned the area ferociously until Lenny pointed her in the direction of the dance floor. After tracking them down, she snatched Azia away. "Why you letting this nigga dance all over you?"

"He said he missed me," Azia smiled, tugging at his shirt. "He also said he can treat me better than Mike can," she slurred, then burst into a sloppy laugh.

Sasha didn't find anything funny. "Listen, you had too much to drink. It's time for you to go home and sleep that shit off. Mike's on his way." She rolled her eyes and Rashaud smiled in return. "And you might wanna be gone when he get here," she warned.

■ ■ ■

Rather than stop her oral assault on Mike's man of steel, Kyla continued to bob up and down on him while he took Sasha's call. She cradled his sac with one hand and fondled it with her fingertips. Coming up for air, she kissed around the head of his shaft then slid her tongue along its full length.

Meticulously enjoying the pleasure that radiated from down below, Mike gripped her hair vigorously as his eyes rolled to the back of his head every time she took him deeper into his mouth. Overwhelmed by the pleasure of her tongue and drunken off of pure bliss, he struggled to comprehend right from wrong. He cupped the back of her head just as his body started to tremble in response to the actions he was receiving.

Kyla brushed her tongue in a circular motion around the tip of his penis, licking away the bead of moisture that had already begun to form at the top. She gazed up at him briefly and murmured, "I love you Mike," and then took a part of him back into her mouth, lubricating every bit of it with saliva.

Mike's body stiffened as she continued to suck him hungrily. Minutes later, a burst of semen shot down the back of her throat. "Aww shit girl…" he grunted. "FUCK!" His body began to jerk wildly.

As she felt the warm thick semen fill her tongue, Kyla squeezed her lips tighter and quickened the pace, sliding every inch of him in and out of her hot little mouth, the head tapping the back of her throat while her nipples teased his thighs with each bob. She continued to lick him clean until every drop was accounted for. Now even more anxious to find her own sexual haven, she pulled her weight up from the floor and started to caress his chest, but he stopped her and began to collect his things. It was very clear that their plans for the night were on the verge of being ruined.

"I thought you were gonna chill with me tonight," she screeched, in her soft squeaky voice.

"I got shit to do," he said, slipped his pants back on. "Something came up." He walked over to a chair that was cattycornered against the wall and grabbed his shirt.

"Yeah, you always got shit to do. Everything but what you need to be doing."

"Fuck that 'pose to mean?"

Kyla rolled her eyes, stormed out of the room and into the bathroom, slamming the door behind her. She knew her position and knew not to question it, but that didn't mean she had to like it. She wanted to be Mike's woman and after the paternity test stated that he was the father of her son, she thought she'd won. How silly of her.

Mike stared momentarily in the direction she headed then continued to dress. Him being there had nothing to do with their son, he knew how to be a father without dealing with her, but decided to continue dipping and dabbing for one reason and one reason only. Kyla had mastered the skill of milking a man dry with her tongue. She gave a toe-curling, leg shaking, eyes rolling kind of head, a kind any man would risk cheating for.

After pulling a wad of cash from his pocket, Mike tossed five hundred dollars on the bed and showed himself out.

Chapter 20

FOR THE GOOD OF THE CITY

Just when DJ Khaled's *All I Do Is Win* blared out of the speakers and ninety percent of the crowd rushed to the dance floor, Sasha received a text from Mike stating he was out front. She waved Lenny over and the two of them helped Azia out the door.

"I can walk," said Azia, tripping over her own feet.

Mike was double parked in front of the place with his emergency blinkers on. Noticing how bent Azia was, he hopped out of the car with his jaw set in the mad position. He looked at Sasha with flames in his eyes.

"I don't know what you looking at me like that for, shit," she yapped, sourly. "She need to learn how to hold her liquor."

Sasha noticed Rashaud standing a short distance away talking to three other guys. She stopped Mike before he had a chance to step off and said, "There go that bastard over there."

Mike turned his head slightly and set his eyes on the enemy. He carried Azia over to the car and laid her across the back seat. He then strolled over to where Rashaud was conversing and cut through the circle. "This is the first and last time I'ma tell you this," he stated, coolly. "The next time you come anywhere around me or my family, I'm gonna make you wish ya mother had a girl instead of your pussy ass." Mike went to walk away but turned back one last time and said, "And I dare you to test me muthafucka."

Rashaud grinned. Any other man would have been embarrassed for getting stepped to like that but not him. He knew if he was able to take Mike off his square, he had to be some kind of threat. "This ya world big tymer," Rashaud shouted, watching Mike walk back to his car. "Don't waste ya energy on lil ol' me." He smacked hands with a couple of his boys. "That nigga scared she gonna want this old thang back," he said, grabbing himself. "He know what it is."

■ ■ ■

The morning after was far from a pleasant one for Azia. She woke up to a serious migraine wishing she hadn't showed her ass the night before. There was very few she could remember, but what she did recall was Mike bringing her to their condo, stripping her naked and throwing her in a tub of cold water, but the images before that were vague.

Locked behind the bathroom door, Azia stood at the bathroom sink struggling to see her reflection through the all the steam the hot shower left behind. She opened the medicine cabinet looking for something to take the edge off. Settling on some pain killers, she popped a couple into her mouth and used some water from the sink. Trying desperately to chase the hangover away, she closed her eyes and let her head fall gently against the mirror.

Mike rolled out of his sleeping position and propped himself up on a couple pillows when he heard the bathroom door open. He started flipping through the channels like he'd been watching television for a while.

I will curse his ass out if he even think about starting his shit the way I feel she thought, never looking his way. He said nothing. She dragged herself over to the walk-in closet draped in a towel and came out wearing one of his T-shirts. She climbed back into bed, turned her back toward him and prayed he'd just let her be.

After some serious contemplating, Mike slid up behind her and began to massage her shoulders. "You need anything?" he asked.

Azia was stunned. She just knew he was going to grill and interrogate her about last night. "I just want to lay here," she mumbled.

With her assistance, he slid the shirt up over her head and tossed it to the side. He then leaned over to his side of the bed, pulled a bottle of relaxation oil from out of nowhere and began to rub her down in it.

■ ■ ■

An hour and a half full body massage, compliments of her Boo, brunch at Souzai Sushi & Sake and shopping at The Pier Shops at Caesars quickly brought Azia back to life. She made sure to hit all the high-end stores taking full advantage of the last minute shopping spree. From Victoria Secret to True Religion, Burberry to Gucci, Michael Kors to Salvatore Ferragamo, Betsey Johnson to Louis Vuitton, Mike sat back and watched as she pranced through every store dropping close to ten grand in a matter of five hours. *If it's gonna get me this kind of attention I need to show my ass more often* she told herself. Her morning had shifted from hell to heaven when he suggested they spend the day in Atlantic City together. No fussing, no fighting, no bickering, no questions, no drama, just the two of them enjoying one another.

On the ride home, Azia looked over her shoulder at him and smiled. She was glad to be back in his company and hopefully he took enough time to get his shit together. She was okay with playing step-mom, but what she wasn't going to deal with was Kyla using that baby to get at her man.

"What you thinking bout?" he asked, looking back and forth between her and the road.

"Something I haven't done in a while," she said, leaning across the armrest to unbuckle his pants. "I missed you."

Mike had one hand on the wheel and the other on the top of her head as she blessed him down below for the rest of the ride home. He had a hard time concentrating every now and then, swerving in and out of lanes her and there, but luckily for him there weren't too many troopers out that night on the Atlantic City Expressway. He loved everything about that girl. The way she walked, the way she talked, the way she smelled, the way she nibbled at her food, the way she bit down on her bottom lip every time she got angry and especially the way she loved loving him.

Just miles away from the Philadelphia-New Jersey border, Mike released all he had inside and Azia tastefully swallowed every last drop. "Damn baby," he muttered, catching his breath. "You know how to thank a nigga don't you," he smiled.

She repositioned herself in the seat and patted her hair down back into place. "I got a lot more to say when we get home," she grinned.

Using his knee to drive, Mike buckled his pants and wiped any proof of an orgasm from his face. "I gotta stop and Lowes to pick up a few things for the new building. After that I'm all yours." Hearing those words felt like music. She couldn't remember the last time the two of them had spent the entire day together. "Hey baby, it's something I been meaning to ask you."

"What's that?"

"The dude Rashaud," he said. "Did you know he was home before last night?"

Azia's heart skipped two beats. She didn't know how to answer that without telling the whole truth about her setting up that meeting with him so she kept it short and simple. "Yeah I knew," she said, wishing she could melt and become part of the leather she was sitting on.

"Why didn't you mention it to me?"

"Cause we were going through all that other bullshit I didn't wanna add heat to the fire."

"And that's all it was about?" He pulled into Lowes parking lot off 52nd Street and stood outside the car so he could finish adjusting his clothes. "Aint no more to ya story?"

Azia nodded her head *no* with believing eyes. She didn't know what he knew or what he heard and was afraid to ask. *Please just let him leave it alone* she wished.

When Mike and Azia entered the store, they became the center of attention. Folks had a tough time keeping their eyes to themselves when one or the other stepped into a room alone, but when they stepped together, it was powerful a sight to see. They were the Will and Jada, the Jay and Beyoncé, of the hood.

You got to be fuckin' shitting me thought Mike, when they turned down the paint isle. Kyla happened to be walking down the same isle with one of her girlfriends carrying some paint and a few brushes. *Now I know I told that girl I would get the damn paint.*

"Just your luck," Azia smirked.

"Don't start that shit up in here," warned Mike. "I mean it Azia. Leave that girl alone."

Mike decided to stop and greet her knowing there was no way to avoid it. The women eyed one another harshly. Azia felt a little overpowered because Kyla's girlfriend was gritting on her too. It didn't scare her one bit. *If these bitches try to make a move on me I'm gonna fuck at least one of them up* she thought. But as if Kyla read her mind, she broke her stare and turned to Mike.

"I already got the paint so you don't need to," she said.

"I told you I'd take care of it, give it here," he said, taking the items from her. "I'll get the rest of the shit just go ahead home." He was pissed, but there was nothing he could say or do about it. It wasn't like Kyla knew they'd be there.

"You gonna meet me there?" she asked, and then winked at Azia.

Azia couldn't wait for her to cross that line so she could have a reason to slide her, again. "See, now this bitch tryna be smart," she snapped, trying to leap over but was stopped dead in her tracks. "You dizzy bitch." She yanked herself from Mike's grip. "I don't even know why I bother." She walked off and went to wait for him in the front of the store.

Nyema

As soon as he walked up to the cashier she asked, "So this who you in here shopping for? I thought you said it was for one of ya buildings."

The cashier along with other pedestrians standing nearby listened on nosily.

"You need to bite ya tongue Azia, you know this aint the time or place."

"You taking care of her now, buying shit to fix her spot up. What you a painter now?" she taunted. "You still fuckin' her aint you?" Mike counted out the money to take care of the balance in silence. "Answer my question."

"Yeah I'm fuckin' her," he responded, stepping in her face. "Now shut ya ass up and go wait in the car."

Azia stared at him with teary eyes before storming out of the store. Mike couldn't believe he'd let her take him there, especially in front of a store full of strangers.

"Thank you," he said, practically snatching his change from the cashier.

When Mike got to his car, Azia was nowhere in sight. He scanned the perimeter then jumped in his car and screeched his way out of the parking spot, vexed. *A beautiful fuckin' day turned into a marvelous fuckin' disaster* he thought. When he got to the entrance of the plaza, he spotted Azia trucking in her Manolo Blahniks. *I should make her ass walk.* He pulled along the curb and rolled down the window. "Get the hell in the car." Azia kept walked ignoring his commands. He drove slowly along the curb to keep up. Cars that came up behind him laid on their horns in an attempt to get him out of the way, but he ignored making them involuntarily go around. "Don't make me get out this car and come get you."

Azia knew damn well she wasn't walking all the way home and stepping onto public transportation in her Chanel wasn't even an option. With her lips poked out, she stepped fluently towards the car only this time the joke was on her. Mike stopped to let her in, but when she went to open the door, he inched up, pumping the breaks.

"Stop playing," she whined, going for the door and he inched up again. "The shit aint funny," she hissed, "You play too damn much."

Neither of them noticed the guy dressed in dark blue baggy jeans, a black hooded windbreaker and a fitted baseball cap. Walking back and forth on the other side of the street, he'd already passed them three times.

Mike finally allowed her to get in. "What you call yaself walking home?" he teased.

Azia stared him down furiously with her beautiful chinky eyes. She had so much she wanted to say but too angry to part her lips to say any of it.

"It's fuckin' me up how you actin' all mad and shit when you runnin' round the city in other niggas faces."

"Whatever--"

"Yeah I bet," he sneered. "That's what you always say to get out of some shit."

Instead of responded and going back and forth, she shut up and started tapping her leg when all of a sudden...*shots rang out.*

The sudden slamming of breaks sent cars screeching and flying in the midst of it all. Azia and Mike ducked as low as they could as an array of bullets connected with the car. He instinctively positioned himself over top of her body as a shield. Luckily for them, after the shooting subsided only three bullets had actually connected with his ride, one shattering the back window and two were lodged in the trunk.

The gunman stuffed the gun back inside of his pants, pulled the baseball cap down to meet his eyes and threw the hood over top of it. In no rush at all, he walked away with his hands in his pockets watching the concrete pass beneath him.

Chapter 21

INSIDE ENEMY LINES

Quadir made his way back to 55th & Wyalusing and hustled inside of the place that he'd been calling home for the last six months. The downstairs was scarcely furnished. There was nothing but a leather sofa, coffee table and 50" Plasma that occupied the living room area, and the Dining Room was completely empty.

Quadir jogged up the squeaky staircase, two at a time. He pulled a key from his pocket and let himself inside of the secured bedroom. The room was immaculate. All the walls were painted red with small bits of black décor to break it up. The furnishings included a King bed, one nightstand, dresser and a 46" flat screen. The room looked like something straight out of a Scarface flick.

Quadir snatched the baseball cap from his head and flung it in the small trashcan located beside the dresser. He then slid the black hooded windbreaker over his head, tossed it in the trash and adjusted his wife beater back into place. There was no doubt about it, he'd definitely been lifting a weight or two lately. After safely removing the pistol from the back of his pants, he placed it under his pillow and fell down backwards onto the bed with his arms folded behind his head. He stared up at the ceiling with a shit-eating grin on his face silently singing the lyrics to a well-known song, but his version. *One two Quadir's coming for you…*

■ ■ ■

After sitting on the scene of the shooting amongst a slew of cops for over an hour and telling them the same thing over and over again, "we don't know who it was", they finally released Azia and Mike, of course keeping the car as so called evidence. It didn't matter though because there was no way Mike was getting back in that whip. They could have it. Azia collected all their belongings and put them in the back of Kane's car.

■ ■ ■

Back at the boutique, Mike and Kane were in the middle of discussing what happened while Azia occupied herself on the phone with Sasha. Mike was leaning against the front edge of the desk listening to Kane try to make sense of everything that been happening. There was way too many loop holes.

"I'm telling you man, I don't buy it," he stressed, standing directly in front of Mike. "Aint no way nobody gonna pop at somebody that many times and only three bullets hit." He shook his head and took a step back. "And it aint like ya wheel was moving, the shit was parked," he reminded, astonished. "I don't give a fuck how bad a shooter you are, that shit just aint happening."

"So what you thinking?" asked Mike, folding his arms across his chest and crossing his feet. He already knew where Kane was getting at because he too had the same thoughts.

"That them muthafuckas," he stated, assuming that there was more than one assailant. "They weren't shooting to kill, it was to either get ya attention or prove a point." Kane was so sure of himself. He threw his hands in the air and said, "I don't think they was tryna get at ya'll for real. Just like I don't think whoever robbed the spot left all them niggas in there alive just for the hell of it. Somebody's definitely tryna say something, maybe the bol' Rashaud."

Mike was impressed. He knew his man was no idiot, but for reasons like this is why Kane was his right hand man. He was good at thinking out the box. In a situation like that, an ordinary ol' trigger happy youngin' would've made a move under pressure. But this was bigger than that, and it was up to them to find out just how much bigger this thing really was.

Nyema

"Make sense," said Mike, moving around to the other side of the desk. "But I don't give a damn who it was or if they meant to hit me or not, my girl was in the car and if something would've happened to her," he said, with squinted eyes.

Kane put one hand up. "I already know," he replied. "I'm gonna follow up wit Sammy and see what he been able to gather up and I'll touch base wit you later." The men smacked hands with a slight hug. He grabbed his keys from the desk and headed for the door. "Ya Denali out front I had Lox bring it over."

Azia got up and followed behind him. "Can you drop me off at your house?"

"You aint going nowhere but home," said Mike, walking towards her.

"I aint going nowhere wit you."

"I aint got time for the petty ass jealous shit, Azia. You think what happened tonight is a game. Ya ass is going home. I don't give a damn 'bout ya attitude."

She turned to Kane and said, "Drop me off please."

"What--"

Kane stepped between them trying to diffuse the situation. "I got her dogg," he advised. "I'll take her straight to the house. Just let her cool off for the night." He gave him the *let it ride homie* stare.

Mike looked at Azia. "Call me when you get to the house," he demanded.

Feeling nothing but bitterness and resentment, she rolled her eyes and left the room.

◼ ◼ ◼

The second Kyla heard the front door shut she jumped up from the bed and flew over to the mirror to make sure she looked presentable. She moved back over to the bed to make sure her son was still asleep then headed downstairs. Following the sound of some footsteps, she made her way into the kitchen smiling from ear to ear. But as soon as she came face to face to welcome her guest, the smile quickly transformed into a frown.

"What the hell are you doing here Quadir?"

"Who you thought I was that other nigga?" he chuckled. "Go take ya ass upstairs and put some clothes on."

"I told you before you can't be walking up in here whenever you get ready. What if I was in here with Mike?"

"Chill the fuck out. I checked for his car before I came in."

She held out her hand. "Give me my damn key back cause you gonna wound up fucking it up for the both of us."

"Damn you aint never got shit in here to eat," he said, looking in the refrigerator. "Whip a nigga something up, I'm starving."

Kyla shook her head and let her eyes roll to the back of her head. "I aint making shit," she said, heading out of the kitchen. "Get off me," she yelled, when he reached in to grab her.

"C'mere, I want some pussy." He was always up front and to the point. No cutting corners, no beating around the bush, he gave it to her like it was. She hated the way he talked to her but what could she do. Nothing! She needed him just as much as he needed her.

A couple years months back when Quadir and Kyla started kicking it, or fucking which is what he called it, Kyla fell in love and was ready to settle down until he flat out told her "aint no strings attached". She thought if she worked on him a little longer and showed him she could be that *ride or die* chick every man wants in his corner he'd eventually grow to love her. But when that didn't happen, she took it for what it was and went back to *doing her*. That was until Mike came along and all she could see was money signs. The only problem with him was that he, in no way shape or form, was ready or willing to commit, especially to her since she had already given the pussy up to half of his boys, including Kane. Nine months and two heartbreaks later, a new baby boy was born and although she had a good idea who the father was, out of shame and humiliation of being wrong she decided to keep the baby under wraps and not press the issue about whether he belonged to daddy #1 or daddy #2.

"Would you leave before Mike decides to pop up," she suggested, in no mood to deal with him or his hard core attitude.

"A'ight. But let me get some head and I'm out."

"No!"

Quadir stood at the sink and gulped down a bottle of water. "I'm tryna be nice. Don't make me make you."

Kyla dragged herself over to him and placed her hands on the sink, pinning him in between her arms. "I can't stand ya monkey ass," she said, dropping to her knees.

"I know but you still gonna give me some head though," he grinned.

Months after the baby was born, Quadir popped back up on the scene questioning the paternity. She never lied to him, told him straight up that it was either his or Mike's. To her surprise he was happy and it wasn't until later did she find out exactly why. Trusting her enough to tell her his plot to get Azia, he knew she would ride with it. Anything to break them two up she was all for, even if she had to use her own child to do it. And finally, all the hard work was paying off, for her at least and Quadir was cool with that because he knew it was just a matter of time before he got his...

Chapter 22

BEAUTY-N-THE BEAST

So what you tryna get into?" asked Quadir, crossing the Walt Whitman Bridge heading into New Jersey with Azia on the passenger side.

When her call came through, he wasn't surprised. And just to make her feel special, he put on a big front like he dropped everything he was doing to come and holler at her.

"You driving like you already know where we going," she responded, sarcastically.

"I don't know where I'm going, but I know it aint safe for us to stay in Philly, right?"

What he call his self looking out for me she smirked. Azia's conscience had been messing with her ever since she got in the car. She tried to talk herself out of the date, but after thinking about everything Mike's been putting her through lately she gave in to the temptation. "This way is cool. I know this new spot over Deptford, we can chill over there," she directed, leaning her seat all the way back and smiled because Quadir couldn't keep his eyes off of her. She watched him slip in *John Legend's* CD and closed her eyes when the beat to *Ordinary People* played softly through the airways. *Umm, let me find out this nigga a smooth criminal* she laughed to herself. *Damn he fine.*

■■■

Vipor made her way through a nice-size crowd of horny hustlers and a slew of promiscuous women just as Nelly's *Tip Drill* came on inside of D's Gentleman's Club. She saw Sammy and Deuce in the middle of a pool game out her peripheral view. They had been playing for a couple hours already and the loser had to take a shot of Hennessey.

Nyema

Although Deuce talked a good game, he was no pool shark and Sammy knew this. Five games later, Deuce was five shots in and drunk out his mind. Sammy glanced over at her and winked his eye. Game on!

"This nigga cheatin'," slurred Deuce. "C'mon chump, play me again."

"Nah! How bout we go blow some money on these hoes."

"I want her," Deuce said, grabbing the arm of one of the dancers that was walking by.

She flung her skinny arm in the air. "You can't afford me," she advised, and then strutted her thin curve less frame towards the next potential client.

"Don't worry bout her, I got somebody way better for you."

As if on cue, the music suddenly switched from one song to the next and the DJ gripped the microphone. "Alright fellas," he said, "I know ya'll been waiting for this one." The beat of Akon's *I Wanna Love You* filled the speakers. "Don't be stingy, go ahead and get dem dollars together," he coached. A female's silhouette appeared in the shadows of the stage. "Here she comes. Go get 'em Vipor."

Vipor appeared under a florescent light and slow danced her way across the stage, seductively and with confidence. She was wearing a red one piece bodysuit with rigged rips throughout. All the regulars swarmed the stage making it rain money without hesitation. She crossed over from one to the other, men and women, allowing them to fill any available opening. Unnoticeably, she worked the stage with her eye on one person in particular. Deuce!

"Now that's a bad bitch," Sammy chuckled. "You see she keep looking at you?" he asked, boasting his ego.

Deuce inched his way through the spectators to get a better view. He positioned himself in a chair without taking his eyes off her. Finally, Vipor made her way over and twirled her bottom in a way she hadn't before. Without saying a word, she squatted in front of him and clapped her ass like it was applauding the president.

Deuce was passed impressed, hooked. "Goddamn girl." He stood and tossed a stack of ones at her. "You can have it all." She spun around on her knees and crawled towards him. He pulled a twenty from his stack and said, "You gonna have to work for this one."

Vipor grabbed hold of the brass bar along the stage and used it to prop herself up on her head like a pro. In position, she rocked her hips to the rhythm of the beat then released herself landing backwards on his lap. The sweet scent of cherry blossom attacked his nose.

"Look good, smell good," he whispered, while his hands roved her body.

Vipor allowed her head to fall back on his chest for their faces to meet. She replied, "I taste good too."

"How 'bout you let me be the judge of that." Her body was talking and he loved what it was saying.

Vipor licked his nose and twirled her twenty-four inch waist around like it was spinning a hula-hoop. Deuce stuck the twenty between her chest and she made her way back up on stage.

Sammy appeared with two drinks in his hands. With his eyes glued on Vipor, he took a seat next to Deuce and passed one of the cups to him. "She the truth aint she?"

Deuce took a sip from the cup and nodded his head at her. "She want me."

Sammy sucked his teeth. "Get the fuck outta here. You always on some ol' King of the jungle type shit," he giggled.

Sammy watched Deuce recline back in the seat like he was a King but he couldn't wait to wash that smirk clean off his face. He'd been trying for days to get some information out of Deuce about the robbery without him becoming suspicious. All he'd been able to find out was that Deuce was working on the side for someone else. Who that someone else was he had no idea. It was like the guy had him under some kind of secret alliance or something. So after talking it over with Kane, they came up with plan B.

Nyema

Sasha told them she had somebody at the club that would be able to work the information right up out of his weak ass in no time. And her name was Vipor!

Chapter 23

PROTECTION FROM THE TRUTH

Mike sat in Georgio's fancy million-dollar mansion sipping on Grey Goose and watching the NFL highlights on ESPN. Through the large glass window he noticed three half-naked women playing around out back by the in ground pool. He shook his head and smiled waiting patiently for Georgio to join him. Not long after Georgio presented himself wearing nothing but a pair of Speedos. Mike couldn't help but laugh at the man's oversized potbelly, the nerve of him.

Mike sat his drink down and stood to greet him. "I see some things never change," he smiled, as the two men hands collided.

"Hey, you know me," he replied, with a smile as well. "Ladies love meat, they don't want just skin and bones no more," he chuckled. "That was ol' school my man." They both sat and made themselves comfortable. "How's things out there in the real world?"

"A little shaken up right now but aint nothing I can't handle," said Mike. "I've seen worse."

"I'm sure you have."

"You said you had something you needed to holler at me about. Got anything to do with the stick-up at my spot?"

"Nah...Nah...Nah...Got something a little deeper than that to bring to your attention," he smiled, as he prolonged Mike's curiosity.

Mike shifted his position in the chair and braced himself for whatever Georgio had to say. When he received the call from him a few days back advising he wanted to meet, it alarmed him at first. But after thinking it over, he knew the man too well than to assume negatively. "Well you got me, I'm all ears."

After a few more minutes of the small talk, Georgio said, "Mike, I want you to meet an old friend of mine. We go way back."

Again Mike shifted positions in his seat. With everything he had going on lately, he didn't know who to trust or what to expect. He had no idea who the *friend* was, but he was wishing he'd never agreed to let the guard confiscate his gun before entering the home, which was one of the rules for any visitor of Georgio's. There wasn't anything he could do about it now but roll with the flow. He watched Georgio's beer belly lead the way out of the room and within seconds, he was back, but he wasn't alone.

"Mike," he said, both men heading his way. "I want you to meet Omar." He turned to Omar and said, "I'm sure you two have a ton to discuss." He left the room to give the men some privacy.

Mike stood and faced Omar, inquisitively. His eyes scanned him thoroughly with intent. He knew he had never seen the man before, but something in his face was all too familiar.

Omar extended his hand and said, "I'm glad we finally got the chance to meet." Their hands collided. "Might as well have a seat because we're gonna be here for a while."

■ ■ ■

All was quiet inside of Sasha's living room, but outside the neighborhood was still very much alive. Sasha was glued to her sofa, motionless, staring up at the ceiling with a blank expression on her face. Something heavy weighed deeply on her mind. She slid a piece of paper from under her leg and looked it over for the nineteenth time hoping something would change, but it read the same thing it did just five minutes ago. Positive for Chlamydia!

"Damn, that muthafucker," she shouted. "I can't believe this bullshit." She sat upright on the edge of the sofa and dropped her head in her lap, knees bouncing with anticipation. Never had she thought about causing Kane any kind of harm until that very moment.

Almost a half hour later, Sasha picked her weight up from the sofa and grabbed some tissues to clean her face, then headed for the kitchen. Seconds later, she was on her way upstairs with a small bottle of hot chili pepper and a steak knife.

The loud snoring coming from their bedroom jerked her attention as she glided across the Persian carpet that dressed the floor. She stopped and stared his way for a moment. Kane was sleeping like a baby, so peaceful it made her cringe. She used the light glaring from the television to guide her over to his bedside. *You like fuckin' around on me muthafucka,* she thought as she lifted his pants and boxers from the floor. *Let's see if you can handle the consequences, you dirty bastard.* She damn near poured the entire bottle of hot chili pepper in the crotch of both garments, and then as quiet, as she could she tiptoed to the closet and pulled the iron down from the shelf.

Without a second thought, Sasha walked back over to his side of the bed, plugged the iron in and brought it to life. It took only seconds for the steam from the water to start brewing. "You wanna feel my pain Kane?" she said aloud. He didn't budge so she moved the iron closer to his face, only inches away from his skin. "I said do you wanna feel my pain?" she repeated.

Between the heat coming from the iron and the bass in her voice, Kane woke up and in one swift motion; he slid up and backwards to safety. "Girl put that fuckin' iron down," he demanded. "Are you crazy?"

Her eyes begged to differ. "I'm pass crazy you rotten bastard," she winced. "Ya ass better be lucky I aint insane or you'd be peeling ya face off of here," she said, raising the iron.

Kane slid across the bed and jumped to his feet making the bed his barrier. "Fuck wrong wit you?"

"I'm asking all the questions."

Nyema

"Sasha, seriously, what the--"

Before he could complete his sentence, she hauled the iron at his head, but he ducked, missing it by only inches. The iron crashed into the wall forming a dent then falling to the floor.

Kane focused his attention on Sasha. The darkness in her eyes was something he had never seen before. "Are you gonna say something?" She didn't respond. "You standin' over there like you ready to hunt me," he said, swinging his arms in the air. "Wassup?"

She shrugged her shoulders. "I don't know, you tell me," she said, coolly.

He pointed down to where the iron had fallen. "You just had a hot iron at my head. Don't you think you need to be the one talkin'?" Sasha cocked her head to the side and stared, strangely. "Girl you done lost ya goddamn mind," he said, walking over to gather his clothes from the floor.

She stepped around the bed, slowly and said, "You think!?!"

Kane didn't know how to take her attitude. He tried to remain cool but it was hard because he had no idea what was going through her mind. "Fuck wrong wit you Sasha?"

She pulled the piece of paper from her pocket. "This is what's wrong wit me," she barked, raising it chest high. She bawled the paper up and pitched it at him like she was throwing a homerun.

Kane opened it up and scanned over it quickly. "Damn Sash," he said, tenderly. "I'm sorry--"

She had heard that word one too many times. It wasn't going to be enough to ease her mind this time around. "Do I look like I feel like hearing ya weak ass apology?"

He slipped into his boxers, shirt and pants. "I'ma just leave and let you cool down so we can talk about this," he said, carrying his boots with one hand.

"Nigga I wish you would try to take ya ass up out this house." She stepped aside to let him by. "Go head, I dare you."

Kane dropped the boots and went to grip her up to gain control but Sasha wasn't having it. She dodged his hand and came back around with the steak knife aiming straight for his inner thigh. She broke through the skin and turned.

In a panic, Kane reached for his penis to check and make sure his goods were still in place. "Ahhh...You bitch! I can't believe you stabbed me?" he said, pulling the knife out of his thigh. He snatched a shirt that was lying on the back of a chair and applied pressure.

"Fuck you and ya dirty ass dick," she yelled, scratching and kicking at him.

Kane felt bad for her. He knew he couldn't retaliate because he was the cause of it all. But she wasn't no light-weight and he didn't know how else to get her off of him so he smacked her and she stumbled back.

"Oh you wanna fight muthafucka?" she yelled, gunning back towards him and punched him in the face as soon as the opportunity presented itself.

■■■

Mike sat speechless trying to process the earful that Omar had just given him. Bilaal of all people was out to get him, and he was the one responsible for the death of Azia's mother. Unbelievable! The things money will make people do. Mike wasn't sure if he could trust everything the man was telling him, he had to have an angle for being there in the first place. So what was it?

"And for this information, what are you expecting in return?"

Omar smiled and secured a thick cigar between his lips. "Nothing!" he advised, lighting the tip. "It's already been taken care of."

"Are you saying I don't need to be concerned?"

Nyema

Omar exhaled some smoke and threw his right foot across his knee. "I wouldn't say that. There's still someone in ya circle that's gunnin' for you. Whoever it is that Bilaal sent here or what their motives are is something that I can't explain."

"If you handled Bilaal the way I assume you did, it may flood 'em out."

"Possibility…"

Mike stood from his seat and extended his hand. "I appreciate the heads up. You need anything you know how to get in contact with me."

Omar stood and their hands collided. "How are things on the home front?"

Mike smiled, stiffly. "Is that your way of asking about your daughter?"

"How is she?"

"I think that's a question you need to ask her yourself."

"I plan on it, but for now I'd appreciate it if you didn't mention my return."

"She still believes you're responsible for her mother's death," he said, taking back the last of his drink. "Don't you think it's about time she knows the truth?"

Omar was hurt behind all the lies that were placed in Azia's head. He couldn't wait to look her in the eyes and tell her that he did everything in his power to protect her mother and would live the rest of his life blaming himself for it. He walked over to watch the sun set over the city of brotherly love. He smirked. There was nothing brotherly about it. Just a city filled with big dreams and broken promises.

"You just worry about finding out who the inside man is. I don't know what his beef is with you, but he out to get you for a reason. And from what Bilaal told me, he's going to do whatever he got to do to bring you down."

■ ■ ■

Azia could hear the ruckus before she walked into Kane and Sasha's home, and when she stepped foot inside she couldn't believe her eyes. The place was a wreck, tables turned over, pictures broken, stuff everywhere, but what concerned her most was the blood on the floor. She heard Sasha and Kane arguing from the direction of the kitchen so she hurried that way.

"What the hell is going on?" she asked, with wide eyes.

"What the hell you put in my pants?" he squirmed, pushing Sasha aside. It had been almost an hour since they'd been fighting and he was dying to seek some form of medical attention for his thigh that had turned numb and the burning sensation that was blossoming between his legs. "I'm done fightin' wit you girl."

Again, she came at him with all she had. "You need to be lucky all I'm doing is fightin' pussy cause I feel like blowin' ya head off," she screeched.

Azia looked down at the upper part of Kane's pants which was soaked in blood. "Are you cool?"

He threw Sasha into Azia and hurried out the kitchen. "Hold her so I can get the fuck outta here," he demanded.

Azia couldn't hold her down for long. She felt like she was trying to tame a wild beast.

Kane was almost to the front door when Sasha made it to the living room. She grabbed her .22 from the china closet drawer, aimed it at him and pulled the trigger. Fortunately for Kane, it hit the wall instead of him. Three inches more to the right and he would've been going to the hospital for more than just a knife wound.

Azia ran over to shut the front door that he had left wide open, staring over at her friend terrified. "Sasha, what the hell happened?"

Sasha headed upstairs with her finger still on the trigger. "I'm good."

"Sash--"

Nyema

"I said I'm good," she shouted, before slamming her bedroom door behind her.

Chapter 24

CHANGE IS COMING

Hello…Am I talking to myself?" asked Quadir, with the snapping of his fingers. He leaned across the table and clutched the bottom of Azia's chin gently and shook it from side to side. "Baby girl, where you at?"

Azia smiled after being jerked out of her daze. "My bad, I just got a lot on my mind right now."

The two of them were sitting in a popular steakhouse housed in Pennsauken, NJ. It's been weeks since they'd been kicking it and Azia was starting to have a change of heart. It was hard for her not to think about everything that had been going on for the past few weeks. She and Mike were barely speaking. According to him, he was "giving her some space". Then there was Kane and Sasha. She didn't know the reason behind them going through what they were going through, but shit just wasn't right. It wasn't the same. It seemed like everyone was falling distant. And then there was Rashaud. After word got out that things were rocky between her and Mike, all of a sudden he started popping up in places she was going to be and blowing her phone up at all times of the night. Running into him constantly and hearing his voice had triggered some old feelings, but she knew taking a step back like that was not an option. But what made things more complicated was the fact that no matter how much she degraded or belittled him, nothing was enough to get rid of him. And last but not least there was Quadir, who was nothing more than a mystery. She had no good enough reason to be sitting across from him, but there was just something about him that drew her in more and more with every day they spent together.

"That's what I'm here for. To free ya brain from all the stress and aggravation," he smiled.

"Oh yeah," she smiled. "How do you suppose you're gonna do that? I gotta admit I'm a handful."

"I'ma big boy I'm sure I can handle it."

■ ■ ■

Twenty minutes after their entrees arrived, Azia had picked through her food realizing she had no appetite and she was more than ready to go. They requested some take home containers from the waiter and had their plates boxed for the night. Just as they exited the place, Azia took one look towards the parking lot and her heart sank to her toes. It was KoKa and Anthony heading for the entrance. Seeing that they were all caught up in one another, Azia's mind was thinking just *turn ya head and walk the other way*, but that thought was interrupted when Quadir made their presence known.

"Hey," he smiled. "KoKa right?"

OMG thought Azia.

Led by Anthony, KoKa stepped up the stairs puzzled. She knew Azia and Mike were going through some things, but she had no idea to what extent. *I know her ass don't call herself cheating on my baby*. She disregarded Quadir and focused in on Azia. "What you doing here?"

"Getting something to eat," replied Azia, trying her best to remain cool and collected.

"Hmm… Does Mike know you're here with him?"

"I'm sure he will by tomorrow," she said, sarcastically. "KoKa, I don't know what you know or don't know, but me and your son decided to in his words "take a break". So what I choose to do right now is my business."

"If you say so," said KoKa. She turned to continue on into the restaurant. *She damn right I'ma tell my baby her ass was out with another man and she bet not mention I was with Anthony or I'll whip her myself.*

Anthony leaned in and kissed Azia on her cheek. He was always fond of her, probably too fond. "Don't let her get you worked up," he whispered.

Going against her better judgment, Azia decided to go back to Quadir's house for a night cap. They were sitting in his living room watching *G. Garvin* put his thing down in the kitchen and debating about whether or not women were better cooks than men.

"I aint the best cook but I bet I can top you," she boasted.

"A'ight...A'ight..." he giggled. "You win cause my ass aint gettin' in the kitchen to cook a muthafuckin' thing." They shared a laugh. "You want a drink?"

"Yeah I'll take something light."

She waited for Quadir to go into the kitchen then pulled her cell phone from her pocketbook. Noticing that she had three missed calls, she scrolled through to see whom they belonged to. Two were from Rashaud and one was from Mike. *Damn she couldn't wait to call and tell on me* she thought assuming KoKa had spilled the beans. Quadir made his way back into the living room with two glasses of Hennessy on the rocks. She took the glass and sniffed.

"Umm...Umm...I don't mess with that dark liquor," she said, handing it back.

"C'mon now," he teased. "You know you probably a lush, stop playing." He shoved it back at her. "You a big girl, right?"

Azia sucked her teeth and snatched the glass back. "You aint gotta try to sucker me in." She took a sip and said, "You gonna have to get me a chaser, cranberry juice, apple juice, something."

■■■

Three Hennessey and apple juices later, Quadir was ready to make his move. He wanted her so bad he could taste it, and hopefully she felt the same way. He removed his shirt and pulled his wife beater down into place smiling at the fact that she couldn't keep her eyes off him. "Go ahead, you can feel 'em," he bragged.

She wrapped her hands around his biceps and squeezed. "Damn, you strong."

"I'm a'ight," he clowned. "I see you workin' wit a little summtin-summtin over there," he flirted, squeezing hers in return.

"Boy get outta here," she blushed, pushing him away playfully.

Their eyes locked and Quadir used that moment of silence to go in for a kiss. Azia didn't stop him. Quadir rose up and placed her body back on the sofa underneath his without breaking the tempo. They kissed, passionately, for nearly a minute before Azia began to resist.

"Qua," she exhaled slowly. "I can't--"

"Don't fight it," he mumbled, nibbling all over her neck. "I want you so bad."

She allowed him to pull her shirt up to uncover her breast and with the unsnapping of her bra strap he took a handful into his mouth. "Qua stop I can't do this," she moaned, but her body language was saying otherwise. He came up for air and they began to kiss again as she wrapped her legs around his waist and penetrated her hips against his. She felt like she was back in high school having a bump and grind session.

"I know you want me," he said, arrogantly. Her hand snaked down to his thickness and she was on fire. "You got it in ya hand now what you gonna do wit it?"

Azia's mind was saying do the right thing but her hormones were raging and she was having a hard time battling them. But as soon as she heard the amplified unzipping of his pants, everything that was tingling inside of her came to a complete haul. "Stop," she ordered, pushing at his body weight. "Please let me up." Quadir went in for another kiss to call her bluff but she turned away. "I'ma need, you to get up."

Quadir climbed from off of her and brushed his clothes back into place while she did the same. Had it been any other female he would've took it just to teach her a lesson. But he couldn't do that to Azia, she was far too valuable and he needed her to gain his trust. The more time they spent together, the more he understood how she'd won Mike's heart. And little did she know she was on the verge of stealing his too.

"I apologize if I lead you on," she advised.

"It's cool," he lied. "You ready for me to drop you back at ya car?"

Damn this nigga that salty he gonna kick me out she thought. "Yeah I'm ready."

Quadir stood and took back the last of his iced down drink. "Let's ride!"

Chapter 25

THEY CALL IT LOVE

Mike had just left out of Sasha's house after dropping some money off, compliments of Kane who hadn't been home since their fight. He didn't plan on returning until Sasha promised to drop the grudge and agree to work things out. But she was no sucker and there was no way she was taking him back with ease after passing off a STD. Hell no! He was lucky it was Chlamydia and all she had to do was pop a pill because it could've been worse. Just the thought of it made her nauseous.

Seconds after Mike climbed back into his car Azia pulled up behind him and parked. She killed the engine, climbed out and hit the alarm on the Porsche while trying hard to fight pass the tint on the Denali to see if someone was inside but could see nothing but her own reflection. Assuming Mike was inside the house because he hadn't had emerged from the SUV, she made her way towards the front door until he beeped his horn and rolled the window down. "Come let me holler at you for a minute," he demanded. Azia pranced over to the SUV and stuck her head in the window. "Get in!" Mike pulled away from the curb as soon as she secured herself in the seat.

"Where are we going?" she questioned, but he didn't answer. She turned her body around to face him and stared him down hoping it would be enough to make him feel on edge and say something. Anything! It didn't work. "Since you aint got shit to say take me back to Sasha's please."

"You fuckin' that nigga?" he quizzed, finally breaking the silence.

Azia assumed he was referring to Quadir. Caught off guard she stumbled on her words like she was guilty of sin. "Wh-wh—a-t?"

"Azia don't fuck around wit me you heard me."

"No," she said, sucking her teeth.

"Then why the hell is folks tellin' me they seen him all up in your face on several different occasions?"

Azia was confused. She and Quadir had been as careful as they possibly could be, dining and spending time out everywhere but Philly. The only time they slipped was when they'd run into KoKa. So who were these folk he was referring to? Did he have somebody tracking her?

"I don't know what you talkin' about. We were just out grabbing a bite to eat that night we ran into KoKa. Dinner! That's all it was."

"So you ran into my mom?" he asked, puzzled because this was the first he'd heard of it.

Damn did I just tell on myself she thought. It was too late to turn back now.

"And she saw you?" he continued, trying to figure out why she hadn't mentioned it.

"Umm…Yes," she answered, mockingly. "She was with Anthony."

Ding…Ding…Ding… Now he knew why his mother never mentioned the run-in. *I know she aint back wit that punk ass nigga.* He rode in silence for blocks, furiously.

Thought after thought crossed Azia's mind as she didn't mind the silence. *What the hell is his problem? Why didn't KoKa snitch on me I was sure she would've? Where is he taking me? Look at him sitting over there all jealous. That's what ya ass get for fuckin' wit me. Nanananana…*she sang invisibly sticking her tongue out at him. Surprisingly, Mike doubled back to Sasha's block. *What now?*

Nyema

He pulled up to the house with his foot on the break and said, "You need to make time to come collect the rest of ya shit and continue to do you."

"Just like that?"

"You running around here wit a nigga that can't offer you shit but drama. If that's what you want I don't want no parts of it. Come get ya shit and tell that nigga if I find out he got anything to do wit stepping to my team and robbing my spot he better watch his back. And if he got a problem wit it he can come holler at me I aint hard to find."

Oh my goodness, who the hell is he talking about. He can't be talking about Quadir. "Mike what are you talking about?"

"Do I need to spell it out for you?" he barked, veins popping out of both sides of his head. "Tell Rashaud to stay the fuck away from my businesses and since you wanna ride wit him you can stay the fuck away too."

Azia was taken aback. Never had he talked to her that way before. "Rashaud!?!" She repeated the name like she'd never heard it before. "How could you think I would fuck wit him ever again. Who is telling you these lies?"

Mike jerked the lever into park giving his foot a rest from the break. They were definitely not seeing eye to eye, they were on two separate pages. "If you aint talking about Rashaud who the hell you have dinner with?"

"Qua," she hesitated.

"Qua," he repeated, with his face bawled up. "Who the fuck is--" he started to ask but then it hit him. "Quadir? Are you serious?" He jerked the lever back into *drive.* "Good bye Azia."

"I just went to dinner with him, that's it."

"I said goodbye," he repeated, staring straight ahead. Then he gave a quick chuckle. "You done gave the nigga a nickname and all. Qua," He chuckled again. "You need to get ya shit together."

"Don't talk to me about getting my shit together," she advised, getting out of the SUV. She slammed the door and said, "At least not until you finish handling ya own."

■ ■ ■

"Sasha!" Azia yelled, hustling through the front door but there was no response. She headed upstairs to see if she was locked away in her room where she'd been the last couple days. She knocked before entering. "Sash," she called out, peaking her head inside.

"Yeah," she said, spread across her bed eating ice cream from the carton.

Azia made her way inside and sat down. "Was he here looking for me?"

"No he came to drop some money off."

"Kane still aint bring his ass home yet. He probably scared the next bullet might not miss."

"I guarantee you it won't," she warned, just before a spoon full of ice cream hit her mouth. "Did you catch 'em before he pulled off?"

"Yeah I talked to him. Somebody told him I been kicking it wit Rashaud."

Sasha threw her nose in the air. "Who told him that?"

"Probably some lame ass broad of his. I don't know."

She stuffed a load of ice cream into her mouth. "I know damn well he aint believe no shit like that," she stated, her voice barely audible.

Azia sighed and threw her body back on the bed. "But I done snitched on my damn self and he is pissed," she said, sitting upright. "You hear me." Sasha put the ice cream aside knowing she was about to get an earful. "He was questioning me about Rashaud and the whole time I thought he was talking about Quadir."

"Why the hell would you think that," she said, smacking her in the face with a pillow.

"Cause we ran into KoKa the other night when we were leaving out of *The Pub* and I swore she ran back and told him."

"Umh…Umh…Umh…" she said, shaking her head. "You done fucked up now."

"I know," she screamed, using the pillow to shelter the pitch. "What am I gonna do?"

Azia wanted to cry but not one tear would fall. She jumped up and started pulling out clothes from the drawer and threw them at Sasha. "C'mon, get ya ass up. I need to go get some air before I kill myself."

■ ■ ■

Mike was in the gym, shirtless, pumping iron and blowing off some steam. After leaving Azia, he was so upset he could've punched a hole through a brick wall. Quadir! How the hell did she end up at dinner with him of all people? He was already upset after believing it was Rashaud who was occupying her time, but to hear that she done found some fresh meat, somebody he knew nothing about, bothered him even more. He laid back on the weight bench and started to do some sets. "Ughhh…." he groaned, using his arms to force close to two hundred pounds up and down until he couldn't take it anymore. "Ughhh…" He rolled the bar back onto its base and laid there for a moment trying to catch his breath. Beads of sweat poured from his face and chest. Ringing from his gym bagged grasped his attention. He got up and grabbed his towel from the back of the bench.

"Yeah," he roared, into his phone while wiping his face. "I'm busy you gonna have to find somebody else to handle it." He paused. "I'm not ya man Kyla. If you aint calling about my son then you need to get off my phone." He paused. "Hello." He brought the phone away from his ear to check the screen. She was gone. He threw the phone back into the gym bag with the feeling of pain and frustration gnawing away at him as he headed over to another bench to release some more stress.

■ ■ ■

Azia pulled in front of Pimp My Tee on 4th & South and lucked up on a parking spot right in front of the store. She and Sasha were on a mission. They had just come from doing some shopping downtown in Center City. Spending money didn't permanently rid them of all their problems, but it sure did help some for time being.

Sasha climbed out of the car first and looked up at the sign. "I should go in there and get a shirt made that says *anybody got an ice pack cause by balls burnin'* with an arrow pointing down towards 'em."

This was the first time Sasha started to open up about what her and Kane was going though. She never mentioned it and Azia never pried. Now that she had opened the can of worms, Azia wanted to know more. "Why the hell would you get that on the shirt?" she asked, climbing out of the driver's seat.

"Cause his ass is hot like fire," she smirked.

Azia threw her hand over her mouth in disbelief. "Don't tell me--"

Sasha cut her off before she could complete the sentence and have her business float into the ears of one of the South Street groupies. "You bet not even say it."

"Oh my gosh!" Azia exclaimed, shaking her head. "Them dirty bastards deserve each other. I don't blame you for shooting at his ass. I'm mad that you missed."

The girls headed up the block to *Ishkabibbles* Eatery to grab a bite to eat. Azia felt bad for her friend. She couldn't help but think about if the shoe were on the other foot how she would've reacted. It was a scary thought and she made a mental note to get on her knees and thank God for watching over her after all the nonsense she'd put her body through in the past years.

"You know what they say. When you sleep with a man you're sleeping with everybody they chose to sleep with before you, and whoever she slept with before him, and on and on and on."

"That's alright 'cause I'm sure I taught his ass a lesson."

"You gonna take him back?"

They found a couple seats inside the eatery and made themselves comfortable.

"You know damn well I aint leaving that man. Not after everything we've been through. Girl, I don't even remember what life was life before Kane," she said, delicately. "He was there when I hit rock bottom and he was there when I came back from it. It's so much you don't know about. Ya'll know the street side of Kane, but I know the best part of Kane. He may be a killer, but he knows how to love and understand me in a way no one else in my life ever could."

"Sound deep."

"I have no family Azia. My mom gave me up when I was like, what, a week old, and my dad never gave a shit about me. I been with man after man since I can remember hoping to fill that void, but it never happened because I was looking for all the wrong things. I wanted someone to love me like my mother and father was supposed to when I should've been focused on loving myself first."

Although they didn't share the same exact story, it still felt familiar to Azia. Tears formed in her eyes. "Damn, that's crazy," she said, catching them before they fell.

"I aint mean to make you all emotional and shit," giggled Sasha.

"Little do you know you just hit home inside of me."

Sasha took her cheese steak and started to dress it with condiments. "I know you told me a long time ago that your mother was killed," she said, hoping she wasn't out of line for bringing it up. "And your father, he's in jail right?" Azia nodded. "You ever try to contact him?"

"For what?"

"I don't know," she shrugged. "To sit down with him and discuss what happened to your mom."

"I don't need to ask him nothing. I know all I need to know."

"Sometimes when we're younger we tend to take things the way we want to take them. And then when we get older, that's when we really start to analyze certain situations and wish we would've done things differently. But by the time we finally decide to do something about it, it's already too late--"

Azia listened to Sasha go on and on. She thought about her mother often and how thing's would've been if she were still alive, but it was very seldom that she thought about her father. What was there to think about, him being the reason that her mother was no longer there to give her advice and see her through life? The thought of it all put an ill taste in her mouth. She pushed her chicken cheese steak aside and nibbled on Sasha's fries.

"Where is all this coming from?" Azia asked, curious.

"Growing up, I didn't have a choice. My parents didn't want anything to do with me. I would've killed just to have a relationship with them, but they made the choice for me. But you on the other hand," she said, looking Azia square in the eye. "You got a choice. Remember that."

■■■

"**D**amn, that steak was right on time," said Sasha, rubbing her belly. "My niggeritis bout to kick in I can feel it already."

Azia laughed as they made their way back to the car. "Greedy and lazy. I'm almost ashamed to be your friend."

Sasha laughed weakly. Her eyes were glued to the familiar face heading in their direction. The woman was carrying a couple shopping bags with her eight-year-old daughter trailing closely behind. "I knew I should've kept my ass in the house."

Nyema

"Why? What's wrong?" asked Azia, following the path of Sasha's eyes. When she realized Kane's baby mother was heading their way she got worried. "Please don't cut up down here Sash. You know how these cops are down here."

"I aint gonna cut up. I just got one thing to say," she advised, passing the car and heading straight for the woman.

Odessa caught sight of Sasha before she walked all the way up on her. She stopped dead in her tracks and pushed her daughter slightly behind her. She raised her hand up chest high and said "Don't come at me wit no bull--" but was cut off by a punch in the mouth that landed her flat on her ass.

Bystanders stopped to gather around, some laughter, some whispers. Then out of nowhere the small angelic looking eight-year-old jumped over her mother and punched Sasha in the stomach.

"Don't be hitting my mom you bitch," she raved, as her skinny bawled up fist tried to hit her a second time.

Azia looked at Sasha in disbelief and grabbed the little girl off of her feet. "You need to calm your little butt down." The girl kicked and screamed to get loose until Azia let her go.

By that time, Odessa had made her way off of the ground, embarrassed, and with a mouth full of blood. She lunged at Sasha while a stranger held her back. "You mad 'cause ya man want me back," she shouted. "But he was never yours to begin with, he was borrowed."

"I aint worried 'bout him wanting ya trifling ass. That hit was for passing off that hot shit you whack ass herpes having whore." Sasha watched the man that was holding Odessa back off of her after hearing that. She knew the girl didn't have herpes but it sounded good. "Aint nobody holding you now," she boasted, gathering all the spit from the back of her throat and spitting it in her face.

Odessa snatched her daughter up and dragged her through the crowd. She knew all about Sasha and a battle with her was something she was not prepared for.

Azia yanked Sasha by the arm. "C'mon, the damn cops coming."

"Fuck the po-lice," she shouted.

Azia tossed Sasha into the passenger side of the car, ran around to the driver's side and got the hell up off South Street as quick as traffic would allow her to. "I should kick ya ass," she huffed.

Sasha checked herself out in the small overhead mirror. "You saw that bitch mouth?" The girls burst into laughter. "Kane can come back home now. I feel so much better."

Chapter 26

CAUGHT ON THE SPOT

KoKa's block cast long shadows of routine activity; some neighbors walking their dogs, some washing their cars, some were jogging and some hanging flags. Labor Day was right around the corner and it wasn't hard to tell with all the red, white and blue scattered around. Mike had been sitting in his SUV for almost forty-five minutes staring at the back of Anthony's car which was parked a few doors down from KoKa's house. He was debating whether or not he should go in and confront his mother for hiding the fact that she had taken him back. After contemplating for ten more minutes, Mike backed down the block and pulled into his mother's driveway. He made sure to make his tires screech just to give her a heads up that he had arrived. He used his key to enter the house like he normally does. No sooner than he stepped both feet in the door, KoKa appeared to greet him. She looked like a nervous wreck, patting her clothes into place.

"Hey baby, what are you doing here?"

Mike shut the door behind him. "I came to check up on you. Aunt Val said you stayed home today 'cause you wasn't feeling good."

"Oh yeah," she said, fidgeting. "But I feel a lot better than I did this morning. Where are you on your way to?"

"Here!" He headed for the kitchen. "Why you want me to leave?"

"Well I was gonna lay back down and get some more rest," she said, following his every move. "Something I haven't done in a while."

Mike made a sudden turn and startled her. "What you jumping for? You cool?"

"I'm fine."

"Oh alright," he said, grabbing a beer from the refrigerator. It was a brand new six pack with only one bottle missing. "You drink beer now?" he asked, popping the top.

"That beer been here for a while," KoKa flagged. "I just took 'em out the pantry to make some room."

He took a few gulps and sat the half empty bottle down on the counter. "I gotta take a leak."

KoKa watched him walk pass the half-bathroom that sat between the living and dining room and head upstairs. "What you forgot it's a bathroom down here?" she asked, following.

"I rather use the one up here," he stated. "What you following me all around the house for?"

"Because it's my house, that's why."

"You acting real suspect right now. Wassup wit you?"

KoKa walked pass him and headed for her bedroom. "Boy please. I'm going to lay down. Make sure you lock my door when you leave out." Mike trailed her towards her bedroom. "Where you going?"

"In here wit you so I can see what got you acting so strange."

She held up her hand against his chest to stop him. "Go on Mike. I want to be alone right now."

He stared into her eyes dramatically. "Who in there?"

KoKa laughed it off. "I'm about to be in there. That's who in there now go ahead to the bathroom and I see you later." She turned her back to walk inside.

"Tell him to come out here and face me like a man."

KoKa's heart was beating uncontrollably. She had wanted to tell Mike that she'd forgiven Anthony and took him back. The only reason she did in the first place was because he took the initiative to seek help for his addiction. Seeing that he was trying to get himself together, there was no way she could turn her back on him. The only problem was she never found the right time to mention it to Mike.

"Mike, listen--"

"How could you take him back? He aint nothing but a broke down weak ass drunk," he yelled, loud enough for Anthony to hear.

Anthony appeared at the doorway and shot daggers at Mike. He knew how protective he was of his mother, but she was his old lady and he was just going to have to deal with it. "I'm gonna let all that shit talking slide cause I know you still bitter--"

"Let it slide? Fuck you think you gonna do to me if you chose not to let it slide ol' head?"

"Ya'll stop it now," KoKa intervened, standing between the two.

"Hey Mike, my man, I aint drunk tonight so it aint gonna be no repeat ass whippings up in here," he warned. "You need to watch how you talk in front of ya mother--"

"You think you got the right to chastise me after the way you treated her. What you so high and mighty now--"

"I said stop it," she cried, staring deeply into her son's eyes. "He's here cause I want him here and aint nothing gonna change that." She hated to see the two men she loved most in the world going head to head, but it was up to her to put her foot down. "I love you baby but you gotta let me live my life how I see fit."

"I aint gotta do nothing. This ya life so live it. I don't want nothing to do wit this fagot, I'm out." He turned to head back down the steps.

"Mike," KoKa yelled after him but he ignored. "Mike--"

Anthony ignored the insult and touched her shoulder. "Let him go baby. He'll come around."

KoKa's sank into Anthony's arms. Her heart sank when she heard the front door slam shut. She just hoped that Anthony was right because if Mike didn't come around and find a way to accept their relationship she'd be devastated and there was no way she could live life without the only man in her life that never once let her down.

■■■

Deuce escorted Vipor out of his car and leaned in to kiss her goodnight but she resisted.

"Unn...Unn...Just glossed my lips up." She blew him a kiss and turned to walk head into her apartment complex. After weeks of leading him on and mastering at making him her new puppet, she had finally got the information she needed so there was no need for him anymore.

"You want me to come up?" he asked, looking like a little lost puppy.

"Nah, I'm going to lay down."

"But I thought--"

"Boy I'm cramping I don't feel like no company," she spat. "Just holler at me tomorrow or something."

Deuce watched her disappear into the shadows of the three story building. He wanted to run after her and beg her to spend a little more time with him. The chick had him open. He was officially, like the song say, *in love with a stripper*. He climbed into his car and called from his cell phone. She didn't answer so he left a message. "Hey it's me I was calling to make sure you was cool. Guess I holler at you tomorrow or you can call me back, if you want." He drew the message out as long as he could then pulled out of the apartment complex hoping to get a call back.

■■■

"Ay hunny, I got something for you," Vipor stressed, into her phone. She wound up having to put up with Deuce longer than she'd expected, but after all the sweet nothings she had to whisper in his ear and orgasms she had to fake it had finally paid off. "Alright I'll see you at the club tomorrow." She laughed. "I'm just glad that now I can get rid of his lil' dick ass. See you tomorrow girl." Vipor walked across her studio apartment and checked herself out

Nyema

in the full length mirror. She rubbed her hands up and down her curves thinking *damn I'm good.*

Chapter 27

HOME SWEET HOME

Kane found himself sleeping with one eye open. It was unusual for him to beat the rooster up in the morning, but he tossed and turned all night long. Even though Sasha forgave him and let him come back, he knew that what happened would be something she'd never forget. The vibration of his cell phone jerked his attention. He looked towards the floor to locate it then eased the arm Sasha had locked around his waist to the side and snuck out of bed. After grabbing the phone, he tiptoed across the room like he was walking on egg shells.

"What are you calling me so early in the morning for?" he whispered, stepping into the hallway. "You can't be calling me whenever you get ready my girl aint having it." He paused. "I told you before if the shit aint got nothing to do wit my daughter I don't wanna hear it and this my last time tellin' you that. We done, you hear me. Done!" He ended the call and turned to head back into the bedroom only to come face to face with Sasha. *What the fuck is she a ghost now.*

She was standing in the bedroom doorway with her arms folded. "You think she got it this time?" Kane nodded his head. "I hope so because if not I won't be held liable for what'll happen next." She turned and switched back into the room.

■ ■ ■

Later on that day, Azia made her way downstairs and found Kane and Sasha hugged up on the sofa watching *The Game* on BET. It instantly brought back memories of when her and Mike would turn their phones off and cuddle all day long. How she missed those days. "Ya'll so corny," she said, crashing their alone time. She flopped down on the same sofa where they were laying and pushed Kane's feet out of the way.

"Oh you done really made yaself comfortable up in this joint huh?" he grilled.

"I been made myself comfortable," Azia giggled. "You late." She grabbed the popcorn from the table and began to stuff her face. "I've been tryna get a hold of Mike. Where is he?"

"I don't know."

"You don't know," she repeated. "Just say mind ya business. That sound'a whole lot better than you don't know."

"Don't worry 'bout him," he advised. "He cool. He just needed to get away for a little while."

"Away with who?"

"Calm ya ass down. He needed some time alone to figure some shit out."

Azia wasn't buying it. "Whatever," she said, placing the popcorn back on the table. "Sash, call me if you need me." She got up, grabbed her keys and headed out the door.

"Where he go?" asked Sasha. "And don't give me that you don't know bullshit."

"Damn, why ya'll all on my nigga head like that?"

She smacked him playfully. "He went away with somebody didn't he?"

"I told you he went somewhere to relax and clear his head. End of story."

"Vipor called me last night she said she got some info for me. I'ma meet her at D's later on tonight."

Kane sat upright and swung his feet to meet the floor. He cupped his head and began to massage it rhythmically. "I hope she was able to get something out of that nigga."

"Knowing Vipor, I'm pretty sure she did," said Sasha, sitting up to rub his head for him. Besides their own issues, she knew he was dealing with a lot more on the merciless streets of Philadelphia. And although he had hurt her in a way that she always told herself she would kill for, that was her boo and she was going to ride it out with him until the wheels fell off.

■ ■ ■

It didn't matter what Azia occupied herself with, anything was better than sitting in the company of Sasha and Kane playing footsies. After paying a visit to the salon and having Lenny touch up her hair, she found herself sitting in Mike's empty condo. She searched the residence for any sign of another woman but came up empty handed. She made her way to the bedroom thinking that maybe, just maybe, she could luck up and find some kind of hint as to where he could've gone and with whom. Nothing! She spread across the bed that she missed so deeply and sucked in the scent of his cologne from his pillow. It made her tingle inside. *Damn I miss that man.* Feeling the desire to go through her wardrobe, she hopped up and headed for the closet. Getting rid of all the old stuff was something she'd been wanted to do but could never find the time. Now with nothing but time on her hand and Mike unable to interrupt, she slipped into something more comfortable and got to work knowing that the Salvation Army could use the items more that she could.

■ ■ ■

A little over three hours later, pocketbooks, shoes and clothing filled two large trash bags in the back of Azia's Porsche. She pulled in front of the Salvation Army on 55th & Market and ran inside to ask for some help with the bags. On her way out, she got the shock of her life. She stood with her mouth wide open knowing her eyes had to be deceiving her.

It was the first of the month so all the crack infested corners were pumping with hustlers and fiends of all shapes and sizes trotting back and forth. But there was only one in particular that stuck out of the bunch. Azia stood at her truck and opened it slowly with her eyes set on a young woman buying coke from one of the corners. *Keemah! It can't be* she thought. She hadn't seen her cousin since she snuck off to LA with Rashaud and left her in the hospital fighting for her life. "Keemah," she yelled, but the woman didn't budge. "Keemah," she yelled again, and then her suspicions were confirmed.

Keemah spun around trying to pin point who was shouting her name like that. Azia locked eyes with the only family she had left before she decided she wanted to stab her in the back and screw her man. Although Keemah hadn't reaped all the benefits of being a crack addict, she still looked all used up and worn out. Embarrassed that she'd just got caught with her hand in the cookie jar, she paid for her dope and skipped off in the opposite direction.

Azia pulled both heavy bags out of her trunk, slammed them into the cart that was provided and watched the volunteer roll it away. She climbed back into her car and circled the block a couple times to see if she'd bump into Keemah, but her cousin was nowhere in sight. She reached for her ringing cell phone and scanned the caller ID. The call was marked private. "Hello," she barked.

"Why you aint been answering my calls?"

"Rashaud would you pa-leaz leave me the hell alone."

"Who you talkin' to like that?"

"You," she shouted. "Goodbye!" She ended the call and shut the power off. "GOODNESSGRACE!" Her mind was spinning in different directions. She pulled to the side of the road for a minute and let her head rest on the steering wheel. A moment later, she powered her phone back on and punched some digits in. "Hey, you busy?" she spoke, softly. "I'm on my way over I'll see you when I get there."

■ ■ ■

So much noise and commotion rang out inside of D's gentleman's club. There was a bachelor party in motion and Sasha was on stage twirling to The Dream's *Rockin' That Thang* giving a hell of a show. She had on a bikini g-string with a bunch of bills filling the straps, and her bikini top was pulled down allowing both breasts to rumble free. She and Vipor's eyes connected briefly when Vipor entered the club and winked at her before heading back stage.

■ ■ ■

After the third song came to an end, Sasha collected all her money from the stage and wiped down the pole with disinfect for the next dancer. As she made her way back stage with two plastic grocery bags full of money, she crossed passed with Danger, the only female up in that joint that loved to hate. *Bitch!* The two of them happened to lip at the same time. Great minds do think alike.

Vipor was changing into her outfit for the night when Sasha approached and took a seat on the bench beside her. "I can't stand that whore."

"Who?" Vipor asked, curious.

"Danger!"

She sucked her teeth. "Oh, Queen of the haters," she giggled. "Just make sure you watch ya back 'cause that bitch act like she got it in for you."

"I'm done talking 'bout that hoe. What you got for me?"

Vipor looked around to make sure their conversation was marked private. "The bol' Deuce been flossing lately, blowing money like crazy. So you know me, I like to get in where I fit in. So I gave 'em a little summtin-summtin and made the nigga take me shopping," she huffed. "Well when we was out, he was running his mouth about how he bout to be running shit and he rockin' wit a new team and a whole bunch of other nonsense like he was Big Willy or some shit so that was my cue to pick his head." A few dancers made their way into the dressing room so Vipor straddled the bench and slid closer to Sasha. "I grilled him and ya'll was right. He's definitely a snake and after I convinced him to let me roll out wit him to make a run, I got a chance to see who he fuckin' wit now."

Nyema

Sasha's ears were ringing. She felt like she was waiting to hear the last number to be called out so she could scream *bingo*. "Who he dealing wit?"

"The nigga Pooch and them that hang out on 56th street, and the other dude, Q or Qua, something like that."

"Quadir!?!" Sasha exclaimed. "Get the fuck out of here."

Sasha didn't feel good about hearing none of it. She felt like someone had stood over her and caved her chest in. Here the whole time everyone suspected Rashaud assuming he was on a mission for some payback. Although no one knew too much about Quadir, they didn't find a reason to suspect him, and Pooch, he always betrayed like it was all love whenever he and Mike crossed paths. Sasha was worried. What kind of game were they playing? And now Quadir had Azia wrapped up in the middle of it all. She hopped up from her seat and jumped into her clothes. "I gotta go," she said, throwing what she didn't need in her locker. "Let me holler at Kane and I'll make sure I have that fee for you by tomorrow."

Vipor didn't know the extent of what was going on, but she was down for whatever when it came to making money. A thousand dollars for giving up a little bit of coochie for some information was cool with her. But she forgot something. "Oh, Sash," she called out, hurrying over to her. She stared deep into her friend's eyes and said, "I don't know what they planning but something is in the works because Deuce told me that by the end of the year, a lot of shit was gonna change. Make sure you tell Kane to watch his back."

Chapter 28

TAKE IT OR LEAVE IT

How about you take a trip with me," suggested Quadir, behind the wheel of his car. "Let me get you away from all the bullshit you been going through lately. It'll help you clear ya head before school start back up."

The offer sure did sound good but there was no way she was going to pull that off without Mike finding out. Taking that chance was not even an option, she'd wound up losing him forever. "As bad as I can use a vacation now is not a good time--"

"Make it a good time."

"I can't just pick up and leave, just like that. Nah!"

"You can't or you won't?"

"Listen Quadir, I enjoy spending time with you and all but you already know who has my heart and that aint change."

"I'm not asking for it to change I'm asking for you to live a little. I want to spend some more time with you, get to know you better. With all the distractions here in Philly that aint never gonna happen." He scooped up her hand and brought it to meet his lips. "Come on Ma, go away with me."

"I can't," she stated, without hesitation.

"Now would be a good time to ride out. I mean, he giving you the cold shoulder anyway. When's the last time you hollered at him?"

"I haven't."

"Where he been at?"

Nyema

"Your guess is just as good as mines," she said, quickly changing the subject. "Where are we getting something to eat from?"

Azia tried to keep the conversation moving but Quadir kept bringing it back around to Mike. "His homies aint tell you where he went?"

She looked him over, strangely. "Why you keep questioning me about him?"

"I'm just tryna figure out why you feel as though you can't ride out wit me for a few days if the nigga aint nowhere around anyway," he lied, digging for information.

"Can we just get to where we going I'm tired of talking about it." Quadir made a sharp u-turn and headed towards his house. "I thought we was gonna get something to eat?"

"I planned on ordering in. You got a problem wit that?"

"I will if you keep talking to me reckless."

"How you expect me to feel? I'm starting to feel like you using a nigga."

"I'm not using you. If that's the impression I'm giving then maybe I'll just fall back 'cause I got enough aggravation to deal with."

His tongue wanted to say one thing but his mouth said another. "It's cool baby girl. I'm following your lead." He grabbed his cell phone and placed a call. Azia watched curiously from the passenger side. "What up?" he spoke, into the phone. "You got that for me?" He paused. "A'ight cool I'll meet you at the store in fifteen." He ended the call and looked back and forth between Azia and the road. "You cool babe?" he asked, trying to clear the air. She nodded. "You feel like some Chinese?"

"That'll work."

Quadir pulled in front of the Chinese store that sat a couple streets down from his block. He hopped out of the car and jogged into the store while Azia waited in the car. Attentively, she watched him embrace another guy that was already inside of the store. He saw the man pass him something small enough to fit in Quadir's front pocket which is where he stashed it. Then she directed her attention on one of the boosters from around the way. He was selling merchandise out the back of his trunk. Just as she thought about walking over to see what the Mike Vick look-a-like was offering, she spotted Keemah walking up the block skitzing. *Damn it must be meant for me to bump into her ass* she told herself. Not wanting to spook her off again, Azia waited until she was damn near at the car before she jumped out on her. The first thing she noticed was the two black eyes her cousin was sporting.

"What happened to you?" asked Azia, leaning in to touch her face but she resisted.

Keemah was embarrassed. This was the first time the two had bumped heads since the big argument they had over the infamous Rashaud. She started to pat her nappy weave down and straightened her clothes like it was going to make her look better. Neither did her any justice. "Don't act like you give a damn about me."

"I'd be lying if I said I did before seeing you like this," she admitted. "You still family. I would never wish this on you."

"Wish what on me," she hissed, rolling her eyes. "There you go thinking you know everything like you always do," she spat, raising her voice. "You aint better than nobody Azia," she said, fidgeting. "I don't care who you fuckin'."

Azia stared her down with sympathetic eyes. "Keemah, we may not be the best of friends after what you did to me but I hate seeing you fucked up like this."

"That karma, it sure is something aint it," she twitched.

Quadir came out of the store with two bags of food in his hands. "Yo, come on we out."

"Hold on," she said, walking over to him. "That's my cousin. Can we at least give her a ride home?"

"Her junkie ass aint gettin' in my wheel."

"You aint gotta be so disrespectful," she told him. "I know you heard me say she's family."

He took a good look at Keemah who was standing on her tippy-toes trying to see who was in the Chinese store, skitzing for another hit. "Aint that the same cousin that fucked ya man?"

Azia looked back at her briefly and sucked her teeth. "Give me a second," she advised, walking back over to Keemah. "Where you headed?"

"I'm cool Azia," she squirmed. "But can you loan me a few dollars? I really need to feed my dog he aint ate in days."

Azia searched through the clutter in her pocketbook to locate five dollars. The disgust she once possessed for the girl was replaced with disappointment. "You need to get some help," she suggested, passing the money over.

Keemah snatched the money and said, "This is all the help I need right now, thanks cuz," before the wind blew her boney frame away.

Azia climbed back in the car and sat in silence. That was not how she'd imagined her first run in with Keemah. Seeing her cousin turned out on drugs made her feel ill. She'd never wish that on her worse enemy.

"You keep spending so much time dwelling on the bad you gonna miss out on the good," advised Quadir, speeding down the street.

Azia looked at him and smirked. He didn't have to be so cold. Her attention was jerked by the vibration of her cell phone. She retrieved it from her pocketbook and screened the call. "It's Sasha," she said, aloud.

Quadir quickly placed his hand over the screen before she had the chance to answer and slowly guided it back down to her lap. "I done shared you enough for one day can I at least get a night with no interruptions or is that too much to ask?"

Azia secured the phone back inside of her pocketbook. "If that's all you want, you got it."

■■■

"Azia I need you to call me as soon as you get this. It's important," Sasha demanded through Azia's voicemail. This was the second message and she was frustrated. She turned to Kane and said, "She still aint answering."

"She probably wit him just give her a minute to call back."

"What if he did something to her?"

"If he wanted to hurt her he would've did it by now. Evidently he using her to get at Mike so let the nigga keep thinking he ahead in the game."

"Were you able to reach Mike?"

"Naw, I left a message I'm waiting for him to call me back."

"Who the hell is this dude and where did he come from?"

Kane crossed to the window with his phone to his ear and peeped through the blinds. "I don't know who the hell he is but, I'm damn sure gonna find out."

■■■

Mike gripped his cell phone from the table and screened the call. This was the fourth call from Kane, but whatever he needed he'd just have to handle it on his own. He sent the call to voicemail and finished putting a dent in his food. Attempting to take his mind off of all the madness that's been going on, he decided to head down Florida to clear his head. But that wasn't the only reason for his trip. He was there on business as well.

He was sitting outside of *Big Willy's* staring out into what seemed like a picture perfect world. South Beach was always popping no matter what time of the year it was. There were hoards of people moving about, locals, tourists, children, everyone moseying along in a worry free way. He zoomed in on the shore and listened to the sound of the waves construct its own music. It was refreshing, relaxing, something he'd been missing for quite some time. Packing up and leaving everything in Philly behind crossed his mind, but only for a moment. That would always be home for a hustler like Mike, at least for the time being.

The sound of someone's voice jerked Mike out of his daze. He turned slightly in his chair and saw Omar standing two feet away from him. He turned back around as Omar walked over and took a seat across from him.

"Glad to see you made it," Omar said, staring out into the sun. "It's so peaceful out here isn't it?"

"I agree," he replied, wiping his mouth.

"If only the whole world was this in tune."

Mike chuckled. "That's a world we'll never know."

The two men sat silent for a couple minutes taking in the beautiful greenery.

"So I hear things are still a little rattled on your end."

"You heard right."

Omar chuckled and secured his cigar between his lips. "Got any idea who the snake is yet?" he asked, lighting the tip.

Mike shook his head. "Whoever this lil' nigga is, he's good. I gotta give him that much."

Omar exhaled some smoke and threw his right foot across his knee. "I'ma tell you now, what I'm about to present you with aint gonna work unless your backyard his clean. I can't risk dealin' wit no bullshit."

"I know you been out the game for a minute, but let me remind you that the streets always gonna be the streets. Aint nothing gonna change that, ever!" Mike stressed. "What matters the most is if I'm man enough to handle it."

"Are you?" Omar quizzed.

Mike leaned forward and looked Omar square in the eyes with a smirk across his face. "Ask ya daughter..."

Omar giggled, lightly at first, but then it turned into a big laugh. Mike had to laugh himself. Although he meant for his comment to be sarcastic, he had to make sure Omar knew that testing his manhood was not an option. If anything, he should've been the one questioning him. I mean he was the one that just came home after spending over a decade in prison. Suddenly, Omar felt someone come up from behind and wrap their arms around his neck. He smiled when Gisele planted her soft lips on his cheek.

Noticing the awkward look on Mike's face he said, "I would introduce you, but from the look on your face seems like you don't need an introduction."

Mike smiled weakly. What the hell was Omar doing with her? The longer he stared at Gisele, the more he remembered about her. Azia's madam! *I be damned* he thought. "You're right, we don't need an introduction."

Gisele wasn't sure how much information Azia spilled about their relationship, but by the look on his face she knew it was enough. "It was never a formal introduction," she smiled, extending her hand.

Because Omar never mentioned her before, he assumed she never told him that she and Azia were friends. "I heard you were down here now," he smirked.

"I'm sure you did. How are things back up *North*?" she asked, referring to Azia.

"Fantastic!" he said, blatantly.

"Glad to hear that," she smiled, pulling the oversized sun hat further down on her head. "I'll let you two get back to whatever it was you were discussing." She bent down and gave Omar another peck on the side of his face while staring into Mike's eyes with a look that said *you better not even think about it,* and then she switched her bottom across the street towards the ocean sun.

"Do I even want to know how you two know one another?"

"Nope!"

"Then I won't ask…" said Omar, shaking his head. He was under the assumption that they may have had a fling or something in the past. If that was the case it still didn't bother him none. He was old school, and in his book one man's loss is another man's treasure.

"Do you know her well enough to trust her?"

Nyema

"Is there a reason I shouldn't?"

"When it comes to women of that caliber, you can never be too sure."

Omar turned in the seat and sat upright. "You got that right," he grinned. "You know what Mike, I respect you. I haven't been around long enough to say I like you, but I do respect you. I heard a lot of positive things about you too. All I ask is that you continue to look out for my daughter. "

"I hear that!"

"Well now that we got that established, let's talk some business."

Chapter 29

YOU MAKE ME WANNA

The beams from the sunlight couldn't be any more crucifying to Azia's face the next morning when she awoke. She cracked her eyes open slowly and every bone in her body stiffened almost instantly. She had never seen the room before. She sat upright against the headboard and studied the place. It was nice, but it was unfamiliar. She snatched the sheets from her body and her mouth hit the floor. *What the hell happened to me* she thought. She stared down at her naked body trying hard to remember the events that could have possibly led up to it last night. But she could remember nothing. *Where the fuck are my clothes?*

Unable to find her clothes, she grabbed a T-shirt from the drawer and slipped it over her head. Again she tried to make sense of her night. *What did I do?* She was almost in tears. As cracked the door open with ease and crept down the long hallway. The sound of a man and female's voice lingered from the kitchen and bounced off the walls. Azia went to tip down the stairs and the third step down squeaked. She froze.

Quadir and Kyla were in the middle of a heated debate. They never heard a sound.

"I'm tired of doing everything you ask me to do and I keep getting the short end of the stick," she whined. "You said--"

"Did I ask you to repeat what I said?" he asked, stepping closer. "Keep ya fuckin' mouth shut because if you even think about tellin' a muthafuckin' soul," he warned, sticking his 9mm in her face. "I'ma make this gun the last thing you ever suck again in life."

Nyema

Kyla was in tears. She felt foolish for allowing Quadir to use her. "The plan was never for you to fall for that bitch," she cried, using the wall to slide down to the floor.

"What part of what I said didn't you understand," he said, yanking her up on her feet. He smacked her across the face with light force. "You need to get ya shit together." He smacked her again. "Get ya shit together." He delivered a third smacked. "You got it together yet?"

"Get off of me," she yelled, trying to break away.

Quadir snatched an envelope of pictures from her hand and dragged her into the kitchen. "Shut the fuck up," he ordered, between clenched teeth. "You gonna wake her up."

She elbowed him in the chest and broke away. "I'm telling you now I be damned if you the only one gonna walk away a winner," she spat. "I better get what I want."

Quadir found himself caught between a rock and a hard plate. "Just take ya ass up outta here before I forget why I need you."

Kyla knew she had him by the balls. She eyed him devilishly for another moment before turning to walk out, then turned back and said, "And what about ya son?" She could see the flames in his eyes. "Yeah I thought so."

■■■

Azia had made it down to the fifth step without causing a distraction. When she heard him tell Kyla to get out she crept back up the stairs, but only after hearing her say something about a son. Because the stairwell was a little ways away from the kitchen, it was difficult to hear every word that was exchanged verbatim. She desperately tried to make it all the way down but the squeaking stairs wouldn't allow it without her cover being blown. She tip-toed all the way back to the bedroom, shut the door and hopped back in the bed. Her heart was racing. *Oh shit* she thought jumping back out of the bed. She pulled the shirt off and placed it neatly back in its place. So many thoughts clouded her mind. She tried to relax so her heart rate would go down but it wasn't happening fast enough. Quadir was going to be up there any minute. She closed her eyes and took a long deep breath. It helped. Seconds later, the door swung open and she flinched, but not enough for him to notice.

Quadir walked over to the bed and stood over top of her. Was he really falling for her? Kyla was right, that was not the plan. He pulled a small brown bottle from his pocket and held it up towards the ceiling. *Damn this shit really work* he told himself.

Azia had been knocked out cold since nine o'clock the night before. After Quadir met one of his boys at the Chinese store to get what they called "a ruffie" also known as Rohypnol, a powerful sedative that causes drowsiness, loss of inhibition and judgment, dizziness, confusion and with a high dosage amnesia, it was game time. In the midst of them eating and making short talk, he stepped into the kitchen to make them both a drink and poured all of the contents into hers knowing the drug's effects are intensified when used in conjunction with alcohol. That's why she had no recollection of what happened and that's exactly the way he wanted it.

He used two fingers to brush hair from her face so he could get a better view of her beauty. She used that moment of disturbance to turn her back towards him as if she were trying to find comfort. "You up," he whispered, softly into her ear.

Azia acted as if she was adjusting to the sunlight, and did a hell of a job at faking it. She turned back towards him and sat up hysterically. "What happened?"

He smiled. "What I aint good enough to remember?"

She jumped out of the bed with the sheet wrapped around her. "Where are my clothes?"

"Down stairs where you left them," he said. "How 'bout you calm down for a second."

"Calm down," she spat. "Why don't I remember what happened? What did you do to me?"

"Nothing you aint want me to do."

Nyema

"You lying," she shouted. "What you do to me?"

Quadir walked retrieved the pictures from his pants. Thank God for the one hour photo shops, at least in his case. He tossed the pictures on the bed. "See for yourself."

Azia sorted through all the photos, shocked. It was pictures of them, naked, in all different kinds of sexual positions. "This is bullshit."

"It felt like much more to me," he whispered, in her ear then slid his fingers through her hair and guided her face to meet his. "I would've preferred a video but this'll do. I know you would hate for them to reach the wrong hands, right?"

"You wouldn't do that--"

"I will do anything to get what I want, and what I want is you." He stuck his tongue down her throat and kissed her aggressively. She snatched away and he smiled. "How about that trip now?"

■ ■ ■

The entire day was a drag for Azia. After leaving Quadir, she went back to the condo and sat in a tub of scorching hot water wishing it could erase whatever happened the night before. The tracks on Mary J's *No More Drama* CD that normally made her feel better for some reason was making matters worse. The images on the pictures played over and over again in her head giving her a headache and a half. She knew Mike would never forgive her if he found out. She soaked her wash cloth in the water and placed it across her swollen eyes hoping it would help the migraine she'd been battling. Not too long after, the sound of banging upon the door echoed down the hall.

Dripping wet and draped in a towel, Azia hurried to the peephole to see who it could be. When she saw Sasha, she spun around and rested her head back on the door. She wasn't in the mood for company. How did she get past security anyway? Azia made a mental note to have a talk with the doorman for letting her up without warning. And again, a knock came from the door only this time harder than the first.

"Please stop all that banging," said Azia, letting her inside.

"What the hell wrong wit you? Why is your phone off? I been trying to reach you since last night. Where you been? Why you aint return my call?" Sasha went on and on. Azia made her way back to the bathroom ignoring the shrieking of her voice. "I'm glad I thought to come here I aint know where the hell you was at."

"Sasha please, not right now," she whimpered, stepping back into the tub of water. She wet the wash cloth again and swung it over her face.

"What's the problem chick and don't give me no bullshit." Azia nodded her head so Sasha snatched the cloth from her face. "I said don't give me no bullshit."

Azia's eyes began to water and seconds later the tears came full force. "I don't know what happened to me," she cried.

Sasha took a seat on the side of the tub. "What you mean?"

"I woke up in Quadir's bed, naked, and I don't remember what happened."

"Did that muthafucka rape you?" she asked, jumping up. She grabbed her clutch in search of her cell phone. "We gotta call--"

Azia jumped to her feet, suds racing from her body. "No! You can't call Mike. Please don't tell him," she begged.

"Is you crazy?"

"He gonna leave me Sasha. Please don't tell him."

"Did the bastard rape you or did you participate?"

"I don't know," she shouted. "I told you I can't remember but he took pictures and he said if I don't do what he tell me to do he gonna show them to Mike."

"Fuck that," blurted Sasha. She continued to dial Kane's number.

Azia hopped out of the tub and stopped her. "Sash please. At least let me be the one to tell him first."

Nyema

Sasha put the phone away. "You better tell him or I will. He probably drugged ya ass, that's why you can't remember."

That made a whole lot of sense to Azia. The last thing she remember is eating and Quadir making her a drink. Everything after that was fuzzy. "It's my fault I should've never been over there."

"It aint ya fault," Sasha advised, trying to be sympathetic. "Dude had it out for you anyway."

Azia picked the towel up from the floor finally deciding to cover her nakedness. "What you mean had it out for me?"

"I don't know the extent of it or what he planning but he tryna get at Mike and you aint nothing but collateral."

Azia dashed out of the bathroom to find something to throw on with Sasha on her heels. She jumped into some pants and grabbed a shirt trying to make heads or tails out of everything. "None of this is making sense."

"It makes a lot of sense. Bottom line is he the one been causing the ruckus while we all assumed it was Rashaud."

Rashaud! Damn! And all this time she'd been treating him like shit. Her legs felt weak. "I can't believe I fell right into his game and gave him the upper hand. Mike is gonna kill me." *Wait a minute.* "But what Kyla got to do with all of this?"

Sasha was confused. "Kyla?"

"Yeah, I heard them in the kitchen arguing about something this morning. I tried to eaves drop from the steps but I couldn't really hear."

"Damn you aint hear nothing?"

"I heard her say *this wasn't a part of the plan* and something about her son or his son. Something like that." Azia sat on the bed to collect her thoughts. "I tried to hear, I tried, why can't I remember anything?" She went into a panic frenzy.

Sasha wrapped her arms around her friend to calm her. "Just calm down we'll figure this shit out together, alright?"

It felt so good to have someone there in her time of need, only Azia was wishing it was Mike with his arms around her saying everything would be okay. "How did things get so messed up?"

"Because we got too comfortable, that's how."

Chapter 30

FLYING UNDER THE RADAR

The line outside of D's Gentleman's Club was ridiculous. Every Thursday drew a thick crowd because all drinks were half price, but that night the number seemed to triple and the women out numbered the men, most of them wearing next to nothing like they were waiting to be interviewed for a spot. Sasha and Vipor arrived together and shook their heads after seeing the crowd. They cut their eyes at anyone who looked like money. It was always good to size their clients up before they officially became a client.

"Girl its some money to be made up in here tonight," shouted Vipor, ecstatic.

■■■

Danger was up on stage working her middle like she had never done before. Pooch passed her with his eyes glued on her ass. She came down off the pole and did a split bringing him to a complete halt. He strolled over with a light bop and pulled some ones out of his pocket. He started to toss them onto the stage one by one when he noticed Deuce heading to the men's room out the corner of his eye. "I'll be back for you," he told her.

Deuce was at an open stall doing his thing when Pooch entered the bathroom, passing two other brothers on their way out. He took the open stall next to Deuce, never making eye contact.

"What you got for me?" asked pooch.

Deuce shrugged. "I don't know where that nigga went or when he coming back."

"Just make sure you keep ya eyes and ears open," he ordered, walking over to the sink to wash his hands. "We gonna hit that nigga spot again in a few days."

Deuce nodded his head, zipped up and joined him at the sink. "Better make it sooner than later cause them niggas starting to get suspicious."

"What you calling the shots now?" Pooch said, stepping up in his face.

"Naw Pooch, I'm just saying--"

"You aint saying shit just shut the fuck up."

Deuce felt chumped. He was starting to realize he had no real place on either team and would always be the dub of either organization. He was a fool for thinking they would treat him any better after seeing how easy it was to turn him against Mike, the one person that gave him a real chance at life after finding out his mother was struggling to make ends meet. Although what he put him on to was no ordinary nine-to-five, it was a job and it damn sure helped keep his family afloat. Whatever happened to *never bite the hand that feeds you.*

The two men cut their conversation short when a short cocky fellow made his way in and over to a stall. When Pooch and Deuce exited the room, Lox stopped rolling his blunt and stepped from behind the door of a personal stall. It didn't matter that they never mentioned anyone's name because he knew exactly who they were referring to. Mike! He rushed out to go and relay the information to Kane hoping that he would give him the go ahead to do what he been dying to do, take the weak link out.

■■■

Kane was sitting at a private table in the back with Sasha on his lap. When he saw Pooch and Deuce enter the bathroom around the same time he knew what it was hitting for. He started to buss in there on them but decided against it at the last minute remembering Lox was in there so he played it cool.

Nyema

Lox scanned the room to see where Deuce positioned himself. When he saw him across the room talking to Sammy and another guy, he made his way over to Kane's table. "Yo, it's time for that fool to go. He definitely passing info on to them 56th street niggas."

"You heard something?"

"Him and Pooch was in there bussing it up. They aint know I was locked in one of the stalls."

Kane nodded his head and turned to Sasha. "Get Vipor on it. Tell her to get him in one of the back rooms." Sasha climbed from his lap and headed back stage. "Tell Sammy to meet us in the back in ten."

■■■

Vipor led Deuce into one of the private rooms dressed in a thong and topless. The room was small but big enough to fit about five or six people comfortably. There were no windows, one sofa and a small table that housed a bottle of Moet on ice. Deuce entered the room trying to adjust his eyes to the fluorescent lighting.

Vipor mustered up a phony smile and pushed him down on the sofa. "You know I missed you right," she said, straddling him.

He buried his head in her chest. "I missed you too baby."

Vipor climbed from off of him and began to give him a show. "What you got for me?"

Deuce pulled a bundle of cash from his pocket and spread five hundred dollars in tens and twenties all over the table. "What you gonna do for that?"

She straddled him again and said, "Whatever you want me to do baby."

■■■

Boom! The sound of the door smacking the wall startled them both. Lox and Sammy made their way into the room first followed by Kane.

"What the fuck," said Deuce, pushing Vipor off of him.

Kane motioned for Vipor to get lost. She picked up her things from the floor, snatched up the money from the table and hustled out of sight. He walked over to the sofa where Deuce was sitting and stared down at his jewels. "You been real jewelry'd down lately my man. Look like you came into some fast cash."

"I-I--" he stuttered.

Lox popped him in the back of his head. "I-I-nothing you clown ass nigga."

"I heard you been doing a lot of shufflin' back and forth. What is it, our home don't make you happy no more?" he asked, pulling his gun from his waist.

"C'mon Kane, whoever telling you that shit is lying," he whimpered. "Tell him Sammy," he coached, hoping Sammy would have his back again.

"Can't do shit for you homie you done fucked up now," Sammy smirked.

Kane started loading the chamber with bullets. "If you wanted out all you had to do was say so."

"Somebody get me the fuck outta here," yelled Deuce, as loud as he possibly could over a Lil Wayne track. Lox punched him in the mouth to silence him. "Fuck you," he said, spitting blood.

Lox stuffed his pistol forcefully into the side of his face. "Let me do it Kane," he begged. "Let me blow the muthafucka out of his misery." Lox knew the plan wasn't to kill the boy, but he just couldn't help himself.

"Don't let 'em kill me," he cried.

"You ready to change ya story?"

"What story Kane? Did that bitch Vipor say something to you? If she did she's lying," he said, assuming Vipor opened her mouth about all the bragging he'd been doing. "She lying man."

"You tryna tell me you aint been swingin' wit those 56th street punks. I dare you to lie to my face." Deuce hesitated. "Yeah you better think before you talk."

Nyema

With Lox's pistol still wedged into his skull he said, "I be kickin' it wit 'em sometimes but it aint bout nuttin'."

"So you tryna tell me these jewelz you rockin' wasn't bought wit our money?" Kane asked, prying for information. He snatched the diamond bracelet and watch from his arms. "Tell me who behind the stick-up and I'll let you ride."

"Naw...I don't know--"

"Since you wanna keep lying for them niggas I tell you what," he said inching closer. "You gonna be the one to take a beat down for 'em." Kane jarred him in the eye with his gun. "And I'ma make sure you suffer muthafucka," he yelled, bashing him in the face over and over again. He flung him on the floor.

Deuce bawled up into the fetal position while Sammy and Lox bashed his face and ribs into a bloody mess with their Timberland boots.

Kane stood over top of his crippled body and smacked his face a couple times to make sure he was alive. When Deuce opened his eyes and started coughing up blood Kane said, "Tell ya boys since they want war they got it." He then sent one last blow to Deuce's head, knocking him out cold.

■■■

Quadir was in the middle of dinner when he got the phone call about Deuce. He was furious after listening to Pooch relay the message the battered boy was told to give. This was not how he had planned it. It was too soon for Mike to start pointing fingers at him. His plan was two seconds away from being out of order. Vexed, he ended the call and waived the waitress over.

"We gotta go," he said, standing from his seat.

Azia knew something was wrong and failed to hold her smile. "Something wrong?" she smirked, already aware of what went down because of a text Sasha sent to give her a heads up.

Quadir looked her shadily and threw a fifty-dollar bill down on the table to cover the tab. "Shit about to get real ugly. You might wanna lose that smile," he warned.

She kindly retrieved her pocketbook from the back of the chair and said, "And let you steal my joy, I don't think so."

Against Kane's advice, Azia decided to continue to see Quadir. She figured that as long as she tagged along she'd be able to keep a close eye on him. Mike was still "away on business" as Kane put it and no one had heard from him in days so he had no idea how heated things had gotten. Taking matters into his own hands, Kane chose to fill his spot and call some plays into action.

On her way out the door she saw Rashaud sitting with Helena. Their eyes met and her heart dropped. Indiscreetly, she shook her head *no* just a little hoping he caught the hint. The last thing she needed him to do was intervene knowing how much of a maniac he was and in Quadir's case he wasn't any better, probably worse.

Oblivious to the prying eyes, Quadir put his arm around Azia's waist and yanked her closer towards him. She continued to snatch away as they made their way out the restaurant doors. Rashaud jumped to his feet and started to advance on it, but he didn't want to play himself. *Who the fuck is that nigga?* She'd been brushing him off since he got out of jail making it seem like she was committed to Mike and there she was stepping out with someone else. *Lying ass bitch!* He was livid and Helena had seen enough.

She stared at him while shaking her head in disbelief. "What kind of hold does that girl have on you? This shit is crazy."

"Shut up before I embarrass you in this restaurant," he advised, through clenched teeth.

"That shit aint gonna keep flying," she said, raising her voice. Onlookers began to whisper. "Go ahead Rashaud," she tempted. "I dare you to beat my ass in front of all these people. Knocking bitches out make you tough right?"

Nyema

The hostess hurried over to their table before they scared the money away. "Can ya'll please keep your voices down."

"Just give me the check," he demanded.

"And please hurry so he can get me home and whip my ass since he act like he can't whip it in front of ya'll," she growled, snatching her pocketbook and storming out the door.

■■■

Kane jumped out of his ride on the corner of 23rd & Oakford. He glanced over at a huddle of guys shooting dice on the side of the mini-mart, but the man he was looking for was not in the mix.

"Yo, Kenny," he yelled out. "Where Monster at?"

Kenny strolled away from the crap game and over to Kane. "He up in the store," he pointed. When Kane went to walk away Kenny stopped him. "Ay, you know word travel fast round the hood, right?" Kane looked at him suspiciously. "I heard them 56th street niggas on some shit right now. If you planning to move on them cats let a nigga know. You know I got ya back."

Kane couldn't help but giggle at the little soldier standing in front of him he was no more than fifteen years old. Although he knew in his mind that he would never recruit the boy into such danger, the kid was alright with him. Kane bumped knuckles with the teeny bopper and made his way into the store. He shook hands with the owner and shuffled his way to the back of the store. Sitting behind some plexiglass was Monster in the middle of conversation with an employee.

"What up?" Kane yelled over the thick glass to interrupt. "I need to holler at you."

Monster tapped Marco, his guy lover, on the butt ordering him to let Kane inside.

Kane followed Monster through a steel door and down a set of stairs. This was not his first journey down the narrow stairwell. He had seen that path many times before. Whenever he and Mike had a situation that needed to be dealt with and didn't want to get their own hands dirty, Monster was definitely the one to call. He was half-Black, half Puerto Rican, with a rich yellow skin tone and soft curls that sat perfectly in place all over his head. Standing at a solid six feet two inches tall, Monster was their best kept secret weapon. Although the look in his eyes remained innocent, the scars that were permanently edged along the side of his chin and the down the side of his neck were definitely war wounds. The three tattooed tear drops under his right eye confirmed it. "What up wit you Kane?" he asked, finally making it to the bottom of the staircase.

Kane was always a little uneasy around Monster because of his sexuality. It amazed him how the homosexual ended up with a name like Monster. But the truth is, when you put in enough work out there in the streets you can call yourself anything you want to be called. "I need you to handle something for me."

Monster walked over to an empty chair that was stationed in a corner. "That can be done, for a fee of course."

"Whatever the cost just let me know."

Monster ran his fingers back through his curls. "Tell me what you need."

Kane stepped forward into the light. "I need you on them dem 56th street niggas for the next couple weeks. I wanna know what they planning to do before they do it. You feel me?"

"Two whole weeks, you know that's gonna cost you Papi."

Kane pulled an envelope from his back pocket and tossed it to him. "That should hold you over for now. Just take care of that for me and keep me posted."

"I thought you was gonna give me something to have fun with," he smiled, twirling the ring on his pinky finger. "You know, like, something to shoot."

"Don't worry," said Kane, spinning back towards him. "I'ma have something nice lined up for you real soon."

Chapter 31

UNLEASHING THE ANGER

Wayne and Hamburger were out of breath by the time they got Vipor down to the basement of a secluded house. She refused to go without a fight. They pinned her down on the filthy floor as she fought, scratched and ripped at their flesh. Sweat flew off both heavy men as they chased her from one side of the room to the other after she broke free. Again, they pinned her face down, took turns running all they had inside of her and did whatever else they could possibly think of doing to degrade her like they were ordered to do.

Deuce stared on piteously, gagged and tied down to an old rusted chair. Her clothes had been ripped to shreds, her body was bloodied and bruised, her face was dressed in dried up tears and her hair was soaked in urine. Then just like that, his stare turned to stone. She was the reason they were in this predicament. If she would've just kept her mouth closed...

Wayne and Hamburger watched the girl manage to use the little strength she had left to crawl towards the stairs. Just as she grabbed hold of the first step, her face connected with what felt like a combat boot.

Quadir was the owner of that boot. No longer capable of seeing out of either eye, she scooted backwards on the filthy compound until landing in what felt like a puddle of water but smelled worse than cat piss. As Quadir's heavy footsteps got closer and closer, she began to feel around for something, anything that would help keep him away. Suddenly, Hamburger and Wayne burst into laughter when they watched her hand dig deep into a pile of human feces.

"Please let me out of here," she cried, through swollen lips and vomited all over herself.

"Pick her ass up," ordered Quadir. He watched Hamburger and Wayne nudge each other insisting that the other do it. "You niggas got to be kidding me." Quadir walked over and snatched the girl up and dragged her down the other end of the room where an old filthy, cum-stained mattress was. He slung the girl down and pulled his gun out ready to pull the trigger, but first he needed some answers. "What the hell did you tell Kane?"

She shook her head nervously. "Nothing, I swear--"

He took his eyes off her for a split second and aimed his gun at Deuce. "You see why I told you not to trust these bitches. Now look at you."

Deuce looked down at Vipor with ice in his eyes. She turned her head towards the wall and willed herself not to cry again. All she wanted was to get outside to breathe some real air or to just be taken out of her misery. Too embarrassed to look any of them in the eye, she bit down on her bottom lip and prayed softly with both eyes closed.

Quadir stepped behind the chair and mugged Deuce with the gun. "Fuck was you thinkin'?" Deuce uttered something but the gag made it barely audible. "Fuck you say?" he asked, mugging him again. "I can't hear you speak up."

"Umm, he can't talk cause the thing--" Hamburger started to explain before Quadir cut him off.

"Do I look like a muthafuckin retard to you?" he asked, sarcastically, ripping the gag from Deuce's mouth. "What you got to say lil homie?"

"She set me up."

"Is you slow or just plain ol' stupid? We established that much now we tryna figure out how much you told the hoe."

"Nuttin' bout the big shit Qua. I swear man, the shit I told her I was pump faking about."

Nyema

"I don't give a fuck what you was doing. Now you got them niggas pointing the finger my way and that wasn't the plan," he reminded him, and mugged him again.

"I promise if you let me go I'll make shit right."

"And how you plan on doing that?"

"Whatever I gotta do."

Quadir looked into Deuce's eyes and saw nothing but fear and regret. At that moment he decided that Deuce would live, for now. He had another job for him to handle but after that, he would definitely be preparing to meet his maker. Without looking, Quadir raised his weapon at Vipor and pulled the trigger twice. Two bullets connected with her head and she was dead before her body hit the floor. He untied Deuce's hands, held the gun to his temple and fingered the trigger. "Time to show ya loyalty my man." He let the gun swerve upside down and dangle from his finger.

Deuce retrieved the weapon and studied it like he was studying for an exam.

"You know what you gotta do, right?"

Deuce never realized it would come down to this. He knew the bad blood between Quadir and Mike would surface, but he had no real intention on participating in a gun battle. Mike had been there for him when he wasn't man enough to hold shit down on his own. But Sammy, he never dreamt of the day that he would ever stab him in the back, but he did and the more he thought about it the more his stomach turned. He nodded his head slowly and cocked the trigger like he was a born professional.

Quadir turned to Hamburger and Wayne. "Get her up outta here," he said, and then nodded at Deuce. "And make sure he handle his business before the sun come up and I bet not see none of ya'll 'til the shit get done."

■ ■ ■

"I aint lying man, the chick be on me. I can't brush her. I guess my stroke is just that magical…" Sammy sang the three syllable word. He flipped the collar of his Polo shirt and dusted around the edges of it with his fingers just as smooth as you would the brim of a hat "What can I say, ya brother got game."

Lox was filled with laughter, almost in tears. He loved the way his little brother swore he was a pimp. He had definitely grown to make him proud. Growing up in the system wasn't fun for either of the boys. When they were separated after their mother passed almost ten years ago, Lox promised himself he would do whatever he had to find his brother. It took over two years, but he never gave up and because of that the hunt finally paid off. Convincing Sammy that the only way they could be together was to run away, Sammy didn't hesitate. All he wanted to do since the tender age of ten-years-old was be just like his big brother and Lox knew it. They found a way to stay out of the forefront until they were over eighteen where the state couldn't touch them. Aware of their situation, Mike put them up in a two-bedroom apartment rent free for one year and food in their stomachs until they got good and on their feet. The blood of the streets ran thick through Lox's veins, but it was never something he predicted for his younger brother. It just happened that way. But Lox figured as long as they had Mike who kept things loyal, safe and secure, there was no need for worry.

"I don't know what you laughing at I aint lying."

"You must'a forgot I birthed ya lil ass so I know what's good."

"Ay Lox, stop saying that shit man, you aint birth me," he said, offended.

"Get ya soft ass outta here."

"Fo'real though." He hopped up from the chair and slid a baseball cap on his head backwards. "I'm running across the street to the store you want something?"

"Nah, just hurry ya ass up so we get finished choppin' up dis work."

Nyema

Sammy gathered all his munchies and collected his change from the small man behind the counter at the corner store and made his way out the door. He stopped and smacked hands with one of the locals that strolled across the street. Tamar was blacker than the heel at the bottom of a shoe. Instead of being called by his government name, the hood labeled him with one more suitable.

"What up Tarbaby," Sammy grinned. "I aint seen you on this end in a while." They swapped a brotherly hug.

"Aint shit, on my way to my girl house."

"Oh yeah," he said, cracking his Pepsi open. "Round this part?"

"Yeah, up the block," the guy pointed. "You probably don't know her cause she a stay at home body. She don't really come out like that. "

"What's her name?"

"Tarissa--"

Sammy choked on his soda. That was the same girl he was just bragging about to his brother. "Not short Tarissa—gap in her teeth—ass like--" He caught himself. "I mean--"

"So you know her," the boy quizzed. "Is she as quiet as she claim to be?"

"I don't know about all that. But don't just go by my word homie, I aint one to fuck up nobody's home."

"You aint fuckin nuttin' up--"

The guy went on and on but something more detrimental captured Sammy's attention. His body tensed up when he saw a car slowly driving down the block. His first instinct was to drop everything and break but decided against it. *There's way too many folks around for it to be a jump off* he thought. He loosened his grip on the plastic bag just in case he had to break out and run. By the time he saw the gun appear out the backseat window followed by Deuce's face, he knew it was too late and he had made the wrong choice. He stared into Deuce's eyes and felt like he was staring at Satan himself. His mind was ordering him to run but his legs wouldn't budge. If it was his time to go then so be it. He just wished he had one last time to tell his brother goodbye.

As if on cue, shots rang out and everyone began to scatter and dive for cover hoping not to end up being collateral damage. Sammy used the guy he was talking to as a human shield. The impact of the bullets that shattered the man's rib and punctured a lung sent him flying back forcing him and Sammy to the ground. The car came to a screeching stop and Deuce darted over to where Sammy had fallen. His nerves were shot and the twitch in his trigger finger proved it. But he knew he had to pull the trigger or Quadir would be the one to make him suffer the consequences. By the time Sammy rolled the guy's dead weight off of him, there was no time to make a move.

"I bet the next time you take sides it'll be the right one muthafucka," Deuce spat, and sent a bullet through his skull, center mass. "And ya brother next."

■■■

Lox had already made his way out of the apartment building when he heard the first couple shots. With everything that had been going on lately paranoia had become a constant thing with him. He jumped down the stairwell, three and four steps at a time, and sprinted towards the store where folks had gathered in an uproar. People were crying, screaming and falling all over the place. Something inside felt very wrong as he pushed his way through the crowd of spectators. He caught sight of the stopped and caught sight of his baby brother lying dead in the street, motionless. He kicked the open Pepsi bottle that had made a puddle beside his brother's bloody head and bent over, cupping his knees, to catch his breath.

"Muthafuckas," he screamed. "Fuck! Ya'll just gonna stand here, go get some fuckin' help," he raved.

■■■

TyTy stood in front of the University of Pennsylvania hospital smoking a cigarette. When he got the call from

Nyema

Lox, he flew down there to see what was up. He decided to take a breather and go have a smoke while the surgeons finished up in the operating room. For so many years, they had trailed along drama and incident free. Now everything was falling apart.

Kane's car pulled up with Camel sitting behind the wheel. Kane swung the passenger door open and hopped out. "What's the status?"

TyTy tossed his cigarette and shrugged, "Waiting for him to get out of surgery. I don't think it's looking too good, he took one to the head."

"Fuck!" Kane yelled, spinning around. He wished there was something around for him to punch. "Where Lox at?"

"He up there you know he aint leaving until--"

Before TyTy got a chance to complete the sentence, Lox came storming out of the emergency room doors drenched in tears. Both Kane and TyTy dropped their heads. After seeing, the state Lox was in they knew it couldn't be good. Camel was still sitting behind the wheel but when he looked up and saw Lox he jumped out to help console him.

Lox was on a mission. He walked right pass all three of them like they were stone until Kane jogged around and stopped in front of him. "Move out my way Kane I got somewhere I need to be."

"I know you mad homie, but let's talk about this."

"Talk about what," he jerked away. "They killed my fuckin' brother man."

"We don't know that yet."

"What I do know is my brother in there fighting and if he don't make it," he yelled, throwing his arms up in the air. "It's on me cause he trusted me to have his back and I wasn't there." He broke down. "He all I got Kane. Them niggas gonna pay for this."

Kane clutched on to him again. "Don't do nothing stupid. We gonna sit down and map this thing out young blood.

C'mon now," he begged, feeling the deepest of sympathy for his soldier.

"Stupid!?!" Lox backed away, staring Kane down with his good eye. "Doing nothing is stupid. All them niggas gonna pay." He turned his back and stormed off to nowhere in particular.

Kane called TyTy over and told Camel to get the car. "Yo, stay with him and don't let him outta ya sight. I'll be back in a few." He climbed in the car and Camel sped away.

Chapter 32

GETTING BACK TO US

Azia was flying down the expressway doing damn near twenty over the speed limit trying to get home as quick as she possible could. She hated being out in the street without a phone. While running some errands, her cell phone battery went dead and she cursed herself for leaving her car charger in Sasha's car. It had been a long, dreadful, day and everything was beginning to become too overwhelming. As much as she wanted to do whatever she could to help Mike out, she had no clue where he was and he hadn't been answering any of her calls, so she was almost to the point of giving up. If he didn't want to be bothered then so be it. She never was into keeping a brother that didn't want to be kept. So many negative thought clouded her brain. *Maybe he busy playing daddy with Kyla and her son. Maybe he tired of all us heffas and said to hell with us. Maybe he left and he aint never coming back. Maybe he doesn't love me like I thought he did...*And the thoughts went on and on.

Azia whipped into her assigned parking spot, grabbed her bags from the seat and shuddered to the elevator never paying attention to the rental car that was parked beside her in Mike's spot. On top of wanting to check her messages, she had been holding her bladder for over an hour and it was on its way out any minute whether she agreed or not. She rushed through the front door, flung her bag on the floor against the wall and gunned for the bathroom missing all signs that made it evident that she was not alone.

By the time Azia finished up in the bathroom, Mike had moved himself from the sofa to the kitchen. He grabbed a beer out of the refrigerator and stood in the hallway leaned up against the wall. She rushed out of the bathroom ready to jump into her homework assignment but instead got the surprise she was least expecting.

"Oh shit," she blurted, clutching on to her chest like she was trying to pull the shock out of it. "You scared me."

They just stared at one another for a while without saying a word. Things began to feel a little uncomfortable for Azia. She felt like they were meeting for the first time all over again, awkward. She looked him over a couple times. He was dressed in linen and it wasn't that nice out. *Where the hell he been* she wondered. Knowing Mike wasn't going to make the first move she decided to break the ice. Walking slowly towards him, the two lovers stared each other down. She wanted to cry, jump in his arms and places kisses all over his face but instead, she just placed her head on his chest hoping he would in turn throw his arms around her. She needed to feel that security. She was dying to know that he still had love for her. But when the hug never came, she took two steps back and looked him square in the eye.

"So, should I take that as a hint?"

"Where you been?"

"You care?"

"Don't answer my question with a question." He took a swig of the beer under the assumption that she was out kicking it with Quadir. "I left you two messages. All this bullshit going on and you don't feel the need to answer ya phone when I call?"

To make her life a hell of a lot simpler she told the truth. "I was in school Mike. Where the hell you thought I was at?" Half of her wanted to tell him her concerns about Quadir, but the other half was afraid to admit it because she felt like she was part of the reason for things spiraling out of control. She brushed pass him and headed to the bedroom.

Mike followed behind her. He positioned himself in the bedroom doorway and watched her undress but said nothing.

"Why are you looking at me like that?"

"I don't know." He walked over to her. "You tell me."

"Come on now, you just got home from wherever you was at and the first thing you got on ya list to do is fuck with me. Are you serious?"

Mike saw something in her that wasn't there before. He knew she was keeping something from him but he wasn't sure what it was. The fear shining within her eyes was a dead giveaway and Azia knew it. She felt like a trapped mouse about to be frisked by a hungry cat.

The tears began to accumulate and she was done playing tough. "Stop looking through me like you trying to read me Mike," she cried. She threw her arms around his neck but he sternly pushed them away. "Don't do me like that."

"You doing you right? Fuck how I feel about the situation. And then you got a nerve to bring ya ass back here 'cause you know I was away. What kind of games you playing Azia?"

"I'm not playing games Mike, I swear--"

"Could'a fooled the hell out of me. You running around town with a nigga that's real suspect right now. What you call that, huh? You helping him? Is that what it is? You helping this nigga get at me and my team?"

Azia felt like the ceiling fan that she was standing under collapsed on top of her head.

"These niggas out here gunning for my head and you think this shit is a game. It aint no game," he yelled. His voice was so strong it made her flinch. "You don't even dig the fact that you making shit worse."

Azia eased onto the edge of the bed and aggressively applied pressure to her head with her hands. This was not making sense. One minute he was talking like she was really fucking around on him with Quadir, and the next minute he was talking like he knew she was doing it all for him. She looked at him confused. "I was playing him close for you. Trying to get information for you but he crazy--"

"Crazy!?!" he repeated. "And what am I?"

"If you already know my reason behind dealing with him why are you sitting here putting me though all this extra bullshit?"

"Because you need to be smarter than this, I aint make you my woman for you to get caught up in my street shit--"

She jumped to her feet. "I don't care why you made me ya woman the bottom line is I am ya woman and I made it my business to have ya back. Aint nothing you can say gonna make me believe I did the wrong thing."

At that moment, Mike was at a loss for words, completely tongue-tied.

Azia walked over to him and stroked his cheek. "I should have never let Kyla get between us in the first place. That's my fault Mike and I'm willing to admit I fucked up but I'm human and I apologize. All I'm asking for is another chance. Let me love you like you deserve to be loved and let me be woman enough to make decisions that revolve around having ya back like a real woman supposed to," she said, then wrapped her arms around his back and kissed him softly.

Mike sighed heavily and returned the gesture halfheartedly. There were no words to express how he was feeling. He'd been in the streets all is life, had grown accustomed to making a shit load of money, and managed to keep his hands clean while doing it. Although he may have had one or two clowns test him in the past, it had never been nothing as significant as it had been the last few weeks. Maybe it was time to say goodbye to game and get out while he was still breathing. But first thing was first, he had no choice to find out what Quadir's beef was with him. Dude came out of nowhere and wound up turning one of his own soldiers against him and that troubled him the most. He was always good to all of his people and for one to cross him like that just wasn't sitting too well with him. It was no longer safe for him to trust, but it was so much more unsafe for whoever was responsible for throwing salt in his game.

Nyema

Azia watched him yank his shirt off hoping the next thing he would yank up was her. She drooled over his muscled body realizing for the first time what she'd been missing since they'd been apart. The more she watched him the more she thought about all the duds she'd been with through high school and college. She kept them rolling in one after the other hoping to gain the love she'd lost by not having a father in her life. Never had she found the one to truly fill that void. The longest relationship she'd been in before Mike was Rashaud, but there was nothing about him that gave her that warm sensitive feeling that a father would give a daughter. He showed her nothing more than a dark side. But with Mike, everything was different. He loved her in a way that no man had ever done before. And it was not about the money, she had dozens that wined and dined her in the past. Mike simply made her feel complete.

"Get ready to ride with me over to the hospital," he advised, jumping into something more suitable for the Philadelphia forecast.

She panicked. "Who at the hospital?"

"Sammy got shot."

"Is he gonna make it?"

"For Lox sake, I hope so."

■■■

The following day, Mike made his way into KoKa's Bar & Grill and found his mother standing behind the bar doing inventory. He smiled at his Aunt Val who was setting up some tables and greeted her with a hug.

"You know you aint never too old for a good ass kicking don't you," she joked, happy to see her nephew. "You better not ever stay away that long again without calling nobody. You hear me boy?"

"I hear you Aunt Val," he giggled, making his way over to KoKa. "What up Ma?"

KoKa looked at him with disappointment in her eyes. "You leave without saying anything, ignore all my calls and the first thing you got to say to me is what up?"

Mike walked behind the bar and hugged his mother. "I needed some time to myself. You can understand that right?"

"I can understand you needing some alone time but what I can't understand is how distant you kept me. I was so worried about you, how could you do that to me?"

"I'm sure Kane told you I was okay."

"You think I'm going off someone else's word after all the bullshit that's been going on around here. People getting shot up left and right and my son decide to pick up and leave without saying nothing." She smacked him in his chest, hard. "I'm so upset with you."

Mike watched as the tears formed in KoKA's eyes. He felt bad for leaving without notice but he was upset with her as well. He knew he would never be the only man in her life forever, but he wanted so much more for her than Anthony.

"I don't care what we ever go through in life you bet not ever let anyone or anything come in between the relationship we have. You are my everything Mike. I have never put anyone before you and through the grace of God I never will. But I gotta have a life too. We may not agree on everything, we may fuss and fight but at the end of the day, we all we got."

The whole conversation felt like déjà vu. Back when he was sixteen-years-old, KoKa entered her first relationship since the death of his father. Mike did everything possible to chase the guy away because he didn't feel that he was good enough. He wanted his mother with no one if they weren't the best, and in his eyes her finding that was impossible so he was all she needed and KoKa became content with that. But now things had changed. Her biological clock was ticking, she wasn't getting any younger and being alone wasn't fun anymore.

Nyema

"I aint got no choice but to respect that Ma, I just want you to be happy."

"I'm trying to be happy but it gets complicated when I have to please you and my man."

"No need to worry about pleasing me, go on ahead and worry about ya man."

Speaking those words felt like pulling teeth out of his mouth and KoKa knew it, but she gave him credit for it anyway. "You ready to go shoot yourself aren't you?" she joked. "Let me hear you say it again."

■■■

Aunt Val, Mike and KoKa sat around cracking jokes and filling their stomachs for nearly two hours. Mike glanced down at his watch knowing he had some other business to tend to. He sucked down the last of his drink and slid back off the bar stool.

"Alright ladies it's been fun but I got places to be and people to see," he said.

"You just make sure you stay out of trouble and remember what I told you," Val warned. "Never too old--"

"For a good ass kicking," he blurted, finishing the sentence for her. "I know…I know…"

"You seen Kyla yet?" KoKa asked, collecting the dishes from the bar.

"Naw! Why wassup?"

"Her phone keeps on calling me by accident."

"What you mean by accident?"

"I guess it was an accident. My voicemail picked up a conversation between her and somebody. Sounded like a guy I don't know. I never listened to the whole message."

"Did you save it?"

"Mike, I don't know a thing bout these damn phones. I just hung up--"

"Let me see ya phone," he said, walking back towards her. KoKa retrieved her phone from her pocketbook and handed it over. "What's ya passcode?"

"I don't know I just hit the voicemail button and listen."

Mike skipped through all KoKa's personal messages until he found the one she was talking about. He took a seat on the stool and listened in attentively. It wasn't hard for him to distinguish Kyla's voice but the man's voice puzzled him. He listened as closely as possible.

"The plan was never for you to fall for that bitch."

"What part of what I said didn't you understand? You need to get ya shit together."

Mike heard what sounded like a smack then the man reiterate, *"Get ya shit together."* Then another smack came and them man asked, *"You got it together yet?"*

Mike stopped listening at that point and replayed the message back from the beginning. He was desperate to figure out who the owner of that voice could be. As he listened in further he could hear Kyla yell, *"Get off of me."*

"Shut the fuck up. You gonna wake her."

"I'm telling you now I be damned if you the only one gonna walk away a winner. I better get what I want."

"Just take ya ass up outta here before I forget why I need you."

"And what about ya son?" Mike's eyes grew wide after hearing the question and the last thing he heard was, *"Yeah I thought so."*

He hopped up from the stool. "I need to take ya phone I'll bring it back," he advised, headed for the door.

"What the hell am I supposed to do without a phone?" she yelled behind him.

■■■

Just as Mike was getting into his car, Anthony's pulled up beside him. He tried to hide the bitterness as he watched the man climb out his car. It was easy to tell there was something very different about him but he couldn't put his finger on it. Anthony threw up a finger advising Mike to give him a minute of his time. Mike stepped back out of his car.

"How was your trip?" he asked, making small talk but could tell Mike was not in the mood. "I heard you lost one of your friends, I'm sorry to hear about that."

"Cut the small talk. Wassup?"

Anthony sighed. He was wishing the two of them could find a way to common ground. "I know we don't see eye to eye but I want you to know I love your mother and I'm doing everything in my power to show her."

"Listen, my mom grown. She makes her own decisions and one of them happened to be you so I got to live with that. But all I'ma say to you is if I ever find out you laid another finger on that woman in there," he said, pointing towards the entrance of the restaurant. "I will bury you man, and won't have a problem spending the rest of my life in jail after doing it. That's my word."

"I know it's only been a little while but I'm clean Mike. No more drinking, no nothing. When I tell you I'm doing whatever I need to, I mean that brother and hopefully one day you'll grow to accept me."

"Maybe one day but that day aint gonna be today," Mike spat, climbing back into his car.

Anthony pulled a small box from his jacket pocket. "It may not be today but I plan on being around for while so take ya time." He flipped the box open and there sat a beautiful engagement ring. "I plan on taking her out to dinner on her birthday and asking her then. I hope you can make yourself available, if not for me, for your mom."

"I'll see what I can do," he responded, then sped out of the lot.

Chapter 33

ONCE AGAIN IT'S ON

Azia picked up her cell phone to see who was blowing it up. She had been ignoring the ringing of it for blocks now because she was on a mission, and she had to stay on point. She pulled up to the red light on 52nd & Market and screened the call. Rashaud! She sent him to voicemail and checked her call log to see if it was him that called the last four times and it was. She tossed the phone back into her pocketbook and pulled off with traffic. She continued to glance down every block that she passed in search of someone or something. This was her fifth time circling the area and hustlers on the corners that she was passing had begun to get uneasy.

"Yo," one of them yelled out. He jumped in front of her car like he was built with a bumper. Azia panicked and threw on the breaks. "Wassup baby girl?" he asked, making his way to the driver side window.

Azia made sure the doors were locked and cracked the window wide enough to slip a quarter through. "I'm looking for Keemah," she shouted.

"Who?" He turned back to his boys. "Who Keemah?"

The clique of young hustlers started to voice over one another that they didn't know who she was until one blurted out, "She might be talkin' 'bout fat ass," he said. "The one that be up in that spot over there," he pointed.

"Oh yeah I think that trick name is Keemah," another mentioned. "Tell her she in Spade's spot," he yelled over to his friend.

Nyema

The boy turned back to Azia and pointed to a row home that looked no better than the house that Jack built. "She up in there."

"Can you get for me please?"

"And what you gonna do for me?"

"What you want?"

"You can start by rolling this window down for me so a nigga can holler at you for a minute."

"Sweetheart," she said, tenderly as possible. "If I had a minute to give you it would be yours but I'm on a mission right now so hopefully this'll do." She pulled out a fifty dollar bill and held it up.

"No problem, I'll handle that for you. Put ya money back in ya pocket."

Azia watched in amazement as the boy walked over to the house and let himself in. She was sure he would've at least taken that money. Moments later he came out of the house followed by Keemah. She was looking around to see where the boy was leading her. When she caught sight of Azia's car she sucked her teeth. She walked up to the passenger side window and knocked on it.

"Get in," Azia ordered.

Keemah climbed in and Azia wished she wouldn't have. The stench coming from her cousin's pores was overwhelming. "What you want with me Azia? I was busy."

Azia pulled off. "I can see that," she responded, sarcastically.

"Where you think you taking me?"

"Somewhere you should've thought about going a long time ago."

The two of them drove in silence all the way down City Line Avenue. Ever since Azia witnessed Keemah copping dope from that hustler, her conscience had been bothering her. She felt the need to make things right. Although the girl did stab her in the back, she was still blood and wasn't nothing going to change that. She knew there was no guarantee that Keemah would stay once she dropped her off at the rehab center, but it was worth a try. Azia pulled into a small lot of what seemed like a secluded location and idled the car.

Keemah grinned deviously. She didn't know for sure where her cousin had brought her but she felt it was safe to assume. "There you go still playing captain save-a-hoe huh?"

"You need help Cuz. I know I'm the last person you ever thought would care but I do and I'm hoping you care too."

Keemah dropped her head and watched the tears add to the dirty stains on her shirt. "Why are you fucking with me? Why can't you just leave me alone?"

"Do you really want me to do that Keemah? Look at me and tell me that's what you want."

Keemah hopped out of the car and started to walk her way back to City Line. "You can two-step your way out of my life and leave me the hell alone. I don't need shit from you. I'm good where I'm at."

Azia sat in her car contemplating on what to do. Playing devil's advocate was not something she admired, but it was hard to push herself to care enough to keep trying to talk somebody out of a situation they wanted to be in. *Damn* she thought, jumping out of the car and into the night air. She had to jog to catch up. "Keemah, wait a minute."

Keemah was out. Trying to keep up with a crack head was job all by itself. "Leave me alone Azia," she shouted, scratching her arms. "You brought me all the way up here now I gotta get home. Take me home," she yelled.

"Girl listen, you owe me so you aint got no choice but to take ya ass up in there and do what you need to do. Stop acting so fucking weak all the time. First Rashaud, now this."

Keemah spun around rapidly. "See, you don't really care about me. You still bitter cause I fucked ya man."

"I'm over that," Azia said, sincerely. "I'm trying to help you but if you too hell bent on making me feel like I owe you something then to hell with it." She turned and headed back to her car. "Stay a bum."

Keemah skipped back towards Azia's car just before she had a chance to get inside. "Alright, I'll go in but you got to go in with me."

Hell no, that was never the plan Azia thought, shaking her head.

"If you don't go with me I'm not going in."

Azia killed the engine and snatched her keys from the ignition. "Come the hell on I aint got all day."

■■■

Twenty-five minutes later, Azia came out of that building with a new outlook on life. Seeing all of the recovering addicts battling with their addictions brought tears to her eyes. She was so grateful to be in the position she was in and made a mental note to get on her knees and thank God which was something she'd been failing to do lately. She hit the button to unlock her car door and just as she grabbed the handle to open it, someone came from behind and hemmed her up with their hand across her mouth.

"You got time for that junkie bitch cousin of yours, but you aint got time to answer none of my calls," Rashaud whispered, angrily. "And then you got a nerve to be running round wit another nigga. But you 'pose to be so in love wit Mike right?"

"Rashaud, you don't understand," she tried to explain, under the broken street lights that were fighting to stay alive which made it almost impossible for anyone to see them because of the way he had her pinned to the car.

"Explain it to me then since I don't understand."

"I don't mess with Quadir, I'm just using him."

Rashaud wrapped his hands around her neck and squeezed as hard as he possibly could. "Stop lying to me you whore. You brush me off for another nigga and come to find out you not only fucking him you fucking somebody else too. I told you I play for keeps and I don't do seconds."

Azia tried everything imaginable to gain a little bit of air, but nothing was working. Her eyes felt like they were going to pop out of their sockets any second.

Rashaud gripped her up off her car, dragged her over to his and dove into her face with a hard kiss that got sloppier as time passed. He then pulled her hair violently, spun her around and smacked her face down on the hood as she kicked and screamed. His fingers rustled with her mouth as she attempting to bite them. "Be quiet before I blow ya fuckin' face off. I'ma show you the consequences that come wit fuckin' other niggas."

"No, Rashaud please don't do this--" she gasped.

He ripped her shirt and tugged at her pants. With one strong hold around her neck, he used his free hand to unzip his pants.

"Please don't rape me."

"Shut the fuck up," he said, forcing himself inside and penetrating brutally. "I love the shit outchu girl, this pussy belong to me. You made me do this, it aint had to be this way."

Azia quit fighting and laid there with vacant eyes until she heard the voice of an elderly lady yell out, "Leave that girl alone. I done called the cops you pervert."

Rashaud scanned the area for the onlooker but it was too dark to see pretty much anything. Fortunate enough for Azia she had seen them. He pulled his pants from the ground and tried to force her in the car. "Come on," he demanded.

She mustered up the strength to fight back. "Get off of me Rashaud," she cried.

"Don't worry hunny the cops are on their way," the woman yelled out again.

Rashaud turned his head for one split second and it was one second too long. Azia dropped her weight on the ground and slammed her foot into his balls. He grabbed his jewels as his knees hit the ground. Azia stared at him insanely before she decided to make a run for it. She didn't care if the police was coming. He was definitely going to get dealt with one way or the other.

■■■

"Before you even think about lying to me I want you to take a minute and think about the consequences," Mike advised. "I'm not doing no fussing, I'm not doing no cussing, no hollering or none of that shit. All I want to hear is the truth."

Kyla sat on her sofa trembling like a thief caught in the night. She thought about making a run for it, but the gun that Mike made visible by placing it on the dining room table made her reconsider.

"Take your time I'll wait." He took a seat on the chair beside his weapon and said, "But I aint got all day."

Kyla sat quiet for a moment trying to get her thoughts together. If she told Mike the truth about everything, Quadir would probably kill her. If she didn't tell the truth, Mike would probably kill her. It was a no win situation so she just decided to play dumb. "I don't know what you're talking about Mike. Please hip me to what's going on cause somebody done told you wrong."

Mike giggled. "Somebody done told me wrong huh?"

"Yeah, and I know it wasn't nobody but that bitch you with. She just mad that I found out they was fucking and scared I was gonna run back and tell you about it. I know it was her wasn't it?"

This was the first Mike had heard of Azia and Quadir having sexual relations. He wanted to know more. "So she's lying because they fucking? That's what you trying to tell me?"

"I got pictures to prove it."

Mike escorted her to the kitchen drawer where a double set of the pictures were hidden. When Quadir ordered her to get the film developed she got doubles just in case she needed them for blackmail one day. And boy was she happy she did because blackmail was the last of her worries, she needed them to keep own ass alive. She eyeballed him as he sorted through them one by one but couldn't read any emotion.

"So what else you got for me?" he asked, sliding the pictures into his back pocket.

"Huh? Wha—t you me—an?" she stuttered.

"You got anything else that'll keep me from wringing ya neck for another two minutes?"

"I told you she lying--"

Mike produced KoKa's cell phone and dialed the voicemail then hit the speakerphone so she could hear. He sat the phone on the countertop and crossed his arms wondering how she would go about getting out of it next.

Kyla listened to the voicemail and tears formed instantly. How could she be so stupid? "Mike--"

He cut her off. "Hold on you had a lot more to say." The voicemail ended and the two started at one another for a moment. "So you still gonna stick with ya story?" She didn't respond. "Who the dude talking in the background?" She didn't answer so he yanked her to the side by her waist and stuck his pistol in her chest. "Please don't make me repeat myself," he said, peacefully.

Kyla's tears began to run like a faucet. She wasn't hundred percent sure that Mike would do anything to hurt her, but she was ninety-nine percent sure he had a goon or two that would be willing to take her out in the blink of an eye. "It was Quadir."

Mike let the gun drop to his side. Quadir! He was confused. "So you trying to tell me." He paused and rubbed his temple, gun still in hand. "That's his kid in there?" She shook her head *yes*. He was no genius but it took him two seconds to put two and two together. "I can't believe this shit. Can't be, you fucking with me right?"

Nyema

"He made me do it," she sobbed.

"Made you do what?" he asked, gripping her up. His mind had already started jumping to different conclusions. "Fuck you talking about Kyla?"

"He made me tell you it was your baby but I swear I didn't know he was going to start killing people."

Mike tried to control his anger but it had finally got the best of him. "What about the paternity test? You had that shit made up?" She shook her head *no*. "So spit the shit out Kyla. What the fuck are you trying to tell me?"

"I'm telling you that the test wasn't rigged. It came back a match because ya'll are related." Mike looked at her with stale eyes. "Quadir is your brother."

Chapter 34

RUNNING SCARED

Mike pulled up to KoKa's Bar & Grill with Kyla and the baby boy in the back seat. He was glad to see Camel had beaten him there like he told him to. He climbed out the SUV and directed his attention to Camel. "I need you to take them to the apartment over on Snyder in your car and stay there with her until I call you." Camel glanced in the back seat at Kyla, the baby and an overnight bag and opened the door to let them out. He was not into asking questions, only taking orders. Mike made his way inside the restaurant and to the office where one of the staff members told him KoKa was. He used his key to get in and didn't bother knocking.

"Keep my phone any longer I'm gonna have you start paying the bill," KoKa joked, but Mike didn't find anything funny. "What's wrong with you?"

He tossed the phone up on the desk. "I need to ask you something and I need you to keep it real with me."

"What is it?"

"Do I got a brother?"

The question caught KoKa off guard. "Where'd you hear that at?"

"I'm a grown ass man Ma, don't do that," he said, staring at the protective instinct in his mother's eyes.

"Yes Mike," she huffed. "He had a whole 'nother family on the side," she admitted, taking a seat behind the desk. KoKa sparked a cigarette and took a puff. "What you think all the fussing and fighting was about?"

"Why you aint never tell me?"

Nyema

"I just wanted to protect you from all of his bullshit. He never wanted us to be a part of that boy's life so I left it at that. I thought it was for the best."

"It wasn't for the best. You should've told me--"

"I'm sorry," she shouted, banging a fist on the desk. "Why are you so upset?"

"Because the little nigga's out to get me, that's why." Mike fell onto the lounge chair and let his head fall back against the wall. "He's on some other shit."

"What are you talking about?"

"Quadir's my brother Ma," he said, lifting up. "He's the one been causing all this bullshit." Mike jumped to his feet and looked her square in the eyes. "You should'a told me 'bout dude."

"How the hell was I supposed to know Quadir was his son? You making this out to be my fault because I decided not to tell you ya father was a hoe?" she shouted, offended.

"You missing the whole point," he snapped back.

"Well draw it out for me because evidently I'm too slow to figure the shit out."

He flagged her. "I'm done talkin'," he spat, storming out and slamming the door behind him.

■ ■ ■

Helena looked at Rashaud with disgust when he stormed through the door demanding that she hook him up an ice pack for his nuts. "Who done kicked you in the balls?"

"Just go do what I told you to do."

She sucked her teeth and did as she was told. Minutes later she came back with a sandwich bag filled with ice cubes and tossed it to him. "Who did it?"

"None of ya business," he said, placing the ice between his thighs. "Cut the TV on it's too damn quiet in here."

She snatched up the remote and powered it on with a smile. "Did Azia do that to you?"

"I said mind ya fucking business," he yelled.

"Hmm," she smirked, flipping through channels. "I'm sick of you and that bitch." She jumped to her feet with attitude. "Let her come over here and take care of ya trifling ass cause I aint doing the shit no more…" she mumbled, until her voice disintegrated behind her bedroom door.

■ ■ ■

After squeezing into a tight parking spot just a few doors down from Kane's house, Mike hopped out the car and snatched the pictures from his back pocket. He jogged up the steps and turned the knob but the door was locked so he knocked. Kane opened the door and stepped back away from the door. He had called Mike to let him know that Azia was there and she needed to holler at him about something, but he refused to tell him what happened to her over the phone.

Mike stepped into the living room where Azia and Sasha was on the sofa sitting. He could tell something was wrong but before asking what that was he had something he needed to get off his chest. He tossed the pictures on the coffee table in front of them and they scattered across the table. Azia saw the pictures and broke down in Sasha's arms.

"Mike, I think that right there might have to wait. Something real fucked up happened to her tonight," Sasha advised.

He looked over to Kane and then back at them. "And what's that?"

"Azia, hunny, you gotta tell him," she said, bringing Azia's face up from her arm.

Azia took some tissue she was previously given and dried her face best she could. She looked at Mike and tried to speak, but nothing would come out. When Azia broke into another uncontrollable cry, Sasha looked over at Kane and gave him a slight head nod.

"Yo Mike, let me holler at you brother," Kane suggested.

Mike followed Kane outside. "Would somebody tell me what the fuck's goin' on…"

"Pssshhh…" Kane used two fingers to wiggle his nose. That was something he'd grown to do whenever he had real bad news to deliver, and with Mike being his closest friend he knew this.

"How bad is it?"

"Real bad homie," he sighed. "Rashaud done got to ya girl."

"What you mean got to her?"

Kane shook his head afraid to come out and tell him.

"Did he touch my girl Kane?" he asked, with blood in his eyes. "What he do to her?"

"He raped her man."

Mike's blood turned to ice and his adrenaline was pumping. Nothing else needed to be said. He walked away from Kane and headed to his SUV. Kane followed without hesitation. He didn't know what the next move was going to be, but whatever it was he was sure he'd have his man's front, back and side. Whatever he needed, he was going to be right there.

■■■

Boom! Helena's front door flew wide open so hard had it not been for the wall it would've flown off the hinges.

Rashaud made the mistake of coming to the door without checking to see who it was. As soon as Mike heard the locks turn and the door crack open, he kicked the door in sending Rashaud flying back onto the floor. He was pissy drunk, barely knew what hit him. Mike and Kane stepped into the house without invitation and made their way over to where Rashaud had landed. Without explaining or complaining, Mike stood over top of Rashaud and drilled his fist into his face repeatedly until blood began to submerge from his nose and mouth.

Helena didn't know what was going on. The first thing she thought was someone had busted down the door to rob them so she grabbed her son and hid under the bed. After a few minutes, she crept down the hallway to see if she could hear anything and she did. She heard what sounded like the wind being knocked out of her man. She ran down to the middle of the staircase screaming from the top of her lungs.

Kane didn't feel the need to jump in the fight because Mike was doing just fine on his lonesome. Had he been a willing participant the two of them may have beat the man to death. Irritated by the woman's scream, he looked over at Mike whose eyes were inflamed with rage. He showed no signs of letting up. Kane pushed Mike back from Rashaud's battered body. He wasn't moving but it was evident that the man was still alive, barely.

"Please don't kill him. Just leave," Helena cried. "Just leave…"

Kane looked at Helena with a mortal glare in his eye. "You try to enjoy the rest of your night sweetheart," he winked, then managed to snap Mike out of whatever zone he was in and pushed him out the front door.

Chapter 35

WHEN DEATH COMES UPON US
𝅘𝅥𝅮 𝅘𝅥𝅮

Sammy's funeral was filled from front to back and wall-to- wall with mourners who stood over the closed casket grieving and saying their final goodbye to the young man that had been taken out of the world at the tender age of nineteen. But out of everyone, Lox had to be the one taking his loss the worse. He hadn't stopped blaming himself for letting Sammy go out alone that night. Had he been there his little brother may still have been alive, even if it meant he had to give up his own.

Mike sat in the front row accompanied by Azia, Camel, Kane, Sasha, TyTy and three of his other Capos, but Lox refused to take a seat. He stood at the head of the casket in the praying position for the entire service. Mike gazed at the golden pearl casket that had cost him nearly twenty-five hundred dollars and shook his head. He still couldn't believe his little homie was gone. He glanced around the room to check out the rest of the items that his money had bought. The funeral director definitely did a beautiful job with the flower arrangements with the small amount of space. He continued to scan the room as the preacher concluded his sermon and watched all the high school teeny boppers ramp and rave about losing their man. It brought a smile to his face. His protégé was definitely a ladies' man.

■■■

After the services ended, Koka made her way over to where Lox was being consoled by his clique. The last place she wanted to be on her birthday was at a funeral, but

Sammy and Lox were like family so there was no way she would have ever missed it.

"Hey baby," she said, hugging Mike first and going down the line. She stopped at Lox and hugged him a minute longer than the rest. "You need anything you know where to find me."

Lox shook his head. KoKa may not have been his mother by blood but she was the closest thing he and Sammy had to one. "Appreciate it," he said, softly.

Mike thought briefly about the last meeting he had with his mother which wasn't a nice one. Being at the funeral opened his eyes a little more. Life was definitely too short for dumb shit and grudges. Now he understood why some people treated everyday like it was going to be their last. You just never know. He made a mental note to sit down with KoKa and sort the ill feelings out about her denying him the knowledge of his brother.

Anthony stepped up to Mike with KoKa's hand locked unto his. He leaned over and whispered into his. "I'm taking her to the Moshulu tonight for dinner and to pop the question. I really hope you to be there man."

Mike looked Anthony square in the eye for nearly ten seconds before responding. "I'm there," he said, with two stiff pats on his arm.

KoKa freed her hand from Anthony's and wrapped her arms around Mike's neck. "I love you baby."

"Happy birthday Ma."

■■■

Fifteen minutes later, the funeral director's assistant began to hand out the orange funeral tags for everyone to place on their dash boards while instructing them to line their cars up on Federal Street in order to head down to the burial site. Lox, Mike, Azia, Kane and Sasha were the only five occupying the family limo. They headed up Federal towards 20th, climbed inside and positioned themselves comfortably. Kane was the last to get in. He had turned his phone off while in the service and decided to check his messages. When he heard Monster's voice, he got a very bad feeling. He listened to the message thoroughly then jerked his head towards Mike. "Something's up," he said, getting back out of the limo. When he began to further explain, someone opened fire amongst them all.

In a panic, everyone started to disburse in all different directions. Some folks yanked their levers into *drive* in an attempt to get the next car out of their way causing nothing but a pile up. It became completely chaotic in a matter of minutes. After hearing the gunfire die down, Mike leaped out the limo like it was on fire. Because he was at the beginning of the recessional line it was hard to see what was going on at the other end of the block. He, Kane and Lox hurried down the block back towards 19th street in the direction of what sounded like a violent car collision. The air echoed the sound of breaks locking, metal crunching, tires skidding, cars spinning, horns blaring and gravel spitting. And then there was silence.

Monster hopped out of a car that had smashed into a fire hydrant. He started running up the block to meet Mike and them. "I gotta get the fuck outta dodge man. Holler at me later," he huffed, and darted the other way.

By the time the men made it to the corner, the street had turned into a madhouse. Babies were crying, mothers were screaming and hustlers were scrambling. The car that Monster had abandoned was still in gear and kissing the hydrant with smoke rising from under the hood. Mike looked to his right and saw another car with the driver, a familiar face, slumped over the wheel unconscious. It was Hamburger and he was barely breathing. The passenger side of their car was massively dented and the face of Wayne was covered in blood, his brains had been disengaged thanks to Monster.

"Aw shit dogg," Kane said, clutching his head with both hands.

Mike turned to his left and followed the path of his friend's eyes and when he did, his heart felt like it crushed into a million pieces. There were motorists jumping out and coming from all directions to gather around Anthony's car. Mike power walked across the street and pushed his way through the crowd. With a heartbreaking expression of pain etched across his face, Mike stared down at Anthony's limp body smothered in blood, lifeless. His heart warned him not to look any further but his mind forced his head to the left. And there she was, KoKa, in the driver's seat bleeding out of her chest and wincing for air.

Before Mike could say or do anything, the Police and Paramedics popped up on the scene ordering everyone back. Mike stood frozen as he watched them put his mother on a gurney and rush her away in the back of an ambulance. Azia appeared at his side in an uncontrollable cry and secured her face in his chest. She didn't know what form of fate the future held for the only family that she'd ever grown to love, but she knew deep down inside that after that day her world would never be the same. As soon as she lifted up for some air, she noticed a familiar face climbing out of his squad car and their eyes met.

Detective Joseph looked at her with sincere regret. He didn't know how she tied into the incident that had just occurred, but seeing that she was a part of it at all sickened him. Even after she buried herself back inside of Mike's arms he continued to stare.

"Can you believe this mess," said Marks, his partner. "Nothing but animals out here in these streets," he barked, shaking his head. "In the middle of a damn funeral."

Joseph took his eyes off of Azia for the first time since he arrived. "I'm not too sure animal is the right word to define whoever's responsible for this one." They moved across to the car that belonged to Hamburger. "And right around the corner from the damn precinct, unfucking believable!"

Marks shook his head. "So what're you thinking?"

Joseph surveyed the crowd of mourners that had turned chaotic, and then turned back to his partner and said, "I'm thinking that it's going to be a hell of a night."

Nyema

∎∎∎

The next few days in the hood were tense. Mike stood in the basement of the small Spanish bodega where Monster called home listening to his side of the story. "If Kane told you to keep an eye on them niggas please explain to me how my mother ended up with a hole in her chest," he asked, respectfully. Had Monster not been there at all she might've been denied the opportunity to fight for her life which she was currently in the process of doing.

Monster wasn't into being interrogated, but because he had the upmost respect for Mike and felt sorry for his mother's situation he felt that he owed him an explanation. "I feel so fucked up bout ya mom's Papi. I tried to diffuse the problem before it got outta hand but dem little niggas Pooch sent was vicious--"

"Hold up," Mike interrupted. "You trying to tell me Pooch sent them niggas to off my mom?"

"Naw," Monster said, shaking his head hastily. "Pooch sent them to stir up the funeral, ya man Quadir's the one laid out the hit. I'm sure Pooch didn't know about that."

Mike stared at the concrete beneath him in silence while Kane stared at him curiously. For as long as he's known Mike he was never into setting up anyone for the kill. He'd always been nothing more than a respectful businessman, never took nothing from no one. Money was the last thing he wanted to be in the streets fighting over because it was more than enough in the pot to go around. Being greedy just wasn't a part of his character. He was the most humble person one could ever know. But the more Kane read into his eyes the more concerned he'd became. It had been a while since he'd seen that look and knew exactly what it meant. Them niggas done released a dragon.

"By the time I caught up with them they had already started popping so I rammed my car into theirs and got a few shots off. I don't know if I hit 'em or not. It was too many witnesses for me to go check it out but that was my bad Papi."

"I heard the medic say one was DOA but I don't know bout the other," Kane advised.

Mike broke out of his daze. "I want them niggas handled, every last one of them. Kane will line you up with whatever you need. Handle that nigga Pooch first. I don't give a fuck if he didn't order the hit. Since his ass wanna be a part of the bullshit he gonna get dealt wit too. But hold off for a few more days, let them niggas think things died down so they can slip up." Mike turned his back and stepped towards the stairs. "I don't want nobody to touch Quadir. Nobody! I'ma handle that one myself."

■ ■ ■

KoKa lay in her hospital bed with an oxygen mask attached to face, needles in her arms and all types of wires all over the place to keep track of her condition. The week she'd been confined to the small hospital room felt more like months and she'd gotten very good at staring at walls. It was not the way she had planned on spinning her fiftieth birthday, but at least she was alive.

Mike had been sitting at the side of her bed for over three hours waiting for her to gain consciousness. The pain medication that the doctors prescribed made it hard for her to stay wake. Finally, KoKa was jerked out of her sleep by a nightmare. She stared around the room wild-eyed as if she was seeing it for the first time until reality kicked in. With heavy eyes she turned and looked at Mike strangely while trying to remove the oxygen mask.

"I hate this damn thing," she slurred.

Mike smiled. It wasn't what he was expecting to hear but just hearing her voice was enough. "Stop complaining old lady."

Azia walked through the door with a bag full of fast food for her and Mike. She smiled after seeing KoKa was awake because she didn't know how much longer she could survive sitting in that small closed in space for one day. The whole thought of being in the hospital around a bunch of sickly people made her uneasy, but what other choice did she have. Her man needed her and there wasn't anywhere else in the world she'd rather be than right by his side.

"Don't bring ya ass in here with all that junk knowing damn well I can't have none."

"C'mon Ma, stop acting so grouchy."

"That's that *over the hill* attitude," Azia giggled.

"Both of ya'll can go to hell," KoKa smirked. She wanted to laugh but it would hurt too much. "Give me a bite."

"The doctor said--"

"She can have one bite Mike, dang," Azia whispered, pulling one of the burgers from the bag. She peeled the wrapper back and fed it to KoKa. "Come on before you get us caught."

Mike took a seat back in the chair. "When that nurse walk in here I don't want no parts of it." He watched the two women in his life laugh and bond in a way they had never done before. It gave him a moment to think to himself about how the tables had turned. Things had definitely gotten too out of hand. Robbing him was one thing but shedding blood on his family was something totally, different.

"I want some of that apple juice they be bringing you. Where they keep it at?"

"Go out and ask one of them nurses and bring me back a lot of 'em cause they always bringing me two like them little ass juices gonna cure my damn thirst."

Azia giggled and moseyed on out the door. KoKa turned her head slightly to face her boy whose mind was obviously nowhere in the room. "I know what you over there thinking about."

"Hmm…" Mike said snapping out of it. "What you say?"

"I aint say nothing yet but I'm gonna say this. I'm still here baby and we got to be thankful for that." The thought of Anthony brought tears to her eyes. "That could've been me sitting in that passenger seat but because of the grace of God it wasn't."

"I'm not up for the lecturing right now--"

"Mike," she said, cutting him off. Her voice was still weak but he could still decipher the authority in it. "You listen to me. I don't want you out there doing nothing that will cost you the rest of your life, whether that be laid up in a coffin or locked behind up behind bars."

"I hear you--"

"Don't just hear me son. You're not going to find the happiness you're looking for by bringing misery to another person's family. I don't want you to become a monster. You're way better than that."

Mike wanted to respond but his tongue wouldn't budge. And just in the nick of time, Azia came skipping through the door with one of those pink trays filled with a variety of fruit juices. He used that as his cue to get up out of there before KoKa tried to keep talking his ears off. "I got some business I gotta handle I'll be up to see you tomorrow," he said, kissing her forehead.

"Go ahead and run," she smirked. "I aint gonna be down forever."

Mike kissed Azia goodbye and exited the room. "Where's he going?" she asked.

KoKa shrugged her shoulders and shook her head from side to side. "Let's just hope it aint to hell."

■ ■ ■

Quadir sat behind the wheel of his car barking into the phone. "You aint gonna keep talking to me like I'm some kind of chump. I don't give a fuck that Bilaal's dead, I'm 'bout to make shit happen. Fuck what you heard."

"Quadir, my man, I'ma need you to stop talking to me like that before we have a major misunderstanding," warned Pooch.

"I was born misunderstood my dude. This shit I'm dealing with is some real life shit, personal shit. While you and

Nyema

Bilaal was plottin' on the nigga's money, I was plottin' to revenge my father's death so aint shit you can say to me right now gone make me do otherwise. Ya'll might'a thought ya'll was runnin' something, but Quadir don't run homie. Save that shit for them corner boys you got sniffing up ya ass."

"Alright kid, if that's the way you want it you on ya own," advised Pooch. "I don't want anything to do with it."

"It is what it is ol' head. Fuck it!"

Chapter 36

UNDER THE GAYDAR

Monster on the loose...

There that nigga go right there," Kane pointed. He and Monster pulled across the street from the Checker's on Lancaster Avenue to stake out their intended victim. After Monster ran up on the corner of 56th Girard Avenue with two metal poles in his hands, the three young hustlers that Pooch left in charge until he got back didn't hesitate to give his whereabouts. With three swings to their heads and a few more body shots, Monster hopped back into the Mustang Kane had rented for the week and they were off.

Monster threw his hood over his head and hopped out the small little racecar. He strolled across the street as the autumn leaves fell from out of nowhere and swam along with him. He stood under the over-the-top checkerboard squares on the red neon sign and eyed Pooch as he flirted his way into some free food. He grabbed the bag from the girl behind the counter, went over to take a seat at one of the tables and poured the contents of the bag onto the table. Just as he stuffed a mouthful of the chicken sandwich into his mouth, Monster appeared and took a seat across from him.

Pooch stared him down carefully until he was able to swallow. He knew Monster well and knew that he wasn't a huge fan of his. "What brings you to Checker's?" he asked, arrogantly. "I thought ya thing was beans and rice," he snickered.

Monster grinned. He wasn't offended because he was about to enjoy the pleasure of sending the rude boy to meet his maker.

Nyema

Pooch pushed his food aside. "What you want fool?"

"Nah, don't let me interrupt you," he said, sliding the food back in front of him. "Finish ya meal Papi. Aint nothing like a dying on an empty stomach." Pooch went to stand but Monster ordered him back down. "I won't mind blowing ya dick off first if that's the way you want it done," he said, knocking on the roof of iron table with the barrel of his desert eagle. "C'mon sit and finish ya food homie."

Pooch lowered himself back onto the seat slowly. He wanted to call the man's bluff but was too afraid to risk it. He knew Monster was sent by Mike, and the thought of explaining that he had nothing to do with what happened at the funeral, but it wouldn't do him any good no way. He stared around at the few folks that were coming and going and tried to convince himself that there was no way Monster would pull the trigger while people were around. Bad mistake!

"If you gonna kill me go on and shoot me you mu'fuckin' homo."

"Eat the fucking sandwich," he said, making his weapon clearly visible. He used it to slide the food towards him again.

At that moment, Pooch knew there wasn't an ounce of concern in the eyes of the beast that was sitting in front of him. He looked down at his sandwich, put it to his mouth and just as he bit into it Monster sent a bullet through the center of the bun. It took less than a second for the bullet to rip through the sandwich and out the back of Pooch's throat. The man was gone before his senses had the chance to feel any pain.

Monster secured the weapon and snatched a few fries from the table. "Who's the homo now?" He stepped over the man and walked away as calmly as he had arrived.

■■■

Azia sat in the middle of the bed drawing up some sketches with books scattered all around her. It was hard for her to concentrate because her mind kept wandering back to the comment KoKa made about Mike going to hell. It actually bothered her more than she let it be known. She climbed out of the bed and went to find Mike. He was stretched out on the sofa watching the Eagles put a hurting on the Giants. She positioned herself comfortable on his chest and he secured her in his arms. "Do you want to talk about it?" He shook his head. "You can't keep all that anger bottled up inside Mike. It's not healthy."

"I'm good--"

"You're not good. You're angry and you want somebody to pay for all this pain they've caused. You can lie to me but you can't lie to yourself."

"Not right now--"

"Well when is it ever going to be the right time Mike? It's always *not right now*. Say something, scream, yell, turn a table over, do something."

With a sudden lift he knocked her off of him and jumped to his feet. "What the fuck do you want from me?"

"I want you to cry. Let it out, it's okay."

"What you want me to cry about? Seeing you butt ass naked on top of another man's dick, huh? Is that what you want?"

Azia's mouth hit the floor. He'd never mentioned the pictures of her and Quadir since the night of the rape. She wasn't happy about what Rashaud had done to her, but a small part of her jumped for joy because it deterred Mike from the pictures. But it was only a matter of time before he threw them up in her face and that time was now.

"Close ya mouth before something fly up in it."

"Mike--"

"Mike what?" he growled. "You aint think I forgot did you?"

"You're mad at everything and everybody else right now but please don't let me be the--"

Nyema

"You wanted me to react right? Well this is me reacting." He backed her into a wall and hovered over her. "How was it?"

"I don't know," she cried.

"You had the nerve to step out on me and you aint even enjoy the shit."

"He drugged me Mike."

"Oh, I see. That's your story and you sticking to it huh?"

"It's the truth," she shouted, pushing him out of her face. "If you don't believe me then that's the fuck on you."

Mike sent his fist through the wall to keep from hitting her, but afterwards he knew he'd made a big mistake. Rage and anger had completely taken over.

Azia flinched at the sound of the punch and turned slightly to examine the damage. She looked down at his bloodied knuckles disappointedly before storming into the bedroom and slamming the door. A few minutes later, she heard the front door slam. She dashed out the bed and ran out to stop him. He was too angry and unfocused to be out on the streets, but by the time she got to the door Mike was already on the elevator heading down and out into whatever the night had in store for him.

Mike stepped off the elevator with his cell phone up to his ear in an irate state of mind. "Where you at?" he asked, stepping into the garage. "Don't move, I'm on my there."

■■■

Deuce strutted down 52nd street glancing back over his shoulder every other step he took. Hamburger was in jail, Quadir was missing in action, Pooch, Wayne and two other members of the squad were dead, and three others were in the hospital in critical condition. He knew it was just a matter of time before a hit was placed on his head. After all, he had already been labeled a traitor and with all the bad blood he and Lox had for one another he was sure he'd be coming to avenge his brother's death. The loud honking of a horn startled him. Just before he took off running, Quadir made himself known.

"Get in," he ordered, with his head out the window. Deuce exhaled and jumped inside. "Fuck you out here for, you know how hot it is right now."

"I'm going over to the spot to fall back. Where you been man?" Quadir looked at him like he was speaking Greek. "I'm just saying man, shit is crazy right now. Niggas getting popped left and right."

"You think you schooling me like I don't know what the fuck is going on?"

"What we gonna do?"

Quadir wished he could blow the weak link to pieces, but with Pooch dead and a handful of his team down, he needed him. "We gonna handle it, that's what we gonna do. When we get to the spot you gonna round up every nigga capable of pulling da trigger. This shit ends tonight."

■■■

"**Y**o, Mike, you know I respect you to the fullest but a nigga hurtin'," Lox explained, patting his hand. He was standing in the middle of Mifflin Street amongst Mike, Kane, Monster, Camel and TyTy trying his best to convince Mike to let him loose. He wanted to lay Deuce to rest so bad he could taste it. "You got to let me get this shit off my chest."

Mike stared into the young hustler's eyes with a deep feeling of compassion. Sammy was a good kid and his life had been stolen from him way too soon. "How many times do I have to tell you over and over--"

"What?" Lox intervened. "That revenge is a dish best served cold? You told me that plenty of times before." He walked up to Mike, grabbed hold of his hand and smashed it against his chest. "You feel that heart beat? That right there is as cold as it gets my nigga."

"That's what we got a gun for Lox," he said, pointing to Monster. "Aint no need for you to get ya hands dirty youngin'. I don't want that for you. The situation gonna get dealt with but it gotta get dealt with the right way. I don't know about you but I don't wanna see no more bloodshed over this way. If I send you out there who's to say you gonna come back. I aint trying to bury two brothers in one month, is that what you want?"

"To be honest wit you big homie, none of that don't even matter to me."

"Well it matters to me--"

Just as the sentence left his mouth, a slew of bullets ripple through the night air. All six men dove for cover from what sounded like thunder, the gun power was vicious.

Kane cursed himself for leaving his gun in the car. He knew better than to get caught slipping. "Give me ya heat," he yelled over the commotion. "TyTy, give me ya fuckin' gun."

TyTy crawled his way alongside a car towards Kane and tossed him the 9mm.

"Fuck this shit, cover me," Monster yelled. Using a car as a shield, he scooted up off his knees and opened fired. "Ya'll niggas want war?"

Quadir, Deuce, Black Stan and Henry ran and took cover. When the gunfire came to a halt, Mike attempted to sprint back towards his ride where his heat was stashed under the front seat. When Quadir peeped Mike, he opened fire while jogging in his direction. Mike ducked back behind a car and whistled over to Kane who in turn sent a shit load of bullets Quadir's way to slow him down. Camel guarded Mike the rest of his way to the car, weaponless. He was ready and willing to take a bullet for his man if the need presented itself.

■ ■ ■

Lox had discreetly made his way up the block to where he'd last seen Deuce. With his back up against someone's car door, he rose up just a little to get a better view. All he could see were flashes from the side of the street where a gun was being fired, but the owner of that gun was not visible. "Shit," he snapped, crawling closer.

■ ■ ■

Monster managed to slither his way onto the other side of the street where Henry was located. As soon as the boy shot his last round and turned away to reload, Monster appeared behind him with his gun aimed at his head and pulled the trigger. Henry was gone before he even knew what hit him at the early age of sixteen. Just as Monster turned to his left Black Stan appeared from out of nowhere and fired his first shot. The bullet connected with Monster's right shoulder which made him stagger back into a car. He managed to stay on his feet but dropped his gun.

■ ■ ■

Black Stan was no gangster. The only reason he was there in the first place was because Quadir asked him to come in a demanding kind of way. But after being in the mix of all those bullets, he promised himself that if he made it out alive, tomorrow he would turn back into plain old Stanley and Black Stan would be nothing more than an afterthought. Seeing that the bullet didn't take the monster down, he aimed to shoot his second shot but before he could get it off a slug ripped through the right side of his neck and exited out the left. He used both hands to bandage the holes, but the blood continued to leak like water from a faucet. Too bad for Stanley, tomorrow would never come.

■ ■ ■

TyTy stood on the side of Monster with his pistol still aimed on Black Stan. Monster was so glad to see his face that he almost kissed him on the lips. And just like that, two bullets sounded back to back sending TyTy to the ground on top of his own victim. He laid motionless with a bullet to the back and head.

■ ■ ■

Lox ran up on Deuce and kissed the back of his skull with his pistol five seconds too late. TyTy was already gone. He watched his friend hit the ground and it brought back memories of his brother. "How you want it pussy?" he spat, between clenched teeth. "High or low?"

Deuce dropped his weapon and stood firm as urine trickled down the right side of his pants. He may have walked into the gunfight like he was a lion, but he resembled nothing more than a lamb. "Lox man, I swear--"

"Don't cry you bitch ass nigga. Take this shit like a man," he said, and pulled the trigger. He then stood over top of the dead man's body and pumped all the remaining lead through his insides. "You weak ass bitch," he spat, firing his last shot.

■■■

Quadir turned back briefly and realized he was alone. The only thing he had on his side was the police sirens that filled the air. As soon as he heard Lox, Monster and Kane's footsteps scrambling in the wind, he fired a couple shots in the air to throw them off and darted around the corner.

"The nigga ran," yelled Kane, catching sight of one of the squad cars. He panicked. "Leave the fuckin' cars cuz. We get 'em later."

The five remaining men dashed into three different directions. Monster went his way, Camel and Mike went one way, and Lox and Kane went another. Less than a minute later, more shots filled the air. Mike came to an abrupt stop. He spun around fiercely and headed back until

Camel grabbed him. "The cops back there man. They cool, let's go."

"Nah," Mike said, shaking his head. "Something aint right."

Chapter 37

GETTING DOWN TO BUSINESS

Azia busied herself with drawing in order to keep her mind off Mike. She was in the middle of completing a sketch when her cell phone rang. It was Sasha crying and screaming in her ear. She could barely understand a word the girl said. "Slow down girl I can't hear what you saying." When she finally grasped what Sasha was trying to tell her, she jumped off the bed in shock. "Oh my goodness I'll be right there."

Kane had been shot and rushed to the emergency room. Azia began to cry until she felt ill. She was afraid to think about how life would be if Kane didn't make it. Both Mike and Sasha would be devastated. She slid into some sneakers and ran out the door, almost forgetting to lock it.

■■■

Omar pulled into the garage and parked his car in the first available parking spot. For the last couple, days he'd been trying to convince himself that it was time to face his daughter and tell her the truth about what really happened fifteen years ago. As bad as he hoped she would jump into his arms and forgive him, he knew it wasn't going to be that easy, but it was definitely worth a try.

Just as Omar went to get out of his car, Azia came storming out of the elevator and into the garage. Her feet were moving too quick for her body to keep up. When she made it to her car, the keys fell from her shaky hands. Her heart was racing. She couldn't stop thinking the worse. She felt around for her keys on the ground and just as she went to stand, a hand landed on her shoulder. Startled, she spun around swiftly damn near jumping out of her shoes.

"Rashaud," she muttered, staring into his swollen face with shock. Though she never asked, Azia was sure Mike and Kane killed him after what he'd done to her. "You're alive?"

"Don't sound so surprised."

"But how'd you know--"

"What? Where you live?" he snarled. "You aint too hard to track. Ya dude need to throw in a few more safety classes, but luckily for me he too busy for that."

Azia closed her eyes and let the tears sprinkle down her lonely face. She didn't know what Rashaud planned to do to her but whatever it was, it couldn't be any worse than the horrible thoughts and feelings he'd left her with after the rape. She just wanted it all to be over with. "Do what you gotta do."

"Oh I am," he said, dragging her over to his car.

"You cool shawdy?" a stranger shouted, quickly approaching to help Azia until Rashaud waved his weapon in the air.

"Mind ya fuckin' business ol'head," he roared, backing the man away and slinging her through the driver side all in one motion

Omar had started to intervene but decided against it. His blood was boiling and the things he wanted to do to Rashaud after seeing him man handle his baby girl couldn't happen there in that garage. He planned to rip the man apart and didn't want any witnesses so instead, he planned to tail closely behind.

Oblivious to the wondering eyes, Rashaud jumped in the car before Azia had a chance to climb completely over into the passenger seat. With the trigger fingered, he sped out of the garage in a hurry. Omar pulled behind them.

Azia battled with the passenger door for blocks, but it wouldn't budge. She sat nervously as he ran three red lights with no set destination in mind. "Where are you taking me?" she shouted.

"Stop screaming before I use this gun to shut ya ass the hell up," he threatened, pulling onto a deserted block and up on a curb to gain some kind of order. Azia pressed her back against the passenger door and tried kicking her way to freedom. "Girl you gonna make me--"

All of a sudden, the driver side window exploded and a pair of strong manly hands snatched Rashaud out by his head. It was Omar!

"She gonna make you do what tough guy?" Omar mocked, smashing his head into the hood of the car.

Azia and Omar locked eyes through the front windshield. She quickly studied his face and everything else about him. She hasn't always been good with names, but she'd always been good with faces. *I remember this man!* Realizing that het was the same man that was in the garage staring her down a months back, she panic and hopped across to the driver's side, leaped out and sprinted up the block towards traffic.

Omar used his power to peel Rashaud's gun from his hand then hammered his nose into the ground with his size twelve boot, and then hauled him over towards an old filthy green rusted dumpster.

"Muthafuck," Rashaud slurred, through broken teeth and a busted nose. "Fuck is you?"

"Ya worse nightmare muthafucka," he growled, slamming him into the dumpster with his left hand, and with his right hand he pulled the trigger twice sending Rashaud to hell with his own gun.

Omar stared down at him briefly. The left side of Rashaud's face was blown apart. With one stiff kick Omar sent Rashaud flying into the shadows with a pile of old garbage, walked away and never looked back.

■ ■ ■

Mike crossed over to Sasha who was seated in the ICU waiting area with her head buried in her lap. "He's going to pull through, just stay positive," he said, squatting in front of her. He began to rub her back for comfort.

"He can't leave me, I need him," she cried.

Sasha just didn't know how bad Mike needed him too. Kane was more than a friend, he was his brother. "That's a soldier in there he aint going nowhere."

Lox entered the room with distress written all over his face. This was the first time Mike and Lox had seen one another since splitting up after the gunfight. Mike whispered something in Sasha's ear and exited the room with Lox shadowing behind him.

■■■

"**W**hat the fuck happened?" Mike asked, trying to keep his voice at a minimum. "Why is it that my man is in there fighting for his life and the nigga that did it is still breathing?"

Lox looked back over his shoulder to make sure no extra ears were around after they stepped into a room filled with nothing but vending machines. "He came from out of nowhere Mike."

"Who?"

"It was Quadir. We thought he was gone but the nigga was still there. He just started blasting at us."

"And you just left Kane there alone bleeding to death?"

"I aint have a choice," he advised, throwing his arms out to the side. "Five-O was coming. I had to go get rid of the heat. I'm sorry man--"

Mike punched the soda machine so hard the lights began to flicker then leaned his head against it. "My nigga…"

■■■

Azia hopped out of the cab in front of the University of Penn hospital and forgot she had no money. "I just have to run upstairs and get some money," she spoke, through tears. "I promise I'll be right back."

"No…No…No…" the foreigner shouted. He jumped out the cab and ran around to the passenger side where Azia was standing. "I need money now."

Azia though about making a run for it until she heard someone call out her name. She turned around and saw Detective Joseph heading her way.

"Is there a problem?" he asked, removing the cabby's hand from her arm.

"No," he shouted. "She owe me money."

"I told him I'd be right back down," Azia said, tears still pouring out.

Detective Joseph stared deep into her eyes and saw the same lost little girl he did several months ago. He pulled some bills from his pocket and shoved it in the Cabby's face. "Now get outta here before I book you for assault."

Azia was so grateful that the detective came to her rescue, but she had somewhere she needed to be. "I have to go," she said, shooting inside the hospital like a bolt of lightning. She scanned the room full of cheerless people for minutes but didn't see any familiar faces. Then she remembered Sasha mentioning the ICU so she approached a security guard who pointed her in the right direction.

As soon as Azia stepped foot off of the elevator, she caught sight of Detective Joseph and Sasha talking by the nurse's station. He had a pen and notepad in his hand writing down whatever answers she had for his hundred and one questions. "Sasha," she interrupted.

Detective Joseph wasn't surprised to find out the girls knew one another. He looked at Azia and said, "I'll be finished with her in a minute."

"Mike's in there," Sasha advised, flagging her hand towards the waiting area.

Azia made her way into the room just as Mike ended a call. She ran over to him and threw herself into his arms. "Rashaud--" she whispered.

Mike held her close and tightened the grip. "Shhh…" There was no need for her to explain because he'd already received the call from Omar.

"But--" she said, taking a step back.

He placed two fingers up to her lip and said, "I know." She stared at him curiously. "I have something I need to tell you."

Her heart began to race, there wasn't much more that it could take. With one bad thing happening after the other, Azia had been through enough. Wiggling her way back into his arms she said, "Not right now Mike. Please, not right now."

■■■

Two and a half hours later, Azia opened her eyes and found her head on Mike's lap. She looked up and he too had fallen asleep. Sasha, Camel and Lox had made their own bunks out of chairs on the other side of the room. Mike awakened after feeling her movements. "I'm just going to the vending machines. You want something?" He nodded his head *no* and closed his eyes back.

Azia was standing in front of the snack machine trying to decide what to get when she was approached from behind. "You scared me," she said, with her hand on her chest. Detective Joseph smiled. "I didn't know you were still here."

"Trying to stick around until your friend comes out of surgery. I would love to know who did this to him. You got any ideas?" Azia shook her head. "I would hate to see you all wrapped up in this nonsense after all you've been through. Is this the kind of life you enjoy living?" he asked, sadly.

"Living is living Detective Joseph. I'm just doing what I got to do to survive."

"How's school coming along?"

"Everything's coming along great. I'm not looking to get caught up in any dumb stuff but things happen and these are my friends. All I know is how to be here when they need me so that's what I'm doing."

"I respect that Azia, but I find you to be a lot smarter than this. All the blood that was shed in them streets tonight was serious and somebody's sending a message. This may sound a little cliché for you, but I want more for you. These street kings or whatever you wanna call the guys you keep getting tied up with are not all that's out here. You have other options."

Detective Joseph was right. There were other choices out there, but she had made hers and she was sticking to it. "I hear you," she said, collecting her goodies from the machine. "Thanks for being concerned but like I told you before, don't worry yaself about me 'cause I'ma be alright."

"I pulled the body of a woman out of the Schuylkill River last night. I found out that she used to dance down at that club your so called friends hang out at. Hopefully none of this is tied to one another and I pray that one day it doesn't wound up being you."

As bad as Azia wanted to question who the woman they found was, she felt the need to get far away from the Detective before he continued to lecture her. "Enjoy the rest of your night Detective," she said, walking away.

"I got a job to do Azia. Hopefully your choice," he said, referring to Mike, "Aint caught up in the middle of all this cause I would hate for you to end up alone, again."

Azia turned back momentarily with a weak smile then continued on. By the time she arrived back to the waiting area, everyone was awake. Sasha and Mike stood talking to a Doctor. She froze up and watched in suspense, barely breathing. When she saw Mike shake the Doctor's hand she exhaled and walked over hoping to hear some good news.

"Is Kane okay?"

"He pulled through surgery but he's still unconscious. They removed a bullet from his chest and one from his leg, but they don't wanna chance taking the third one out cause it's too close to his spine. If it shift the wrong way it could paralyze him." Azia could see the fire in his eyes. "Stay here with Sasha. I need to go holler at my mom for a minute."

Azia tightened her grip on his hand and stared up at him as her eyes began to water. "I love you Mike."

He kissed her gently on the lips and replied, "I love you too."

■ ■ ■

Quadir kneeled down and pulled a flat cardboard box from underneath his bed. He pulled the flaps back and dumped all the contents onto the bed which contained over a hundred thousand dollars, a passport and two guns. He knew it was time to lay low. Although he was still a little bitter for not finishing what he'd set out to do, the two people closest to Mike were in the hospital fighting for their lives on account of him, which was somewhat of an accomplishment in his book. But sticking around was way too risky. The streets were too hot. Not only was Mike gunning for his head, the cops were desperate to connect someone to the murders, and he was sure that pretty soon the dots may connect to him.

After stuffing everything, he needed into a book bag, Quadir headed downstairs. He glanced down at his watch to check the time and clicked on the news channel to see if there were any updates about the shooting.

■ ■ ■

Mike stood beside KoKa's hospital bed staring down at her for a while before she finally awoke. Feeling the presence of someone standing over top of her, she opened her eyes and smiled. "I hope you here to take me up outta this raggedy room."

"I wish, but they aint ready to let you go yet."

She rolled her eyes. "Well I'm ready to go."

Mike pulled the white blanket that was neatly folded at the foot of the bed over her. "Just relax and let these people do their job."

"Did you ever get in touch with Anthony's mother?" she asked, sadly.

"Yeah Ma, I took care of everything. Don't worry about all that, just focus on getting better so you can get outta here."

"I just can't believe he's gone."

"What did I just say," he said, brushing the tears away from her cheeks. "Don't put yaself through that."

As much as Mike disliked Anthony, he knew the love his mother had for him was sincere so he decided to leave her with something he knew Anthony would've still wanted her to have.

"The hospital released all his belongings to me," he said, reaching deep into his pocket. "And I'm sure this is something he would still want you to have."

KoKa studied the diamond engagement ring in Mike's hand and cried softly. He elevated her hand and slid the ring onto her ring finger. It was a perfect fit.

Chapter 38

WATCH WHAT YOU ASK FOR

Lox stared down at the text message that came through on his phone and shook his head in disbelief. Things had definitely spiraled too far out of control, and something needed to be done about it.

"What you shaking ya head at?" asked Sasha.

"I'm reading this text," he said, not knowing whether to hit Sasha with some more bad news. "This shit is crazy."

"Why, who's it from?" asked Azia, butting in the conversation.

As if on cue, Mike entered the room. Lox walked over to him and passed of his phone so he could read the text. Mike could do nothing but shake his head as well.

"What the hell do the message say?" both girls questioned, in unison.

Mike took a deep breath and relayed the bad news. "They found your girl's body Sash--"

She stumbled over her words. "Who? What? Huh?"

"Vipor," Lox confirmed. "They found her dead."

Sasha fell to her knees hoping that this was all just a bad dream she had trouble awakening from. Vipor was dead and it was because of her. Had she not presented her with the offer the girl would still be alive and well. Was it really necessary? Did they have to kill her?

With red swollen sleep deprived eyes Sasha looked up at Mike and said, "Please do whatever you gotta do to make it all end. It's not worth her losing you." Focusing on Azia she reiterated, "I'm telling you it aint worth it."

Lox helped her up from the floor and she headed to the bathroom to finish grieving in private.

"Stay here with Sasha and make sure she cool," advised Mike. "I got some things I need to go handle." He grabbed Azia by the hand and escorted her out of the building.

■ ■ ■

Omar was sitting behind the wheel of his rented Chevy Impala in the *Grays Ferry* shopping plaza in front of Pathmark waiting patiently. When he'd received the call from Mike advising for them to meet, he knew the time had come for some skeletons to be released. He played different scenes over and over again in his head wondering how the first meeting with his daughter after all those years would turnout. Nervousness overcame him and the feeling felt so familiar. He began to think back to the day Azia was born, the first time he held her and the last time they hugged. It warmed his heart, but for how long. There was a strong possibility that even after hearing he wasn't the reason behind her mother's death, she still wouldn't forgive him for not being there as a father, for neglecting to reach over the last fifteen years, and for leaving her alone in the cold world to fend for herself. He watched Mike pull into the plaza with Azia on the passenger side. The wait was over.

Mike circled the lot until locating Omar's car. Pulling into the empty handicap spot next to him, he put the lever in park and told Azia, "Sit here for a second I be right back."

Azia watched him climb out of the SUV and jump into the Impala, but the tint made it difficult to see the driver's face. She turned the radio up a notch, let her head fall back onto the headrest and closed her eyes while listening to the smooth sound of Alicia Keys' voice swim through the airways. She cracked her eyes open and glanced at the clock on the dashboard. It had been six minutes already. She leaned up and strained her curious eyes to see what the men were doing, and just as she did, the passenger door of the car flew open.

Nyema

Mike walked around to the passenger side of his SUV and opened the door. He grabbed hold of her hands and stared deep into her eyes. "Remember I told you I needed to tell you something?" She nodded her head. "Do you trust me?"

"Yeah, I trust you Mike. What kind of question is that?"

"I want you to meet someone," he said, helping her down from the seat and leading her over to the Impala. "It's been long enough."

"What's been long enough? Who's in the car? What's going on?" The questions kept coming, but Mike ignored them all. "Mike--" she growled, watching the mystery man's door fling open.

As soon as Omar hopped out and turned to face her, she recognized him right away. Although it was dark the night he came to her rescue, she would never forget those eyes. Her grip tightened on Mike's hand as she stared at him inquisitively.

"Who is he?" she asked, but it was a question that needed no answer. The more she stared at Omar, the more he reminded her of a man she once knew. "How--"

Mike shushed her. "Just talk to him. Give him a chance to make things right."

Azia wanted to yell, scream, punch, kick and a lot of other things, but her mind went numb for a minute. Omar went to reach out for her and she smacked his hand away. She followed that with two more hits, then another, and then another. Seeing him was hurtful, heartbreaking because it only reminded her of her mother.

"Why'd you bring him here?" she whined.

Omar pulled her into his arms and held her tight. He nodded his head at Mike advising it was okay for him to leave. He knew there was somewhere more important that Mike needed to be.

Azia noticed Mike walking off and jumped out of Omar's arms. "You aint leaving me here with him."

"You said you trust me," replied Mike, gripping her into a bear hug. "You need to hear him out. Don't worry babe, everything's gonna be okay."

Chapter 39

I COULD NEVER BE HIS WOMAN

Mike turned onto Snyder Avenue and pulled in front of a two story duplex, one of his many investments. He climbed out of his SUV and was met at the door by Camel. "Where's Kyla?"

"Up there sleep," he pointed.

Mike brushed pass him and made his way inside to the upper level. "It's time for her to get her ass up. She got work to do."

A few minutes later, Kyla was jerked out of her sleep by Mike. She jumped up in a panic and stared up at him.

"Get up and throw ya clothes on," he ordered, tossing a shirt and pair of pants into her face. "And hurry up."

Camel and Mike were standing near the door in the middle of a whispered conversation when Kyla appeared with the baby on her hip. Just as she went to cross over to the sofa, Mike's harsh voice startled her.

"Let's go!"

Kyla shifted the baby up on her waist, grabbed his baby bag and approached the men.

"He's staying here," Mike said, taking the boy from her arms.

"Why can't he go?" she shouted. She was starting to get a very bad feeling. "My baby is going wherever I go."

Mike handed the baby over to Camel. "I said he aint going, now bring ya ass on," he repeated, dragging her out by the arm.

■■■

"How could you leave me here to deal with all your shit," Kyla screamed, through the phone. "He will kill me if he finds out I been lying to him all this time."

"Bitch calm down," Quadir raved. "That nigga aint gonna kill you. He think the kid is his so all you gotta do is play off that."

"He knows I'm hiding something Quadir. I don't want to stay here. I wanna go with you."

"You already know that aint happening. I don't travel wit whores and kids so you need to come up with a plan B sweetheart."

"You's a piece of shit Quadir. This is your son," she barked. "The least you could do is give us some money so we can roll out for a little while until shit die down."

At that moment, Quadir grew a heart. He didn't want any parts of her or the baby, but the least he could do was throw her a few dollars for the extra aggravation. "Where you at?"

"Home!"

"Sit the fuck down and chill out. I'll be there in a minute."

Kyla ended the call and handed the phone over to Mike. She was scared shitless and didn't have a clue what to do about it. "Are you gonna kill me Mike?"

He smiled. "Now why would I do that?"

Kyla turned her head and gazed out of the window wondering how she could allow herself to get caught up in the mess. If she could go back and change it all she definitely would. But it was too late for would'a, should'a, coulda's. At the end of the day, she had no one to blame but herself.

■ ■ ■

Quadir took a swig of Hennessey from the bottle and placed it back on the table. After rethinking, he grabbed the bottle from the table and threw it in the

bag with the rest of his belongings. He cut the television off and jumped to his feet. It was time for him to go somewhere and fall back. After locking up, he banged on his neighbor's door.

A forty-something year elder with grays protruding through his fade and thick beard appeared at the door in his Calvin Klein underwear. "Do you gotta always bang like you the police?"

Quadir tossed him the keys to his house and said, "You know what to do. Sell whatever you can get rid of and I'll be back for my bread later."

"Where you going?"

"Away!"

"For how long?"

"Long enough," he said, walking in the opposite direction.

■■■

A little over an hour later, Quadir was pulling up in front of Kyla's door. He stepped out the car and scanned the area for anything unusual, but nothing seemed out of place so he used his key to make his way inside.

Kyla's heart started to race after hearing the front door slam. She climbed from the sofa onto her feet when he entered the living room.

"Fuck wrong wit you?" he asked, looking at her strangely.

"Nothing! I'm just ready to get out of here."

Quadir's eyes scanned the room. "Where's the baby?"

"I got to go pick him up from my girlfriend's on my way out." She picked up the small suitcase she had packed up and held out her hand. "Can I have the money so I can go?"

He pulled a wad of cash from his pocket that he'd rubber-banned and set aside for her. But something wasn't right. His antennas were definitely up and at work. When Kyla walked over to retrieve the cash, in one swift motion he spun her around and put a gun to her head.

"Who the fuck in here wit you?" he whispered.

"Nobody!"

"I'ma ask you one more time, then I'ma start talking with bullets."

"Please don't let 'em kill me," she cried out.

Mike stepped out of the kitchen and made his presence known. He was hoping that Quadir passed her off the cash and let her go before he made his move, but things weren't going as planned. He knew what his brother was capable of, and after seeing the gun jammed into the side of Kyla's head it was a ninety-eight percent chance that the woman wasn't going to make it out of the situation alive.

"What up my nigga?" Quadir smiled.

"Don't you mean brother?"

Quadir locked faces with Kyla and giggled. "Oh you told him huh?" He smashed the gun deeper into her head. "I should'a known better than to trust ya stupid ass."

"You're hurting me--"

Mike stared into his eyes and for the first time he noticed that Quadir did bore some resemblance to him and their father. "Let her go my dude. This right here is between me and you."

"It was always about me and you. She chose to get involved so she aint got a choice but to woman up and take the consequences. Aint that right baby girl," he taunted, licking her sloppily.

"You wanted me, you got me," he said, throwing his arms to the side. "Let her go so we can deal with this shit and get it over with."

Quadir separated himself from Kyla, aimed one gun at Mike and pumped two shots in her, once in the face and once in the throat. Blood painted the walls before the woman's body hit the floor.

Turning back to Mike and laughed, "I bet she won't run her mouth no muthafuckin' more--"

"You think running round here bringing gunfights to funerals and killing women make you a G nigga? That shit don't make you tough. You just as weak as ya father was."

Nyema

"Oh, so you ready to talk about my father? Had it not been for you I would still have one."

"You aint know that fool like I did. I did us both a favor--"

"You do shit for me but leave me out here alone to man-up and show my own self the way of the streets. Something a father is supposed to do for his son."

"You got ya own son now. Who the fuck gonna show him the way?"

"He mines by accident. That shit don't count."

Mike shook his head with disgust. "You turned out to be nothing just like him."

"And you bleed the same blood nigga so what the fuck does that make you?"

"Vicious," he growled, popping off two shots and ducking back into the kitchen. "

"You missed me brother," Quadir yelled.

"On purpose, but the next won't be. Let's end this beef right now and go our separate ways before shit get too ugly."

"I plan to go my separate way but it won't be before I take ya punk ass down," he shouted, then sent a slew of shots towards the kitchen. "How's ya mother?"

Mike became irate. He slouched down behind the wall and sent some shots back in return. "She'll live which is more than I can say about you."

Quadir laughed. "And ya right hand man. Did he pull through?"

"I hope you aint think a weak ass nigga like you would bring him down."

"Guess I need to sharpen up, and I can start with you," he yelled, running closer towards the kitchen, took cover behind a china cabinet and dumped several shots Mike's way.

The gun battle continued until the sound of police sirens spiraled through the air. Quadir carefully climbed to his feet and tried to catch a peak out the window. "Look like we gonna have to continue this at a later date."

"You hear a few sirens and now you wanna bitch up huh?"

"Call it what you want. If I get knocked I won't get the chance to lay ya ass down. Shit, I done waited this long, I can wait a little longer." Quadir sent some more shots to throw Mike off and snuck his way over to a side window.

Mike eased his way out of the kitchen on his knees. Catching sight of Quadir scrambling out of the window, he opened fire putting a bullet in his leg.

"Muthafuck…" Quadir shrieked, falling head first out of the window.

By the time Mike made it over to the window, he caught a glimpse of Quadir dipping into an alley. Rushing out of the front door in an attempt to catch him at the other end of the block, Mike was met by several officers with their pistols held high.

"Lower your weapon and get down on the ground," they yelled out in unison.

Mike tossed his weapon onto the ground and put his hands behind his head.

Two officers rushed over to bring him down while several others ran up in the house. With his hands secured behind his back, they pulled Mike to his feet and walked him towards the back of a squad car. Detective Joseph met them on the way.

"We got one down in here," an officer yelled.

Joseph watched them stuff Mike into the back of the car with distaste. He grabbed the door before it closed and kneeled down to Mike's seated level. "You care to share what went on in there?"

"Nope!"

Joseph climbed to his feet and said, "Hopefully Azia opens her eyes after this. She's too good of a girl to be held down by you street thugs." He slammed the door shut and yelled to an officer, "Get him out of my sight."

Chapter 40

HIS LOVE IS WORTH THE WAIT

Azia studied the grin that Omar had plastered across his face while talking on a call. It wasn't hard to tell that is was a female on the other end of the line. Nor did he try to hide it.

"When I finish my rounds here in Philly I'll be heading back that way." He paused. "I'll make sure to do that." Another pause. "Sound good to me, I'll see you then." Omar ended the call and buried his head back into his plate.

"Was that your girlfriend?"

He chuckled. "I wouldn't call her that."

"Hmm…" she pouted. "So I take it you're not gonna be here for long."

Omar wiped crumbs from his face and swallowed back the rest of his drink. "There's a lot you don't know about. I'm sure when things settle down Mike will sit you down and explain everything."

"Why can't you explain it? What? You came all this way to look me in the eye and tell me you weren't responsible for my mother's death. Were you hoping I'd feel better after hearing that? I tell you what DAD," she stressed. "Just because you weren't the one that pulled the trigger don't mean you aint responsible. They came in there for you, not her. She just got caught up in the middle of it."

"And look at us now. History does repeat itself doesn't it?"

Azia sucked her teeth and rolled her eyes. He did have a point.

"Baby girl, you're a grown woman and I'm not walking into your life after all these years to play daddy like I've been here forever. And you're not the only one that blames me for your mother's death. I blame me, but it aint going to bring her back. All I ask is that you give me a chance to show you that I do care. I'm not the heartless animal everybody wanted you to believe I was when you were growing up."

Azia stared at his curly hair and looked deep into the chinky eyes she and her fathered both shared and felt his pain. Her heart thumped at the connection and a hidden part of her was set free. "I'm glad you came to find me," she said, through tears.

He took his daughter's hands unto his and said, "Baby, I'm just sorry it took me so long."

Azia's cell phone began to vibrate across the table. "It's Camel," she said, answering the call. "What happened?" She jumped up from the table. Where'd they take him?" Her head began to spin in a million different directions. "Meet me down there, I'm on my way. They arrested Mike," she said, collecting her items from the table and hurried out of the restaurant with Omar hot on her trail.

■■■

After waiting for nearly an hour in the interrogation room, Mike sat firm and straight-faced like he had no worry in the world. Detectives Joseph and Marks stared at him through the two-way glass window trying to make sense of what went down.

"You think he did it?" Marks asked.

"No," Joseph replied, folding his arms. "But I'm sure the cock sucker knows who did."

"Well I hate to say it but he aint going to break. He's been asking for his lawyer for the last thirty minutes."

"Some kind of way he's tied up in all the bullshit that's been going down. He can call for his lawyer all he wants. We still got him on the weapon's charge."

"I already talked to ballistics. His weapon doesn't match the slugs that were pulled out of the girl and it's registered to him. There weren't any more weapons discovered at the scene."

"Somebody else was in that house and I'm going to find out who it was if I got to dedicate my life to it," he howled, so vexed that veins began to pop out the side of his neck. "I'm also sure he had something to do with that prick Rashaud popping up dead, I'd bet my life on it. As a matter fact, get his little girlfriend down here to see if we can get anything out of her."

"You mean the baby's mother, Helena right?"

"Yeah! Her! Maybe she can tell us something that we can make stick before that damn Jew lawyer he got make his way down to claim him. If his gun was registered then I'm sure he's licensed to carry. We got to find something and we got to find it quick."

When Azia spotted Detective Joseph exit the small room and back out into the precinct, she called out to him. She watched Marks whisper something into his ear before heading her way. "Nobody's helping me. Can you please tell me what happened?"

"It's bad Azia, real bad," he said, shaking his head and looking over to Omar. "And you are?"

Omar extended his hand. "A friend."

"Mike is going to be here for a while so I doubt if ya'll want to stick around. We got a girl dead and another suspect in the wind. I don't know what else I can tell you besides you need to pick some better friends."

"Please don't do this to me Detective Joseph. I beg you not to do this."

"I tried to warn you Azia. I tried," he said, sorrowfully walking away.

Azia dropped her head into Omar's chest and he secured her in his arms. She was in pain and watching her made his heart heavy. He escorted her out of the precinct and over to his car just as Camel was pulling up. Omar remembered him from a couple of previous meetings he and Mike had. The two men hands collided.

"What they talking 'bout in there?" he asked.

Omar shrugged. "From what they saying it aint looking too good."

"That's bullshit. They aint got nothing on him."

"They said a girl died--"

"It was Kyla," he advised, looking over at Azia.

She rushed him with wide-eyes. "Who killed her?"

"It had to be Quadir, but he got away." Camel leaned into the backseat of his car and came up with a baby boy in his arms. "I hate to do this to you Azia, but I don't have a choice. KoKa in the hospital and I don't know shit about no babies," he said, securing the boy in her arms.

Azia stared down at the boy speechless. She didn't know any more than Camel did about babies, but the little boy smiled at her and it warmed her heart.

"I gotta go track down Brisco so he can come down here and find out what the fuck's going on," he advised, passing Omar the car seat and baby bag. "I'll call you when I hear something."

■■■

Five and a half hours later, Azia found herself at the condo pacing back and forth in an unsure state of mind. Mike was locked up, Kane and KoKa were in the hospital, and she was stuck with a baby and in the company of a stranger. After watching Omar bounce the baby up and down on his knee desperate to get him to stop crying, her anxiety kicked in full throttle.

"I can't just keep sitting here doing nothing," she blurted, storming towards the door.

Omar laid the baby on the sofa and rushed over to stop her from leaving. "It's nothing that you can do right now. Let the lawyer do his job."

Nyema

Azia scrabbled over to the phone and punched in Camel's number, but it went to voicemail. "Why haven't he called me back yet?" She dialed Camel's number three more times but kept getting his voicemail. Frustrated, she threw the phone down. "Take me back down to the precinct," she ordered.

"I don't think that's a good idea."

"I don't care what you think," she yelled. "Just take me back down there so I can see what's going on."

Omar gripped her by the arms gently. "I'm going to need you to calm down. You going back down there aint going to help the situation."

"You aint in no position to tell me what to do," she shouted, jerking away. "Get the baby and come on."

When Azia swung the door open, she was met by Mike standing on the other side. She jumped into his arms and planted kisses all over his face. He made his way inside with her legs wrapped tightly around his waist. Omar closed the door behind the two and followed them into the living room.

"They let you out?" she questioned, happily.

"I don't pay Brisco all that money for nothing. He dug in their asses cause they aint have nothing on me and got me up outta there."

"When the Detective told me you were caught with Kyla's body, I swore they were going to keep you."

At the mention of Kyla's name, the thought of her baby popped in Mike's head. He scanned the area and found him lying on the sofa fiddling with his bottle. "Damn," he huffed, shaking his head.

Azia's heart went out to Kyla. Although they didn't get along, she never wished death upon her. "What are we going to do with him?"

"I don't know."

Omar walked over to interrupt. "Yo, my man, what's the situation with Quadir?"

"The situation is still a situation..."

Hearing that upset Omar because he was ready for him and Mike to get down to business with the Columbians, but with Quadir still on the loose he knew it would just make things more complicated. "I'm sure he'll lay low for a while so that'll give you some time to get ya shit together. I gotta head back to Florida for a few days to get some things in order, and then I'll be heading back this way for a while."

The two men shook hands. "Cool, I see you when you get back. Thanks for keeping my baby together for me while I was down," he said, referring to Azia.

Omar and Azia stared at one another without saying a word. After reaching out towards her, Azia dragged her weight across the floor and into his arms. Her head landed on his chest and he held her close. Azia didn't want to let go. After being deprived of that paternal feeling of benevolence she'd been longing for the last fifteen years, she'd finally had it at her fingertips and would do anything not to lose it again.

Omar sensed her concern. "I'll be back," he advised, staring into her innocence. "I promise."

And with that being said, he was gone.

■ ■ ■

After a nice hot meal and a long hot shower, Mike made his way into the bedroom to unwind. He stood beside the bed drying the water from his naked body and watching Azia rock the baby to sleep brought a smile to his face.

"You looking like a professional over there," he giggled.

She sucked her teeth and smiled. "Whatever!"

Mike wrapped the towel around his waist, took the baby from her arms and placed him down onto the pile of blankets Azia managed to turn into a crib for the night. He then joined Azia at the dresser where she was slicking her hair back into a ponytail.

Nyema

"Mike," she said dryly, almost inaudible. "Why didn't you tell me about my dad?"

"Because it wasn't my place to tell," he said, planting soft kisses on her neck.

"Are you going to at least tell me what happened to Rashaud?"

Mike looked her dead in the eye and said, "Some things are better left unsaid."

Azia could read between the lines, she was no dummy. Instead of interrogating him further, she started to caress him through the towel. "You're looking at me like you want to eat me or something."

"What if I do?"

"It's something you aint done in a while so I might just let you do that."

He picked her off her feet and sat her on top of the dresser. "Earlier you asked me what I wanted to do about the baby, but what really matters to me is what you want."

"I got what I want standing right here in front of me," she said, gazing into his eyes. "Whatever comes with it I'm all for."

Mike leaned in and kissed her softly. Azia flung her arms around his neck and invited his tongue into her mouth. They kissed passionately as he fondled her breasts. Wrapping her left leg around his waist, Azia leaned back using the dresser mirror as leverage impatiently waiting for his strong body to seize hers as she thrust her hips against his thickness. After easing her nightgown off, he allowed the head of his shaft tease her pussy while his lips found their way to her brick hard nipples. He then slid in and out of her slowly as she dug her fingernails deep into his flesh yearning for more.

"I love you so much," she moaned, biting down on his lip as their bodies moved in perfect synchronization.

Mike smiled against her lips, both of their body temperatures rising. Feeling the urge to cum, he slid out of her and sent his fingers down to her wetness. Azia squirmed while trying to bring his fingers where she wanted to feel them the most, but he resisted her efforts.

"Please...oh...no...put it back..." she inhaled sharply, shifting her tongue to his nipples.

Intense pleasure swept irresistibly over them both, their minds and their bodies, at the brink of a sensual overload. He gripped her by the waist and pushed himself back inside of her, smiling at her sudden lack of communication. Azia drew her legs back a little more and cupped his tight ass, her inner walls clenching him rigidly.

"Mmm...Mike..." she moaned, sucking on his bottom lip trying her best not to scream.

Unable to fight the feeling any longer, he released everything he had inside of her, neither of them able to control their breathing. Then, he pulled out of her slowly as she interlaced her fingers with his and rested her head on his sweaty torso. Eventually their movements came to a cease, and their kisses became less demanding.

Trying to catch his breath, he kissed her face tenderly. "I love you too," he finally replied, rubbing up and down the small of her back.

Azia sighed lightly while staring at him wonderingly, but knowingly. After all the hell they'd been through, she knew this was not their happy -ending. It was only the beginning.

Chapter 41

THE PRICE OF FREEDOM

...One Month Later

Mike entered the hospital room that KoKa had been calling *home* for the last couple of months. He was followed by Azia who was carrying the baby and a handful of balloons, Sasha with a cake and Kane on crutches. After weeks of therapy, she was finally being discharged and was more than ready to go.

"I don't need no damn wheelchair," KoKa told the Nurse.

"We sure gonna miss you around here Ms. KoKa," the Nurse giggled. In her four years at the hospital, she'd never met a patient as witty and charismatic as KoKa. Although they all agreed that she was a piece of work, she had definitely become a favorite. "Make sure you come back and see us."

"Chile please, the only way you gonna get me back up in this hospital is if somebody put another bullet in me," she smirked.

"Woman would you shut ya mouth. I can hear you all the way down the hall," Aunt Val said, busting into the room with more balloons and a bouquet of flowers.

"Pa-leaze just get me out of here before I hang myself," KoKa said, leading the way out of the room. "I need a drink."

Everyone followed behind giggling and snickering to themselves.

Aunt Val pulled her car along the passenger pickup and Mike helped KoKa get in. "We gonna meet at KoKa's right?" Val asked.

"Hell no, we gonna meet at the restaurant. Did ya'll not hear me say I needed a drink?" KoKa snarled.

"She's back…" Azia sang.

"You damn right I'm back. Now bring ya'll asses on."

"Hey Mister," a young boy said, yanking on Mike's jacket.

Mike and Kane looked down on the kid suspiciously. Where did he come from?

"What's up little man?" Mike asked.

"This for you," the boy said, shoving a picture in Mike's face.

Mike stared down at the picture and began to scan the area wild-eyed. "Where'd you get this from?"

The boy pointed to the other side of the street and replied, "Him over there," but there wasn't anyone visible. "A guy paid me twenty bucks to bring it over."

Kane snatched the picture from Mike's hand and recognized the face immediately. It was a picture of Mike's father posing with a gun in each hand. He flipped the picture around and held the back towards Mike. It read:

> *Til death do us part big brother…*
>
> *I promise I'll see you again real soon…*

Mike crumbled the picture into a ball and let it fall to his feet just as Azia and Sasha pulled up with the car.

"You cool my nigga?" Kane asked, before getting in.

Mike took one last look around, then turned back to his friend and replied, "I wouldn't be me if I wasn't."

TO BE CONTINUED…

ALLURE
ERICA KIMBERLY

Allure: to exert a very powerful and often dangerous attraction on somebody

Antonym: Dissuade

Kamryn Mackey is a beautiful and vibrant 19-year-old girl with a heart centered in the city of Los Angeles. She and her best friend, who is gay male, only source of income is through boosting from high-end department stores. But Kamryn soon has a change of heart about her illegal profession and decides to call it quits, so she thought. During a relapse and a lot of persuasion from her crime partner, Kamryn runs into a mysterious and overwhelmingly handsome brother who catches her eye.

When New York native Ricky Wade first visited Los Angeles at 17 years old, he only had ambition and a few hundred dollars. After a connecting with a heavy hitter in the LA drug world, Rick moves from The Big Apple to The City Of Angels and never looks back. Now at age 32, he has it all. With a focused hustle and a tiny circle of trustworthy partners, Rick has managed to evade law enforcement, while building a drug empire, which stretched across the Southwest region. These days, Ricky Wade is looking to expand his business. But first, he finds a love interest in Kamryn and decides to focus on pleasure.

Soon after meeting Rick, life Kamryn once knew changed right before her very eyes. She immediately recognizes the cons of his type of work, and proceeds with caution. From shopping sprees to exclusive vacations, Rick stops at nothing to win her over. Kamryn secretly adores his prolific lifestyle, one she could only dream of having. Within time, their whirlwind relationship takes off and Rick finds his place in Kamryn's heart. After being introduced to his finer way of living, Kamryn unexpectedly drops her guard and falls head over heels for Rick. After introducing her to his world, Kamryn soon becomes Rick's rider and ultimately the couple's relationship soar to new heights.

For Kamryn, things couldn't be better thanks to Rick. She begins to believe that together there is nowhere else to go but up... Until she finds herself in the terrifying center of a man's intrigue. With Rick's fate handed down to him, it'll be Kamryn fighting for her own freedom... And a price will have to be paid for it. The question is... Who will pay it? And how much?

(May 2011)

ROBBERY REPORT
GLORIOUS

(In Stores Now!)

Gerrod Mason, Frank Wilson and Lisa Mathews all have something in common, they're all from a city in New Jersey small in size but big in reputation just off the NJ Turnpike's Exit 9 better known as New Gunswick. Together they contribute to and rep their town's hood monarch to the fullest, giving the streets something to talk about.

Gerrod aka G Millions, the charismatic thug and Frank aka Famous, the trend setter, form a bond thicker then blood brothers and make a pact to get it by any means necessary and that's exactly what they do. From the North, to the Mid- West down to the Dirty South they show the true meaning behind the old street saying, If you can't make it then take it.

Life for the duo was all good but soon gets better after Lisa aka Lady Pink, joins the crew. She becomes the main ingredient missing in the masterpiece the two were chefing up. Equipped with beauty and brains, not to mention loyal and deadly, it becomes evident why Lady Pink is every man's dream and worse nightmare all rolled up in one.

Together, the trio and their band of young hungry wolves become the criminal version of the dream team, contributing to the boost in the crime rate wherever they traveled.

But like all other families in the underworld, greed and lust emerge leaving two fatal questions? Will they be able to maintain their loyalty and reconcile differences so they can continue to break bread together? Or will they fall victim to the saying there are no honor amongst thieves and become just another statistic.

MEMOIRS OF AN ACCIDENTAL HUSTLER
J.M. BENJAMIN

In Stores Now!

Meet the Benson's…A young married couple, with four children living under the same roof in a nice neighborhood. On the outside looking in, one could easily mistake them for an average "Middle Class" family that had moved on up like "The Jefferson's"…But that's not the case. They are far from being in comparison to "The Huxtables" and life as they once knew it comes rapidly crashing down.

Eight year old Kamil, the next to the youngest of the Benson clan, shares how life was for he and his siblings, after being forced to adjust to the conditions of a "New Way" of living. He details what it was like after his mother made a bold and drastic decision to walk away from not only the "Finer Things" in life they had grown accustomed to, but his father as well.

A Brownstone in the Bed-Sty area of Brooklyn New York, traded in for a housing projects in a small town where his grandmother resided in Plainfield New Jersey, Kamil takes you on a journey of how he was exposed to another world and a different breed of people than he was used to in the city that became his home.

Bonded by the absences of their fathers, he and his brother befriend a group of boys from the neighborhood and form an un-breakable bond, vowing not to travel down the same road as their dads, making a pact to stay in school and out of the streets.

Kamil also takes you through his personal experience with the opposite sex, as a childhood crush develops into something much more.

As this story un-folds, walk with Kamil as he transitions from childhood to teen into young adulthood and struggles with the very things his mother walked away from and tried so hard to prevent he and his brother from embracing.

What starts out as a game and a means of survival…Ultimately ends up serious and addictive. This is the memoir of an Accidental Hustler…

Order Form

A New Quality Publishing

_____	**Down In The Dirty**	$15.00
_____	**My Manz And 'Em**	$15.00
_____	**Ride Or Die Chick**	$15.00
_____	**Ride Or Die Chick 2**	$15.00
_____	**Back Stabbers**	$15.00
_____	**Have You Ever…?**	$15.00
_____	**On The Run With Love**	$15.00
_____	**From Incarceration 2 Incorporation**	$15.00
_____	**Heaven & Earth**	$15.00
_____	**Ski Mask Way 2**	$15.00
_____	**Around The World Twice**	$15.00
_____	**The Robbery Report**	$15.00
_____	Total Number Of Books Order	_____

Name

Reg (Applies if Incarcerated)

Address _____

_____

City/State/Zip Code _____

Email _____

WE ACCEPT MONEY ORDERS FOR MAIL ORDERS
WE ACCEPT STAMPS FOR PRISON ORDERS
PURCHASE ONLINE AT
WWW.ANEWQUALITYPUBLISHING.COM